TASK FORCE BATTALION

The flag rose in the air, fluttering in the strong breeze. And now many more men had joined them, all standing and watching as the flag of their country was raised once more on East Falkland. The men saluted and a strange sense of power seemed to fill them. Even Moss felt it. A stirring which he had not experienced before.

'Now we're here, we're here to stay,' said Colonel Clavell, who had joined the little group.

The flag moved gently in the breeze.

The first of the Sea Kings took off, carrying its cargo of wounded. The pilot looked down at the flag for a moment and then guided the machine through the low cloud, away from the bridgehead, the groans of the wounded loud in his ears.

TASK FORCE BATTALION

Tom Lambert

Star

A STAR BOOK

Published by

the Paperback Division of

W.H. ALLEN & CO. LTD

A Star Book
Published in 1983
by the Paperback Division of
W.H. Allen & Co. Ltd
A Howard and Wyndham Company
44 Hill Street, London W1X 8LB

Printed in Great Britain by
Hunt Barnard Printing Ltd, Aylesbury, Bucks.

ISBN 0 352 31325 0

For all the men and women who served in the South Atlantic.
Particularly those who didn't return.

'. . . We are not prepared to compromise
the liberty of the Falkland Islanders'
- Prime Minister Margaret Thatcher

'. . . It is not an invasion, but the recovery
of territory which is Argentina's'
- General Leopoldo Galtieri

GLOSSARY OF MILITARY TERMS

SLR — Self-loading rifle
GPMG — General purpose machine-gun
LSW — Light support weapon
SMG — Sub-machine-gun
HMG — Heavy machine-gun
GTA — Ground to air (missile)
HB — Heavy barrel (usually regarding a machine-gun)
Lance-jack — Army slang for a Lance-Corporal
'Shiny Sheff' — Nickname for H.M.S. Sheffield

One

The landing craft rocked uneasily in the choppy water off San Carlos. Ronnie Moss steadied himself on the rope ladder for a second before stepping down into the amphibious vehicle where a number of other men in his platoon already waited. It was pitch black and Moss could scarcely see a hand in front of him. For him and the hundreds of other men in the nearby landing craft the night had become one of noises: the persistent howling of the icy wind which swept in from the west, the lapping of the waves against the hull of HMS *Fearless* and, above all that, the thunderous roar of cannon fire from the ships further out to sea.

For over two hours now, the night sky had been alive with the incessant roar of heavy guns and the unending plumes of fire which signalled another explosion. The blanket of shells was designed to cover the landing, but Moss was not the only one amongst the Paratroops who felt perspiration run on his forehead, despite the cold. Many still had the terrible vision of enemy troops sitting patiently behind their machine guns just waiting for the British to come ashore.

Moss felt powerful hands pulling him into the landing craft and he found a place between two other men of his platoon. They watched, mesmerised, as the dark sky was lit a vivid shade of orange by the unending series of powerful blasts which pulverized anything beneath them. Shells from the massive 4.5 inch guns on the ships out to sea came hurtling in, the whistle of their arc drowned by the deafening cacophony. The after-shock came like rolling thunder, sweeping across San Carlos bay like an almost palpable blanket of sound, threatening to tilt the very bulk of the *Fearless* itself. The black hills of East Falkland stood out in sharp silhouette against the blazing backdrop of countless explosions. Moss watched the bombardment in awe, wondering if the entire range of low cliffs which masked the beach were going to collapse under the onslaught of so much high explosive. The low cloud which hung over the bay seemed like just more smoke. Great mushroom clouds of choking fumes wafted lazily across the sky, bringing the smell of cordite and burning wood.

It seemed like an eternity to Moss, waiting until the last Paratrooper was safely in the landing craft. He looked up into the darkness, as did many other men, conscious and fearful of the ever-present threat of air attack. Moss swallowed hard and squinted into the night as if expecting, at any moment, to see a squadron of Skyhawks come screaming out of the west, cannons blazing.

'That's some bleedin' firework display,' whispered Steve Fisher. He was about a year older than Moss and, at nineteen, already carried the single stripe of a lance-corporal proudly on his sleeve. He bit a thumb-nail abstractedly as he watched the continuing bombardment.

Moss sucked in a deep breath as he heard the engine of the leading assault craft rattle into action and, a second later, there was a violent lurch as his own vehicle moved slowly through the water. The steady chugging of the engine seemed conspicuous in the silence which had suddenly descended. All the men were immediately aware of the fact the bombardment had ceased. They were on their own now and that knowledge only added to their trepidation.

'Can't this fucking thing go any faster?' asked Bill Turner, anxiously, squinting through the gloom. The beach, more than a hundred yards from them, was almost invisible.

'Are you in a hurry to get there then?' asked Sergeant James, his voice rasping through the darkness.

'No, Sarge,' said Turner.

'Then shut it,' James told him.

One or two of the men giggled nervously. Ronnie Moss gripped his rifle tightly, the bulk of the L1A1 SLR at least reassuring him to some extent. Although, he reasoned, it would do him no good if the Argentinians *were* waiting for them.

Alan Carter stood impassively as the assault craft drew nearer the beach. He had his eyes lowered, his mind concentrated on what he would do when he reached the beach. He knew what he had been told to do, he knew what he must do. Find cover as quickly as possible—if there was none there, make it yourself. Carter stroked his chin thoughtfully. Maybe the Argentinians would be waiting for them. In a way he hoped they were; at least that way there would be no half measures. The men would know what to do immediately. Carter had seen enough of skulking about in darkness during his three spells in Northern Ireland. There, you never knew where the bullets were going to come from; at least out here, he thought, they were facing an enemy on a more equal basis. No house-to-house searches here. From what they had been told, East Falkland was as open and desolate as anything on God's earth. Not the ideal place to fight a war but then, Carter reasoned, there was no such thing as an ideal war. He'd seen plenty of action during his time in the army, both in and out of uniform. Approaching his thirty-seventh birthday, Carter had joined when he was eighteen and, as well as his time in Northern Ireland, had also seen a little action in Aden. But the crescent-shaped scar which he carried beneath his left eye had been a legacy of neither of those hell holes, rather of a pub in Bayswater—and it was a bottle scar, not one made by a bullet. He touched it almost lovingly, the memory of that night suddenly and unaccountably coming back to him. He'd been on leave, enjoying a quiet drink in the pub where he'd been going ever since he could lift a pint pot, when a group of youths, none of them over eighteen, had come in. The landlord, a friend of Carter's, had refused to serve them and the little bastards had started cutting up rough. One of them threw a dart at the landlord and, when Carter stepped in to stop them, the second youth had bottled him. Overcome more by anger than pain, the soldier had floored all four of the youths, breaking a bar stool over one of their heads.

He smiled to himself, wondering why that particular memory should surface at a time such as this.

He looked across at Moss. The kid had barely finished his training and Carter could see the look of worry on his face, his eyes bulging whitely. They were all the more prominent for being framed by the black camouflage grease which the men had smeared on their faces. They looked like heavily armed Black and White Minstrels.

Fifty yards to the beach.

'I forgot to bring my bucket and spade,' said Ossie Morris.

'You'll be digging your own bloody grave if you don't shut up,' rasped James. 'Everyone get ready.'

Forty yards.

The silence was deafening, broken only by the chugging of the engines and the splashing of the water as the assault craft drew nearer. The black hills and small cliffs seemed to crowd in around the men as they approached the beach and smoke could still be seen rising in lazy plumes from the cannon-blasted positions. The men in the assault craft on either side also prepared themselves for the moment when the ramp was dropped, which would signal their arrival on the island.

Thirty yards and the engines were shut off, the assault craft gliding smoothly over the choppy water of the inlet. The only sound now was that of the amphibious vehicles to the rear, the ones which carried the Scorpion light tanks.

Moss tried to control his breathing but it was coming in short gasps. He felt a steadying hand on his shoulder and looked round to see that it was Carter. The older man looked at Moss and nodded, the gesture saying— 'Everything's going to be all right.' Moss wished that he had Carter's faith. He had always looked to the older man for guidance and reassurance, ever since he finished his training. The platoon had welcomed him into its ranks and the youngster had found Carter particularly helpful. He had treated the boy as a father would treat a son and Moss had been grateful. Right now though, no one in the world could have stilled his anxiety. But he was not alone. Most of the men felt that uncertainty, the surge of adrenalin which would, any second, send them racing from the landing craft and up onto the beach.

Into the sights of Argentinian machine-guns?

They could only wait and pray.

Twenty yards and the craft began to slow down. Sergeant James pushed his way to the front of the vehicle, standing close by the ramp. No one uttered a sound.

Turner's stomach rumbled loudly and Morris dug him in the ribs. The two men steadied themselves.

Ten yards.

The ramp was dropped. There was a splash and then, suddenly, everyone was moving. In all four of the assault craft, Paras were suddenly aware that the moment had come. They flooded forward, splashing into the icy water which lapped up as high as their waists. Rifles held high above their heads, they waded ashore.

Moss gasped as he felt the water close around him. His heavy boots sank into the soft sand beneath the surface and, for a second, he thought he was going to go under. A wave buffeted him and he swayed, but Carter shot out an arm to prevent him falling and, side by side, they waded through the freezing surf. Cursing under his breath, Tom Harris struggled up alongside them carrying one of the GPMG's. Behind him came Bill Turner, his chest criss-crossed by belts of ammo for the machine gun. He reminded Moss of something out of an Italian Western.

All along the beach the Paras advanced, led by their officers and NCO's whose eyes were ever watchful for any hint of movement from in front of them. The leading squads finally reached the shallows and quickened their pace.

'All right,' hissed Sergeant James. 'Move it.'

The men tried to run, slowed down to a certain extent by the water and the soft sand but, eventually, they found themselves on the beach itself. They fanned out, looking for cover, heading for the few buildings which were scattered about less than fifty yards from them. Up a slight incline, these looked ominously quiet in the darkness and Moss checked slightly as he saw what looked like a barn ahead of him. But, led by Carter, he ran on, ducked low, the rifle held across his chest. His heart was thumping madly against his ribs now but it was a feeling of relief he felt as well as fear.

Relief at feeling firm ground under his feet after so long on the ship.

The smell of salt water was strong in his nostrils and he could feel it sloshing about inside his boots, leaving a trail of sodden boot marks in his wake.

There was a small embankment just ahead of them and Moss threw himself down behind it, his rifle pressed tight to his shoulder. Other men joined him while Carter and a number of the others scuttled off towards the buildings to check for any signs of the enemy.

Moss noted that the man beside him had an infra-red night-scope fitted to his rifle and he was scanning the area ahead carefully. Through the scope, the man could see the Paras approaching the cluster of buildings which stood at the top of the incline. Of the Argentinians, there was no sign.

Carter and James paused on either side of the doorway which led into the barn. Then, at a signal from the sergeant, they both dashed in. Immediately assailed by the smell of damp straw and wood, the two men ducked low, weapons levelled.

James pointed to the upper loft of the barn and, covered by him, Carter scuttled up the rickety wooden ladder which led to the loft. He hauled himself through the small hatch and lay on his belly, the SLR pressed to his shoulder. A quick glance around told him the building was deserted.

'Clear,' he called down, clambering back through the hatch.

'I reckon they lost their tops,' said James. He kicked at an open, discarded box of ammunition lying nearby. Indeed, as the two men emerged from the barn, they saw that other Paras were discovering the same thing.

The Argentinians had fled.

James glanced at his watch. It was 4.00 am. He turned to see the familiar figure of Colonel John Clavell approaching. The officer drew nearer, his long loping stride making him instantly recognisable. He had a Browning pistol gripped in his fist.

'All right, Sergeant,' he said. 'Bring your men on and I want details sent out to check the surrounding areas.' He stroked his chin thoughtfully. 'I want to know just how far the bastards have retreated.'

James saluted, watching as the officer scuttled off, calling more men to him.

Moss, now up on his feet, turned to see half a dozen more landing craft approaching the beach and, seconds later, more troops were wading ashore. The silence of the approach had been rapidly replaced by the clattering of equipment as men ran into positions and orders were shouted to them.

There was a particularly loud splash followed by the harsh roar of engines and the youngster saw the first of the Scorpion light tanks charging from the landing craft and up onto the beach, sending a fine film of spray up behind them as their tracks churned through the mud and sand. Three of them turned to the left and headed for the open country beyond the small settlement and Moss heard the bleating of sheep as their herds were scattered by the swiftly moving tanks. Clouds of bluish diesel fumes now began to mingle with the salty smell of the air, brought in with the freezing wind. The men shivered as they went about their business of digging in, quickly pulling entrenching tools from their packs as they worked to create slit trenches.

Carter saw a group of sappers hastily carrying forward boxes of ammunition and, away to his right, some artillerymen were preparing a position for the 105mm guns which had also been brought ashore. He saw mortars being carried up the beach, and men carrying heavy machine guns and boxes of ammo.

Moss passed some engineers who were erecting radio aerials and he heard one of them relaying information.

'Ashore safely,' he was saying. 'No casualties. No sign of the enemy.'

The buildings which made up the settlement reminded Moss of whitewashed Nissen huts and he could see the men of his battalion digging in just beyond a group of these buildings.

'Come on, sonny boy,' shouted James. 'This isn't a sight-seeing trip. Get your bloody finger out.'

Moss started digging, the slimy mud making it difficult. Each time a spadeful of earth was removed, the hole would immediately fill up with glutinous mud. Already many of the men were up to their ankles in it.

'If I'd have known it was going to be like this, I'd have stayed on the fucking ship,' said Turner, dejectedly.

'I didn't expect them to clear off without a fight,' Morris offered.

'Bleedin' good job they did if you ask me,' Fisher said, smiling. 'I can't say as I would have hung about with all that shit the Navy were dropping on them.'

'I wonder when we're going to get some food?' asked Turner.

'Jesus Christ,' muttered Vince Jennings. 'Is that all you ever think about, your bloody guts?'

Turner threw a spadeful of earth over his shoulder and grunted indignantly. 'Of course it's not,' he said. 'But I'm hungry.'

'You're always bleedin' hungry,' Fisher told him.

'Shit,' howled Jennings, hopping about on one leg, holding his foot. 'I just hit my bloody toe with that shovel.'

'You should look what you're doing,' Corporal Wallace told him. Wallace, 'Knocker' to the troops, was in his late twenties and was instantly recognisable to all in the regiment because of the horrendous, almost disfiguring birthmark which covered half his face. Purple in places and inclined to grow bright red in the heat, it made Wallace look positively grotesque, but the men of the platoon had come to accept it. Only Moss felt the occasional twinge of discomfort when he looked the corporal full in the face but, he told himself, probably even he would come to terms with it eventually.

Wallace had gained his fighting abilities partly because of the birthmark. He was a Geordie, born and brought up in Sunderland, and the hideous mark had made him the butt of every schoolboy's joke going when he'd been a kid. He'd lost count of the number of times he'd cracked people for making comments about it. It had landed him in jail once. During an argument he'd laughed at another youth when the boy blushed.

'Maybe I'm red now,' the boy had said. 'But at least I won't have it for life.'

Wallace had completely lost control and nearly killed the boy with a lump of wood. He'd got eighteen months in Strangeways for that, and he still thought himself lucky. The other boy had been unconcious for two days and had finally left hospital with 200 stitches.

Now Wallace continued digging, urging the men around him to hurry up. The slit trench would at least give them some cover from the biting wind. It seemed to have increased in severity since they first landed and the men shivered as they worked. A particularly powerful gust blew Turner's red beret off, much to the amusement of the other men. He had to chase several yards to catch it, watched by Sergeant James.

'Fed up with digging are you, Turner?' he said. 'Fancy a bit of exercise.'

Turner finally retrieved his beret, brushed the dirt from it and stood up.

'No, Sarge,' he said. 'I . . .'

He got no further.

'Well,' James began. 'If it's exercise you want, pick your gear up and come with me. Colonel Clavell wants the outlying areas searched. The scorpions are already scouting, they need some men to back them up.' He pointed towards five other men nearby. 'All you lot, move yourselves. We didn't come here for a fucking holiday, we came here to kill Argentinians, now move it.'

The men designated hastily grabbed their equipment and joined Turner and the sergeant.

'You know I think he means it,' said Phil Anderson.

Fisher looked puzzled. 'Means what?'

'That we're here to kill Argentinians.'

Fisher laughed.

'Well what the bleedin' hell did *you* think we were here for?' asked the cockney lance-corporal.

'We're here to regain the islands for Britain,' said Anderson.

Fisher laughed. 'Well, the Argies aren't going to give them back to us on a bleedin' plate are they? 'Course we'll have to kill a few. Anyhow, so what if we do? They shouldn't have invaded in the first place should they? It was our fucking island. This is a piece of England.' He held up a lump of mud in a symbolic gesture. The men returned to their digging.

All over the beach and its surrounding hillsides, the Paras were hastily completing their network of trenches. Anti-aircraft positions and radios were being set up and the men knew that, soon, Sea Kings would be bringing in supplies.

In fact, when Moss first saw the dark shapes moving through the sky towards the beach-head, that was what he thought they were. Against the grey sky of approaching dawn, the oncoming objects moved like black arrowheads. Then he heard the steady rumble and saw that they were travelling at such an impossibly high speed they could not be helicopters.

'Jesus Christ,' he murmured.

The noise of their engines grew louder, finally turning into a high-pitched shriek as they bore down on the Paras.

The leading wave of Skyhawks, four of them, swung in low, their 20mm cannons firing as they approached. The heavy shells spattered across the surface of the water before drilling their way up the beach. There was a series of explosions and, barely fifty yards away, Moss saw three men hurled into the air by the blast.

'Take cover,' roared Wallace but the men needed no prompting. They threw themselves down, trying to bury their bodies in the hastily-dug slit trenches, knowing that if any of the aircraft were on target with either bombs or machine-guns, they would have little chance.

Carter crouched down, watching as the first wave passed overhead, their engines trailing vapour into the chilly morning air, the whoosh as they swept by nearly deafening him.

'Skyhawks,' Robin Brent told him.

It was then that the second wave came screaming in. Wailing like banshees, the Mirages roared in low, strafing the British positions with machine-gun fire. Tracer flashed through the gloom, drawing dotted lines of death across the sand. Moss lay still in a foetal position, his eyes closed. His head seemed to be bursting, as the noise of the Argentinian planes grew louder, filling his ears with their powerful howl.

One of the leading planes released its bomb and the deadly metallic object sped to earth where it exploded. A shrieking geyser of fire and mud was flung fully twenty feet into the air and Carter saw men falling, saw bodies tossed about like leaves in a high wind. And then more bombs were dropping. The ground beneath them shook under the repeated impact. Fountains of water and bloodied sand cascaded over the men and Wallace raised his head in time to see one of the deadly projectiles fall to earth near the barn, less than twenty yards from where they lay. The impact caved in one side of the barn, the wall crumbling inward as if struck by a giant fist. Lumps of wood and metal spiralled into the air, some flashing over the heads of the Paras, missing them by inches.

Brent, chancing a look up, was hit in the side of the head by a lump of shrapnel about the size of a man's fist. It slammed into his helmet, knocking him off his feet. He sprawled headlong in the mud and Wallace hastily scrambled across to him. Brent rolled onto his side, his eyes glazed and Wallace hastily pulled off his helmet to see if the lethal chunk of metal had done any damage. There was no sign of blood. It appeared that Brent was merely concussed.

The Skyhawks wheeled and came roaring back for a second time, but at last the British anti-aircraft crews seemed to have recovered their senses and a solid wall of fire met the second attack. The troops themselves swung their rifles up and began blasting away at the attacking planes, which in turn, opened up once more.

Air bursts dotted the heavens, great clouds of smoke rolling across the beach and, all around, the staccato rattle of automatic fire offered a high pitched accompaniment to the rumble of exploding bombs and the insistent screams of the Argentinian planes.

One of the Skyhawks was hit.

There was a sudden flash of brilliant orange flame from just behind its left wing; then the aircraft cartwheeled in the air, the nose dipping viciously as the pilot fought to keep control. A second later, the plane exploded in a blinding ball of white and orange flame. Lumps of blazing metal showered the troops below. A large fragment landed near Moss, where it hissed angrily on the wet ground. He himself was firing for all he was worth, the heavy sweat of fear clinging to his back. He was pale, his face drained of colour, but he knew what he had to do and, with Carter at his side, the lad fired at the attacking enemy aircraft. Empty shell cases flew from the SLR's, raining down like brass confetti as they fell to earth.

'Where the fuck are our planes?' said Wallace, his finger still tight around the trigger of his rifle. He cursed when the hammer smashed down on an empty chamber and hastily slammed in a fresh magazine.

Then, as if in answer to his question, out of the north, more aircraft could be seen—though none of the men on the ground had any time to watch for them. The Mirages came hurtling in once more, another deadly cargo of bombs falling on the British positions. Carter saw a man decapitated by a lump of burning shrapnel. The body seemed to remain upright for a second, the severed stump of the neck spouting blood into the chill morning air, before it pitched forward into the mud. The head itself rolled for some distance like a discarded football. That same blast tore open the thigh of another Para and Carter had time to glimpse a medic rushing to the man's side, trying to fasten a tourniquet around the shattered limb. Blood was jetting wildly from the wound and Carter realized that the man's femoral artery must have been severed.

A hand on his shoulder alerted him to the fact that a squadron of Sea Harriers had finally reached the battle zone.

'They're ours,' said Brent, thankfully, and now all eyes turned to the swiftly moving British planes as they roared in towards their prey.

The Mirages and Skyhawks may have been capable of greater speed but they lacked the manoeuverability of their opponents. The men on the ground saw the first of the Harriers release its Sidewinder missile. The deadly projectile locked onto the heat left by a fleeing Mirage and raced after it. Moss could imagine how the Argentinian pilot must have felt, trying to outrun the lethal missile. Knowing he was racing death. The Sidewinder hit its target and there was a thunderous blast, the Mirage disappearing beneath a shrieking ball of fire. What remained of the pilot fell to earth along with the wreckage of his plane. The Harrier then turned, looking for fresh prey, its 30mm Aden machine guns blasting away at the nearest enemy plane.

The sky was filled with the whine and roar of aircraft as the British pilots outmanoeuvered their enemy counterparts with a skill that was mesmerising.

Missiles and tracer fire flashed across the grey dawn sky and, time after time, enemy planes were sent crashing to the ground. One of them, hit in the side by a burst of fire, came hurtling towards the beach itself and Carter watched as the men beneath it ran for cover. Still carrying its bomb load, the devastated plane now became a massive missile itself. It hit the beach and exploded with a deafening roar. The heat wave rolled over the men nearby like a blanket and the aftershock sent many of the Paras staggering. A huge cloud of smoke rose from the wreck and mushroomed out like a vast black umbrella, flames leapt high into the air and there was another explosion seconds later as one of the bombs detonated due to the fierce heat.

The air was full of tiny cinders which reminded Moss of those little black flies which infest the countryside on warm summer days. He was finding it difficult to breathe because of the heat and the choking smoke but, as the wind parted it, he kept his eyes on the heavens where the aircraft were still fighting out their deadly duels.

Half a dozen Argentinian planes were blasted from the sky. The last of them, its tail blown off, pinwheeled towards the ground bleeding black smoke into the air behind it. The pilot managed to eject but, even as he began to fall, he saw one of his own planes hurtling towards him. The swiftly moving Mirage could not avoid him and the tip of its wing caught him just below the sternum, slicing the body completely in two. The legs fell to earth but the parachute opened and the severed torso floated gently to the ground, a confetti of entrails dripping from it.

It was with a mixture of triumph and relief that Carter saw the remaining enemy planes finally turn and speed away, chased a short distance by the victorious Sea Harriers. Then they too swung away and headed back to where they'd come from, disappearing through the low cloud like mysterious saviours who, now their job was done, were no longer needed. The troops on the ground watched them go, the shock of what had just happened numbing them momentarily. But then, almost inevitably, it was Wallace who brought those around him back to their senses.

'All right,' he roared. 'The fun's over, let's get back to work.'

Moss ran an appraising eye over the battered British positions, now cratered in a dozen places, the shattered remnants of enemy aircraft still blazing like funeral pyres where they'd fallen. Medics were attending to the wounded. There were men dashing back and forth all around him, orders were being shouted, officers re-organising their men. Moss saw Colonel Clavell walking amongst the men, checking with battalion commanders on their losses, although despite the ferocity of the attack the British had escaped relatively lightly. Moss didn't know how many men in his own platoon had been killed or wounded but, as he helped clear some wreckage from the slit trench, he saw two men being helped towards the beach. One was bleeding badly from a wound in the cheek which had torn away a large flap of skin to reveal the shining white of teeth beneath. The man's face was a pulped mess, torn and pitted by tiny pieces of shrapnel. The second man was being carried by two of his comrades and Moss blenched when he saw that the Para's leg was almost severed. A tracer bullet had hit him just below the left knee, shattering his shin bone, the jagged ends of which protruded through the torn flesh. His trousers had been cut away at the thigh to prevent the material of his uniform rubbing against the terrible injury. He was moaning quietly as the other two carried him past.

By now, dawn had well and truly broken. A dirty, grey dawn which was filled with low hanging cloud and rain-filled wind. Moss shivered as he continued digging the slit trench, turning when he saw the first of the Wessex and Sea King helicopters hovering lazily over the beach, dropping majestically to land. The lad watched as the wounded were helped into one of the Sea Kings. Meanwhile, other men were hurriedly unloading supplies from the three or four Wessex. He watched as Morris, Fisher and the little Scotsman, Jim Robertson, scuttled across to the nearest chopper to collect supplies for their platoon. The steady whirring of the rotar blades sounded like huge rice flails in the stillness of the morning.

'You all right?'

Moss turned to see Carter looking at him.

The youngster looked vacant for a moment.

'I said, are you all right,' Carter repeated.

'Yeah,' Moss said, swallowing hard. 'I must admit though, I thought they were going to hit us harder than that.'

'I'll give them a call if you like,' said Vince Jennings. 'Perhaps they'll come back and do an encore.'

'You know what I mean,' said Moss. 'Didn't you expect that they'd at least be waiting for us when we came ashore?'

Jennings grunted. 'They've probably got something lined up for us when we get further inland.'

Moss nodded, nervously, and looked across at Carter. The older man smiled and shrugged his shoulders.

'I bet they've got every gun they can find ready for us when we move out of this bloody bridgehead,' Jennings muttered.

'It's being cheerful that keeps you going, isn't it?' said Carter.

'Well, what the hell do *you* think they're going to do?' Jennings demanded.

Carter's smile vanished. 'I wish I knew.'

Fisher and the other two returned carrying boxes under their arms and Moss could see from the strain on their faces that whatever they held was heavy. Robertson dropped the two boxes he held and wiped his hands on his trousers.

'Careful, Robbo,' said Fisher. 'Chucking them about like that, the bleedin' things could go off.'

'Ammo?' asked Carter, watching as the lance-jack carefully put down the crates he was carrying.

Fisher nodded. 'Yeah. And medical supplies. Take as much ammo as you can carry. The chopper pilot says that with the weather being this bad they don't know how often they can make drops.'

'That's bloody handy,' said Jennings, dejectedly.

'Wrap up, smiler,' said Fisher. 'Just fill your pouch and stop bellyaching.'

The box lids were prized off, Fisher using his bayonet to do the job, and the men watched as he peeled back the aluminium foil which covered the ammunition. Beneath it lay row upon row of 7.62mm slugs and the men took turns, filling their ammunition pouches, slotting fresh bullets into half-empty magazines.

'I wonder where old Jamesey's got to,' Morris wondered aloud. 'He's been gone for half an hour.'

'Perhaps the bloody Argies *are* waiting for us inland,' Jennings intoned.

Carter looked across at him, his brow wrinkled.

A moment later, the men turned as they heard the familiar rattle of tank tracks and one of the Scorpions appeared over the incline to their right. Behind it came a column of troops, some, Moss noticed, with their hands placed behind their heads. As the column drew nearer, the Paras realized that the grey-clad troops flanked on either side by the familiar camouflage-clad men of their own side, were Argentinians.

'Bleedin' hell,' exclaimed Fisher. 'Looks like old Jamesey's gone and caught himself some prisoners.'

Sergeant James strode along at the head of the column, Captain Palmer at his side. Moss could see that the two men were talking and, as they drew nearer, James and a couple of other paras peeled off from the column and rejoined their platoon.

'Where did you find them, Sarge?' asked Wallace, indicating the dejected looking Argentinians. He scanned the row of sanguine faces and counted nine of them.

'There were about forty hiding out in the hills about a mile from here,' James explained. 'Those lot gave themselves up. The others just chucked away their weapons and pissed off.' The sergeant looked around at the cratered bridgehead, the wrecks of burned out enemy planes, the blood-flecked sand.

'What happened?' he asked. 'We heard the firing.'

'Skyhawks and Mirages,' Brent told him.

'Shit,' murmured the sergeant, looking around. He saw two men lifting the corpse of an engineer onto a stretcher. A blanket was hurriedly placed over the body but, as the men passed nearby, James could see the blood soaking through the thick material. 'Did we lose any men?' he wanted to know.

'*We* didn't,' Wallace told him, referring to the platoon. 'I don't know about the other units.'

'Is there anything moving about out there?' asked Fisher, indicating the direction from which the column had just come.

'There's some more houses,' James told him. 'But no Argies. The captain said that we should move on in about half an hour. The other units, the ones that are going to take the northern route, will be moving out in the morning. But,' he paused, smiling enigmatically, 'there's something we've got to do first—Knocker!'

Wallace immediately began rummaging around inside his pack, and, a moment later, produced a neatly folded piece of cloth. Led by James, the platoon marched over to a nearby flag-pole which stood between two of the whitewashed buildings. There the corporal unfurled the piece of material which the men recognised as a Union Jack. He threaded it onto the cord which hung from the pole and, at a signal from James, pulled. The flag rose into the air, fluttering in the strong breeze. And now many more men had joined them, all standing and watching as the flag of their country was raised once more on East Falkland. The men saluted, watching as the ensign fluttered and a strange sense of power seemed to fill the men. Even Moss felt it. A stirring which he had not experienced before.

'Now we're here, we're here to stay,' said Colonel Clavell, who had joined the little group.

The flag moved gently in the breeze.

The first of the Sea Kings took off, carrying its cargo of wounded. The pilot looked down at the flag for a moment and then guided his machine through the low cloud, away from the bridgehead, the groans of the wounded loud in his ears.

It was 5.30 am.

Two

There were no roads leading out of Port San Carlos. Not even any dirt tracks which, Moss thought, was probably a good thing. The ground was heavy, a thick glutinous mud which made movement difficult, and the men found themselves sinking up to their ankles in it. Every footstep became a battle and it wasn't long before Moss began to feel the muscles in his thighs and calves tightening up. The men of the battalion moved slowly across the barren terrain, buffeted from all sides by a powerful wind which whipped light rain and even snow into their faces. Carter felt the tiny frozen droplets stinging his skin as he walked on, glancing around as he did so.

East Falkland was totally devoid of trees and even, it appeared, bushes. There wasn't a yard of cover to be seen on the low, undulating hills and Carter chanced a quick look upward into a sky thick with rain clouds. He, like many of the others, was thankful for the cover which the clouds offered. To a certain extent it hid them from the view of any passing Argentinian planes which was just as well because, exposed as they were, an air attack could have wiped them out. The column, with Colonel Clavell at its head, trudged along in the wake of a trio of Scorpions which had fanned out ahead of them, watching for the slightest hint of enemy troops. Behind the column, five ton Scania lorries pulled the British 105mm guns which were to be used against any Argentinian positions encountered. Though quite when and where that would be, no one knew. The Paras knew that they were to be the southern arm of a pincer movement which would eventually close on the capital of Port Stanley; but what they would find on the route and particularly the number of enemy troops facing them was still something they had to discover. Moss wondered what sort of opposition they would encounter but, at the moment, he was more concerned with dragging himself through the sticky mud which threatened to tug the boots from his feet.

'Who in their right mind,' said Tom Harris, almost slipping over. 'Would want to invade a place like this anyway? It proves the fucking Argies must be mad.'

'They think it belongs to them,' Anderson said.

'Well, they're bloody well wrong aren't they?' hissed Sergeant James. 'Now shut up and keep walking, save your breath. You'll need it.'

The men trudged on, noting that the land was beginning to slope upward slightly. Perched on the lower part of the slope was a cluster of the familiar whitewashed buildings. Some had clapboard fences around them and, at the sight of the buildings, the column slowed down. Ahead of them, the three Scorpions fanned out. One moving slowly towards the first of the buildings.

'Spread out and keep low' shouted Colonel Clavell, making a sweeping gesture with his arm. He drew the Browning from its holster and scuttled forward. Ducked low, the men of the battalion followed him, trying to find some kind of cover on the windswept hillside. Moss brushed some snow from his face. His lips felt numb from the cold and he could see his breath forming gossamer clouds in the early morning air. Carter was alongside him, the older man holding his rifle across his chest as he ran. The two of them finally found a low dip in the muddy soil and threw themselves into it. They were joined a second later by Turner who hurriedly set up the GPMG, the legs of its bipod sinking into the soft ground. He squinted down the sight, watching as Clavell, Captain Palmer and a couple of other men advanced cautiously towards the house. Moss could see a number of other Paras moving up on the flank of the building, their rifles and sub-machine guns at the ready. Palmer himself carried a Sterling which he cradled in one hand, his eyes open for the slightest movement ahead of him. The Scorpions switched off their engines and, once more, an eerie silence descended broken only by the harsh crying of the wind.

Clavell and the others were less than fifty feet from the front of the house when the door opened.

Instinctively, they dropped, weapons pointed towards the door.

Moss pressed the SLR to his shoulder, peering down the sight.

'They're not Argies,' said Carter softly as he watched the open doorway.

'How do you know?' Turner demanded, his finger still crooked around the trigger of the machine gun.

'Because they would have opened fire before now' said the older man with an air of assurance.

Indeed, as the watching troops looked on, they saw that the man who stepped from the house was in civilian clothes. What was more, he was waving. He walked to the end of his path and leant on the white fence, cupping a hand to his mouth in order to make himself heard.

Clavell kept his hand raised, ready to give the signal to fire but, a second later he heard the familiar tones of an English voice.

'Hello there.'

The man was a Falklander. Behind him a woman emerged from the house and, behind her, a small child. They walked down the path to join the man and Clavell and the others rose up and made their way across the last few yards of open ground which separated them. The Colonel turned to the troops at his back and waved them forward. Orders were shouted and the entire battalion trudged slowly forward.

Harris walked past muttering to himself and Moss could see something akin to disappointment on his face.

'What's the matter, Bomber,' asked Carter.

Harris shrugged. 'I thought we were finally going to run into some Argies' he said.

'Why the big rush?' Carter wanted to know.

'I want to get it over with,' Harris told him. 'All this hanging about gets on my wick.'

'Perhaps they'll chuck it in before we reach them,' said Moss, hopefully.

Carter shook his head. 'No chance. They're more scared of what will happen if they lose.'

The men moved forward, gradually forming up into platoons once again. Moss passed close by the house and saw Clavell talking to the man and his family. The islander was shaking the Colonel's hand and smiling. His wife even leant forward and kissed the officer on the cheek.

'Thank God you're here,' said the man, seemingly reluctant to release the Colonel's hand.

He had already introduced himself as Tom Fenwick.

'How long since the Argentinians were here?' asked Clavell.

Fenwick told him it was a matter of hours.

'What sort of shape were they in?' Clavell wanted to know.

Fenwick shrugged, looking at his wife as if seeking assistance.

'They looked tired. Most of them were kids. The oldest didn't look much more than eighteen.'

'They went in that direction,' said Mrs Fenwick, pointing south.

Clavell looked at Palmer, almost as if it came as no surprise to them.

'Goose Green' said Clavell, flatly.

'It's only about three or four miles from here,' Fenwick said.

'How were you treated by them?' the Colonel wanted to know.

Fenwick shrugged again. 'They didn't bother us much,' he said. 'A few of them asked if we had any food or drink to spare. I think they must be running short of supplies.'

'They looked cold and miserable, more than anything,' his wife added.

Palmer nodded. 'Good,' he said. 'Hungry troops don't fight as well as they should.'

The little conversation rambled on while, meantime, amongst the other houses and buildings, the Paras were being greeted by more islanders. Men shook their hands, some women kissed them. One threw her arms around Harris's neck and hugged him.

'Steady on, love,' he said, grinning. 'I've got a wife back home.'

The other men laughed.

Moss looked around at the small clutch of buildings. Buffeted by the wind and drizzle, they seemed to cling almost defiantly to the hillside. The streets which ran between them had been reduced to liquid mud by the comings and goings of Argentinian troops and equipment and he looked across to see Brent kneeling beside a set of tyre tracks. Dirty water filled the twin indentations but the Para was poring over them as if he'd discovered some priceless relic in the mud. Sergeant James picked his way across to where Brent was crouching.

'What is it?' he asked.

'Cannon tracks,' Brent told him.

'Got any idea what sort of guns?' asked the sergeant.

'Looks like 105's' he said.

Brent prided himself on being able to identify any weapon currently in use in the war, whether it be British or Argentinian. And, since a great deal of the Argentinian equipment was the same as the British, his task was made simpler. However, he knew that the enemy also possessed American, French and Israeli weapons too. A combination which could prove to be lethal. Brent had always been interested in guns for as long as he could remember. His father had been a gamekeeper on a large estate in the South of England so he'd more or less grown up with guns. He'd been taught to shoot at the age of twelve and he still remembered the first time he ever fired a twelve bore. The recoil had nearly knocked him over and he'd carried the bruise on his shoulder for more than a week but, gradually, over the years, he'd become a first class marksman. It was his love of weapons that first prompted him to join the army and his skill, acquired in civilian life, had been honed to a fine art during his years in uniform. Now, at twenty-two, he was probably the finest shot in the battalion and he regularly won the prize of top marksman at Bisley every year. He was one of the men in the battalion who carried the 4.85mm LSW. There were three allocated to each platoon, the weapons given to those men who had proved themselves to be fine shots. Brent carried the weapon with pride: to him, it symbolised his own abilities as a marksman.

He straightened up from the cannon tracks and looked at Sergeant James. Neither of them spoke. They didn't have to. Although the Argentinians were retreating at the moment they obviously intended making a stand sooner or later and, backed up by artillery of that calibre, they obviously didn't intend losing their ground easily.

Fisher, Carter and Moss were shown to an empty house where, they were told, the enemy troops had stored weapons. The lance-jack knelt beside a box of ammunition and scooped up a handful of bullets.

'They really must have been in a bleedin' hurry to get away,' he said. 'Leaving all this lot behind.'

Also in the room were several boxes of grenades, machine-gun belts and even a couple of pairs of boots. Moss looked at them all in amazement.

'Don't touch any of this,' the cockney told the islander. 'The whole lot could be booby trapped.' Then Fisher left the house with Carter and Moss in hot pursuit. The three men eventually found a couple of engineers and Fisher told them about the ammo cache. The two men hurried off into the house and Carter exchanged a knowing glance with the lance-corporal. Both of them had served in Northern Ireland and both knew the risks of booby traps. Indeed, the two of them had seen a man from their platoon lose both his arms when he picked up what seemed to be a harmless cardboard box. It had, in fact, been filled with plastic explosive and steel bolts. After a few moments, the engineers emerged from the house.

'It's clear,' said the first of them.

'They really must be in a hurry,' said Carter.

Fisher nodded and walked away to see what the remainder of the platoon were up to. He found Turner sitting on the front step of a house, a steaming mug of tea in one hand, a huge sandwich in the other. He raised the mug in salute as

Fisher passed him and the cockney couldn't resist a smile as he saw his companion stuffing great lumps of bread into his mouth.

'It was worth the trip,' he said, beaming, pieces of sandwich falling from his cavernous mouth.

All over the settlement, the Falklanders were coming out of their houses to greet the British.

Morris spotted a particularly attractive girl, the thick clothing she wore unable to disguise her fine figure. The Para watched her for long moments, running his eyes over her large breasts and shapely hips. He nudged Jennings and directed his friend's attention towards the girl who, he guessed, was about twenty. She had long dark hair which the wind ruffled, plastering it across her face. She was laughing and talking to a couple of other Paras who, no doubt, were having the same thoughts as Morris.

'What about that then?' he said, lecherously.

Jennings nodded. 'Not bad,' he said.

Morris turned round, flabbergasted. 'Not bad?' he said. 'She's fucking beautiful.'

'That's a bit of an exaggeration,' Jennings said, scornfully.

'Look at the tits on her,' Morris drooled. 'Look, mate, after three weeks at sea I couldn't give a shit if she looked like you as long as she's a woman.'

'Do you ever think about anything else?' Jennings wanted to know.

Morris grinned and shook his head.

'All right you randy little bastard, stop admiring the scenery and get a move on.'

The shout made Morris jump and he turned to see Sergeant James standing behind him.

'Christ, Sarge,' he said. 'You scared the shit out of me.'

'If you don't get in line, sunshine,' James told him. 'You won't be able to shit.' His voice rose in volume. 'Because you'll be wearing your arsehole for a hat, now move.'

The men were already forming up into columns of platoon strength, one on either side of the village, the others in what Moss took to be the main street. They stood in the sticky mud waiting for the order to move on and, when it finally came, a chorus of cheers met their ears as they marched forward. The islanders waved happily to them as they left and the troops momentarily forgot the freezing weather, such was the warmth of their send off. Turner, in particular, felt much happier. He'd eaten five huge sandwiches whilst awaiting the order to move on and the lady who'd made them for him had given him some to take with him. They were tucked away safely in his pack. The islanders followed the Paras to the outskirts of the small settlement, then stood and watched as they climbed the hillside, finally disappearing over the top out of sight.

The rattle of the Scorpions' tracks gradually receded into the distance until there was no sound but that of the familiar icy wind as it hissed and whistled around the tiny dwellings and over the bleak terrain.

'Do you think they'll take it?' said Ruth Fenwick, watching as the last of the Paras disappeared over the hill.

'Take what?' asked her husband.

'Goose Green.'

Fenwick stroked his chin thoughtfully. 'I don't know; but I bet they'll give the bloody Argies a run for their money anyway.'

Overhead, the rain clouds seemed to be swelling, as if waiting for the right moment to let loose their icy load. The wind whipped them into dense masses and the watching islanders shivered, anxious to return to their homes, wondering just what lay ahead of the men who had come as their liberators.

Three

Night brought the rain which had been threatening to fall all day. The Paras, fortunately, were already dug in when the deluge began but the slit trenches which they'd hurriedly excavated and the tents which had been erected offered little protection. Some men slept beneath the lorries, trying in vain to find shelter against the furious onslaught of wind and sleet. No one knew for sure but it didn't take much to guess that temperatures were well down near freezing. Up to their ankles in mud, the Paras broke up the supply boxes and used them to line the trenches. The boxes were made of a material which acted as an insulator and some men even wrapped it around them, finding added warmth in the cardboard.

Charcoal was used to light fires. It burned without smoke and the meagre flames were hidden by tents and pieces of tarpaulin. The men couldn't risk giving away their positions to any Argentinian planes which might try a night reconaissance.

Moss sat sipping a mug of hot chocolate, warming his hands around the steaming receptacle. He was shivering and he could feel the rain seeping down the back of his tunic, dripping from the rim of his helmet.

The crews of the three Scorpions slept inside their vehicles, sheltered from the elements.

'It's all right for those lucky sods,' said Harris, motioning towards the tanks. 'At least they're out of this rain.'

'Yeah, it might be all right now,' said Fisher. 'But I wouldn't fancy going into a fight in one of those bloody crates.'

Harris was puzzled. 'Why not?'

'Because if a bleedin' Anti-Tank shell hits you wouldn't stand a chance,' the lance-jack explained.

'The Argies probably couldn't even get one on target' said Turner, scornfully.

'They seemed to do all right at San Carlos,' said Carter, cryptically. 'Don't underestimate them.'

Harris looked surprised. 'Why the new found respect, Alan?' he wanted to know. 'You know as well as I do the bastards haven't got an ounce of guts among them.'

Carter shook his head. 'You should never underestimate any enemy,' he said. 'All right, they chucked it in at San Carlos and they cleared out of that settlement before we arrived, but sooner or later they've got to stand and fight.'

'Most of them are conscripts aren't they?' said Morris.

Carter nodded.

'I suppose, in a way, you can feel sorry for them,' said Anderson.

All eyes turned on him, almost angrily.

'Why for Christ's sake?' Fisher demanded.

'Well, like Morris said, most of them are conscripts. None of them asked to be here.'

'Neither did any of us,' snapped Fisher.

'I don't mean it that way,' Anderson said, trying desperately to qualify his statement. He could sense the feeling of anger amongst the men. 'I meant, we're all professionals. We volunteered to join the army. They were called up.'

'Sod them,' rasped Harris. 'They started the fucking war, now they're going to pay for it.'

'I looked at those prisoners we took at Port San Carlos,' Anderson continued. 'They looked pathetic, almost helpless.'

'It's a cert those bloody Argie pilots weren't helpless,' said Carter. 'If it hadn't been for the Harriers, they'd have blown the shit out of us.'

'I mean the infantry looked so helpless,' Anderson persisted.

Carter was unimpressed. 'Try telling that to the blokes we left lying on that fucking beach.'

There was an uneasy silence and Moss looked at his older companion over the rim of his mug. Carter had taken a tin of tobacco from his tunic and was rolling a fag.

Brent smiled humourlessly. 'You know, I find this whole affair slightly ironic,' he said.

The other men looked at him, puzzled.

'We're a member of NATO, right?' he said. 'The Yanks, the French, they're supposed to be our allies and yet it was a French missile, fired from a French plane, that sunk the Shiny Sheff. Those planes that attacked us in San Carlos water were Skyhawks. Built and sold by the bloody Yanks. And the other planes, the Mirages, they're French too. The fucking C-130's are Yankee bombers.' He paused angrily. 'The Argies are shooting at us with rifles and artillery that we sold them a year or two ago. Our wonderful Government led by our illustrious leader'—his voice had taken on a savage note of sarcasm—'sold weapons to Galtieri and now they're using them to kill British soldiers. If it hadn't been for Thatcher and her fucking idiots in Whitehall none of this would have happened in the first place.'

'What do you mean?' Harris asked.

'Two months before the Argies invaded,' Brent continued, 'British residents in Buenos Aires had been writing letters home about how the Argies were getting ready to launch an invasion on the Falklands. The captain of a British trawler even reported it to Whitehall but what did they do about it? Fuck all. So here we are, sitting up to our arseholes in mud because of that bloody cow in Number Ten.' He exhaled deeply, his face white with rage. He sipped at his mug of coffee, watched by Moss who had listened to the heated tirade with interest.

'This is a face-saving war,' said Brent. 'For Thatcher and for Galtieri. Both of their countries are knee-deep in unemployed people; inflation's going through the roof. This little lot just provided a convenient distraction for them.'

'You should have been a politician,' said Fisher. 'Not a bleedin' soldier.'

'The politics don't matter,' said Carter. 'The fact is we're here and we've got a job to do. That's all that matters. Our only concern is kicking the bloody Argies back into the sea. It's too late to worry about *why* the war started.' He sucked hard on his cigarette, blowing out a long stream of smoke.

Turner was chewing contentedly on one of the sandwiches which the islander had given him.

'Nice people aren't they?' he said, stuffing in another lump of bread. 'The islanders.'

Fisher laughed. 'You only like them because one of them gave you something to eat, you gutsy bastard.'

The other men laughed too.

Jennings inhaled deeply then sighed. 'Did you see that bird with the big knockers back in that settlement?' He grinned. 'If they all look like that, I think I'll stay here when the war's over.'

He reached into his pack and pulled out a copy of *Men Only*. It was crumpled and one or two of the pages were torn but, nevertheless, he began leafing through, muttering contentedly to himself. Robertson edged closer, trying to get a look.

'Push off, Robbo,' said Jennings.

'Let's have a look when you've finished,' the Scotsman asked.

'Get out. Last time I lent you one it came back with all the pages stuck together.'

The other men laughed loudly, even Brent managing a smile.

'I'll give you a couple of fags for it,' the Scot persisted.

'I'll consider it,' said Jennings, haughtily.

'You know, you must be a glutton for punishment,' said Fisher, pointing at the magazine. 'Looking at those birds in there is like making an alcoholic look at a bottle of Scotch that's inside an electric fence.'

'It might be torture but it's a lovely way to suffer' said Jennings, and once more the men laughed.

'I wish my old woman looked like some of the birds in there,' said Harris, wistfully.

'There's nothing wrong with your old lady, I've seen her,' Fisher said. 'She's nice.'

Jennings lowered the magazine and looked across at his companion. 'I didn't know you were married,' he said.

Harris nodded. 'Three years, this month. We don't celebrate our anniversary, we just have two minutes silence.'

The others laughed, Carter managing a thin smile. His mind suddenly wrenched back eight years, a vision floating unwanted into his mind. It was of a woman, a dark, raven-haired woman standing in the doorway of a house with suitcases in each hand. It had been *his* doorway. *His* wife. It seemed like an eternity since she left him. For years she'd been asking him to leave the army and for years he'd ignored her requests until finally they became pleas. When he returned from Northern Ireland the second time, this time with a sniper's bullet in his arm, she had given him an ultimatum. Either he chose the army or her. The army had been his life ever since he was a teenager and now he realized that he should never have married in the first place. He would not, *could* not leave the army. It had become engrained in him and she had told him so, she had told him that he'd lost the ability to love. And they had split up, leaving Carter with the only thing which really mattered to him. The Army. Eight years. They had been married for six but those years had receded, almost erased from his memory, as if they had never been. Carter could not contemplate life without the army; he knew he would never make it in civilian life and he didn't even want to try. He looked around at the other men in the platoon, all of them in their twenties, Moss even still a teenager. Carter suddenly felt very old.

Anderson was chewing thoughtfully on a bar of chocolate, gazing into space.

'You know, I don't think any of us really thought that things were going to turn out like this when we left Plymouth,' he said.

'Like what?' Jennings mumbled from behind his magazine.

'Everybody seemed to think it was a big joke,' Anderson continued. 'The war, everything. I know I did. I felt as if we were invincible, that the Argies were going to chuck it in as soon as they heard we were coming, but when the Shiny Sheff was sunk I started to wonder if it was all going to be so bloody easy. Perhaps we're not so invincible.'

'That was a missile,' said Carter, scornfully. 'There was nothing anyone could have done about that. Once we get to grips with the Argies it'll be a different matter.'

'You said, a minute ago, not to underestimate them,' Morris reminded him.

'I know, but they're still no match for *us*. No army in the world can match the British Army and we're not about to be beaten by a bunch of fucking cowboys.' He ground out the remnants of the cigarette beneath his boot.

Fisher nodded in agreement. 'That's right,' he intoned. 'Besides, this is our land, it belongs to Britain. The Argies will be sorry they ever bleedin' well landed here.' He raised his mug of tea in salute. 'God save the Queen' he said, smiling.

The other men echoed his toast.

The flap of tarpaulin was pulled back and Corporal Wallace walked in, looking decidedly bedraggled. Rain was dripping from his helmet and his face seemed to glow even redder in the cold. Moss averted his eyes, not able to look at the hideous birthmark. The corporal put down his rifle and gratefully accepted the steaming mug of hot chocolate which was offered to him. He held it between his gloved hands for a moment then took a hefty swallow, cursing when the hot liquid burned him.

'Christ,' he murmured. 'That's hot.'

Fisher grinned, watching as the corporal sucked in hasty breaths to try and cool his scorched tongue. Finally he turned and looked at Moss.

'O.K., Sunshine,' he said. 'You and Carter outside. It's your turn to get a breath of fresh air.' He grinned, watching as the two men picked up their weapons and disappeared out through the flap in the tarpaulin into the freezing rain and wind. The corporal seated himself on one of the torn-up supply boxes and exhaled deeply.

'Anything moving out there, Corp?' asked Turner, taking a chunk out of another of his sandwiches.

'Not a damn thing,' Wallace told him. 'Mind you, it's so bloody dark you can hardly see a hand in front of you anyway.' He looked around. 'Anybody got a fag? I'm out.'

Fisher tossed one over.

'Where's Jamesey tonight?' asked the cockney.

Wallace took a drag on the cigarette and sniffed hard.

'Meeting with the Colonel,' he said, jerking a thumb in the general direction he meant. 'I think they're planning the attack.'

The men fell suddenly silent.

Colonel John Clavell jabbed a finger at the map which lay before him and the dozen or so officers and sergeants grouped around him followed his pointing digit.

'Darwin and Goose Green,' said Clavell. 'Our objectives for tomorrow, gentlemen.' He paused, chewing on the stem of his pipe. 'As you can see we're going to have to go in frontally. We can't outflank the bastards because the isthmus is too narrow.' He exhaled deeply. 'It's the airfield we're after,' he said. 'But, as you can appreciate, we have to knock out the garrison in both towns. We can't risk a push on Port Stanley with enemy troops still at our backs.'

'Any reports on their positions, sir?' asked a tall Major who, James noticed, had the little finger of his right hand missing. He recognised the man as Major Fulton.

Clavell nodded and prodded the map once again.

'They're heavily dug in, here.' He pointed to the open ground just in front of the spot on the map which marked the Darwin settlement. 'And on the Hill of Gorse, just behind the town itself. Also, reconnaissance reports that there are heavy concentrations of artillery on the hills overlooking the airstrip at Goose Green itself. The settlement, needless to say, is very heavily fortified and manned.'

'What support will we have, sir?' asked Captain Palmer.

'Well, we're going in just before dawn at 0.400,' the Colonel told them. 'There'll be artillery support and there should be air support too. Aside from our own mortars of course.'

Everyone seemed satisfied.

'Any questions?' asked Clavell.

There were none.

The Colonel checked his watch. 'Right, well, I suggest we all get some sleep. I know it's not easy in these bloody trenches but we'd better try all the same.'

A ripple of laughter ran around the room.

'Have your men ready to move by 0.345.'

Sergeant James ran a last appraising eye over the map. The officers and other sergeants began to file out of the hastily constructed HQ.

'Something wrong, Sergeant?' asked the Colonel.

'No, sir' said James. 'Just having a look.' He smiled.

'Yes,' muttered Clavell, still chewing on his pipe stem and, for the first time, James noticed that it wasn't actually lit. 'It looks a bit sticky doesn't it?'

'Yes, sir, it does.'

'Like I said, if only we could outflank them. There's too much open ground for my liking; I just hope going in under cover of darkness will give us an edge.'

'We'll be all right, sir,' said James.

Clavell smiled.

'Your men, Sergeant, are they all right?'

'They'll feel better when they can get their hands on the fucking . . .' He paused. 'Sorry, sir. They'll be all right once they get to grips with the enemy, sir.'

The Colonel smiled.

'Yes, waiting around is the worst part of it.' He looked at James. 'Well, Sergeant, you'd better get back and brief your men then get a couple of hours' sleep yourself.'

Salutes were exchanged and James left, walking out into the blustery wind and hammering rain. Alone in the ragged HQ, Clavell leant over the map, the pipe gripped between his teeth. His eyes riveted to the narrow causeway which his men must cross in order to reach the enemy positions. He reached for the hip flask on his belt and slowly unscrewed the cap, removing his pipe for a moment while he took a hefty swig from the solid silver receptacle. It had his initials engraved on it. The flask had been a present from his wife on their silver wedding two years ago. He replaced the cap and returned the gleaming gift to its position on his belt. He crossed to his pack and fished out a piece of paper and a pen. He wrote to Winnie every other day, had done religiously ever since he first set sail from Plymouth on April 5th. He had received just one letter back so far. The mail had been held up or something, they'd given him some tuppenny-halfpenny answer when he'd asked them. God he missed her. He missed their walks through the woods which lay at the bottom of their vast garden, too, which he had come to savour over the years. But now he rebuked himself for letting his mind wander. He had important matters at hand. In just under six hours he was to lead his men in an attack which could have a critical bearing on the entire campaign. Nevertheless, with the rain pounding against the tarpaulin which covered his slit trench, he set about writing:

My Dearest Winnie . . .

Ronnie Moss shivered in the darkness, gripping his rifle tighter as he walked back and forth outside the dug-out where the remainder of his platoon sheltered. The mud was ankle deep and he found it difficult to move freely, simultaneously having to guard against slipping over in one of the many puddles around the trench. The wind howled mournfully around him and he was buffeted mercilessly by its powerful gusts which, at times, threatened to blow him off his feet. He knew that Carter was less than twenty feet from him but, in the impenetrable blackness, he was invisible. Moss might as well have been standing there on his own. The sky was like rain sodden velvet, no moon and not even a star showed through the mantle of night. Moss had never known it so dark. He wandered slowly backwards and forwards like a blind man, scarcely able to see his feet as they were gripped by the glutinous ooze. His breath made clouds in the air as he exhaled and, when his lips began to go numb, he pulled the scarf up around his chin. He stood still for long seconds, listening for some sound of movement from Carter, but the high-pitched wailing of the wind drowned out all other noises. For all Moss knew, the Argentinians might have crawled up to within a few yards of the camp and were just waiting for dawn to open up on it. He shuddered, trying to push the thought to the back of his mind. It refused to go. Visions of enemy troops blasting away at him with rifles and machine-guns filled his mind and, not for the first time, he wondered whether he was going to die in the following days' fighting. He had wondered whether he would survive after the Sheffield was sunk and he remembered the feeling of desolation which had descended over the men for a day or two. He'd seen survivors being brought aboard, men burned almost beyond recognition. One seaman had been hauled from the water, the skin of his face charred black. Moss could still remember how his eyes bulged, so white amidst the mass of raw and blackened flesh. An officer who had been hurt in the initial explosion when the Exocet first hit, his arm torn off at the shoulder, the severed stump still spurting blood despite the thick bandages wound around it. The cook, his white overalls blackened by smoke and drenched with blood which was pumping from the gaping hole in his stomach, exposing the jellied mass of intestines inside.

Those visions now swam into the youngster's mind and he still recalled them with revulsion. Was he going to end up like one of those men? The thought haunted him and, if the truth was told, it plagued many of the men who had made the 8,000 mile journey across the Atlantic to this desolate corner of the globe. Even those who had seen death at close hand before (men like Carter, Wallace, Fisher and many others) must feel that strange twinge of foreboding, Moss thought. He had once heard someone say that a man only truly appreciates the quality of life when he is faced with death. Moss knew the quality of life and he was terrified of dying, but not until the incident with the Sheffield had it truly come home to him.

When they'd first sailed from Plymouth he had scarcely had time to think about 'real' war. There had been exercises all the time to prepare the men for battle readiness but few had thought it would ever come to a shooting conflict. In fact the general concensus of opinion aboard ship was that the Argies would chuck it in before the British even arrived.

Moss stood shivering, thinking just how wrong they'd all been.

He'd written a letter home the day before the landing at San Carlos was due to take place, wondering if it would be the last time he ever got the chance to communicate with his family. He had wondered whether he would die on that beach and, when the Skyhawks and Mirages had come hurtling in, he had prayed. He would pray again tomorrow morning. A prayer spoken inwardly. He knew his mother would be in Church at home, on her knees asking that he be protected.

Home.

He swallowed hard, thinking suddenly about the house where he lived with his parents and younger brother. Moss remembered how proud his father had been when he'd joined the Paras, of how everyone in the street seemed to flock around him every time he came home on leave. There seemed to be a community pride in his achievement at becoming a Paratrooper.

Moss lived in a small town in the South of England, about thirty miles from London. He was a popular lad but, like many of his generation, had been forced to live out a life of wandering the streets. He had drifted aimlessly for the two years after he left school, unable to find work. The army seemed the only way out for him but he could not have dreamed that he would be plunged into open war so quickly. He knew when he signed up for three years that it would include a trip to Northern Ireland, but anything like this was totally beyond his imagination. Indeed, many of the other men in the platoon shared his disbelief. A large proportion had been recalled from leave to rejoin their units but they came without complaint, fired by that curious, indefinable thing called National Pride. Something which Moss himself had felt upon seeing the Union Jack raised at Port San Carlos. Something which belonged to Britain had been taken by a bunch of bloody Argentinians and there was no way the men in the British Army were going to give it up. There was a fierce resolution amongst the troops which had not been dampened by the casualties sustained.

Moss wondered how many would die the following day.

Carter, meanwhile, could hear his young companion pacing nervously up and down in the mud while he, for his own part, stood still. He had his eyes half closed, shielding them from the icy particles of snow which the wind sent lashing into his face. His mind, like that of Moss, was on the following day but not with the same trepidation. He wondered just how tough the opposition would be but it didn't worry him. If he died then that was that. He would die as he had lived. As a soldier. Death held little fear for Alan Carter. When a man's life is as empty as his was, death seemed to lose some of its terror. But Carter was a survivor. He had learned how to survive in Aden and on the streets of Belfast and Londonderry. He'd seen many men, many friends, fall, but always he came through all right. Except for that one time in Belfast; but, he told himself, that was his fault. It could have been avoided. Out there it was a different war. A battle of wits, a war of nerves. But the Falklands was a different matter. It was man to man and no one could handle himself better in combat of that sort than Alan Carter.

In a perverse sort of way, he even relished the next day's fighting, the thought of it sending a surge of adrenalin through his body. It was perhaps relief as much as anything. After being cooped up on the ship for all those weeks, it would be like a safety valve for him to finally get to grips with the enemy he and his companions had come so far to fight. And Carter knew they had no stomach for it. Most were, indeed, conscripts but, nevertheless, it was the British who were the ones forced to do the attacking. Probably, Carter thought, against prepared positions.

He gazed aimlessly in front of him, the entire landscape hidden beneath a blanket of impenetrable darkness. He could still hear Moss's boots slurping in the mud as the youth walked about, but above it all was the constant swirling of the wind as it roared and screamed like a man in pain.

Carter wondered if that sound would be echoed on the battlefield the following day.

Four

Colonel John Clavell checked his watch and watched as the luminous second hand ticked around to 4.00 am. All around him, the paras waited for the order to advance, spread out as far as the narrow approaches to Darwin would allow.

The men had been briefed earlier that morning, told exactly what they had to do and what to expect. Now they stood shivering in the wind and rain, waiting for the order to move in.

Clavell looked up at the dark sky, still full of rain clouds. It would, in thirty minutes or so, be dawn. His men had a large expanse of open ground to cover before they reached the outer Argentinian positions which were still invisible in the blackness.

He chewed his bottom lip contemplatively, feeling the Browning pistol in his fist. Less than half an hour earlier he had received notification that there was to be no air support for the attack due to the appalling weather. Clavell had accepted the decision but it made him feel all the more anxious about the impending assault. He took one more look at his watch and then waved his hand in the direction of the Argentinian positions.

'All right,' he whispered. 'Let's move.'

All along the line, the order was repeated and the Paras began their advance.

The ground which led from the hillside to the neck of the isthmus was even more water-logged than the land which the men had so far encountered and many stumbled in the filthy water, trying not to make a sound if they could help it. Officers and NCO's hissed orders and rebukes as the troops advanced.

Moss, struggling through the sucking mud and water, felt it lapping against his calves, spilling inside his boots and he shuddered.

He stumbled but Harris shot out a hand to support him. Picking their way cautiously through the icy water and glutinous muck, the Paras drew closer to the outskirts of Darwin.

Clavell, at their head, felt the ground begin to rise sharply and also, he thought gratefully, it seemed to be getting firmer. The Colonel glanced once more up at the sky and saw that the first grey fingers of dawn were beginning to probe through the rain clouds. He urged the men to move faster. There were still a couple of hundred yards between them and the first line of Argentine defence. Clavell could clearly see in the half light, the outline of a breastwork and, beyond that, the silhouettes of the houses which made up the settlement itself.

Moss, too, saw the trench ahead of him and like many of his companions nearby, instinctively dropped lower. They quickened their pace, moving as fast as the slippery terrain would let them.

'We've caught the bastards napping,' Clavell whispered to Captain Palmer who was running alongside him.

They were now less than a hundred yards from the trench and, as yet, there was no sign of movement from the enemy.

The Paras following up also quickened their step, guns now held across their chests in readiness.

Fifty yards.

The battlefield was now lit by a dull grey light which made the advancing Paras look like ghosts. Moss could feel his heart beginning to beat hard against his ribs. Carter felt that curious feeling of exhilaration sweeping through him as the men drew closer.

Twenty yards.

A solitary Argentinian soldier poked his head up lazily and looked over the rampart of the trench. He saw the advancing paras and, immediately, the British heard him shouting something in Spanish. More enemy soldiers appeared at the rampart and, a second later, the sharp crack of a rifle shot broke the silence of the morning.

But, by now, the Paras were on top of their quarry. The leading men, Clavell at their head, vaulted the low breastwork and landed in the Argentinian trench. The startled enemy troops snatched up their weapons and tried to fight back.

Clavell spun round and fired twice at the nearest enemy soldier. Both shots hit their target, the second blasting the man off his feet. The enemy troops nearby scrambled to their feet and, behind the foremost trench, the Colonel caught sight of more Argentinians running from houses. Many were firing indiscriminately and stray bullets sang through the air.

Moss saw an enemy sapper rise ahead of him and, quick as a flash, the youth swung the SLR up to his shoulder and fired. The recoil slammed the stock back against his shoulder and he winced but the Argentinian was hit just below the breast bone, the bullet powering through him, splattering those behind with gobbets of flesh and grey-red lung tissue. He toppled over.

Carter swung the butt of his rifle and smashed it into the face of an attacker. The man crumpled up, his nose shattered by the impact. The Para kicked his man onto his back, watching as the Argentinian threw up his arms for mercy. Carter dashed on.

Sergeant James clambered up the other side of the trench, the sten gun gripped in one powerful hand. He shouted in pain as a bullet scythed through his left ear and warm blood trickled down his cheek. Gritting his teeth, he opened up with the Sten, the staccato rattle of the sub-gun momentarily drowning out the shouts and curses of those men fighting in the trench. Half a dozen Argentinians fell as James swept the lethal weapon back and forth. One of them staggered blindly as a bullet tore off his lower jaw. Firing short bursts, the sergeant ran forward, finding Clavell and Wallace at his side. The three men managed to reach the first of the buildings on the outskirts of the settlement and Wallace tugged a grenade from his belt. With a vengeful yell, he tossed it into the house.

A second later there was a dull roar and, from inside, shrieks of agony. A body, propelled by the force of the blast, was hurled from a window crashing in a bloodied heap at Clavell's feet.

And now the men heard the familiar arc of a shell as the British artillery opened up, their fire directed at the enemy positions nearer the settlement itself. The huge shells sped across the sky before falling to earth where they exploded with terrifying ferocity. Argentinian troops were hurled into the air by the explosions and the breastworks of their trenches were torn apart as the fusillade intensified. The ground began to tremble under the onslaught of high explosive and the Paras slowed down slightly, for fear of being caught up in their own artillery fire. The massive shells rained down on the enemy positions and Clavell watched the great plumes of fire shooting into the morning sky as the enemy trenches and dug-outs were pulverized by the gunners' accurate aim.

The British troops were already past the first line of Argentinian defence. Those enemy troops who remained alive had hurriedly thrown down their arms and raised their hands high above their heads. A number of Paras were shepherding them away and Moss got a quick look at them. Most were no older than himself. They looked pale and frightened and one was being supported by two of his comrades. A bullet had caught him in the leg, just above the left knee and blood was running freely down his calf. One of the men didn't even have any shoes on. Rifles had been thrown down, whole boxes of ammo left untouched in the foremost trench.

The rest of the Paras by now had bypassed the frontal position and were trying to find cover amongst the half-dozen buildings on the outskirts of Darwin. They watched in awe as the artillery kept up its thunderous barrage and Carter noted that the enemy weren't replying.

Not a shot had been fired from the second trench.

'Keep low,' said Clavell, his eyes scanning the enemy positions before him.

Then, as the men watched, first one, then two Argentinians emerged from the second line trench, arms held high above their heads. Unfortunately for them, a shell landed less than a foot ahead of them and both men were catapulted into the air by the force of the blast.

Clavell turned to Private Regan, a note of concern in his voice.

'Contact those bloody gunners,' he ordered. 'Tell them to cease firing.'

Regan fiddled with controls of the radio and finally managed to get his garbled message through. Two perfunctory 105's fell to earth and blew another part of the rampart to smithereens. Then the guns fell silent. Fingers hooked around the triggers of their rifles, the Paras watched silently as half a dozen, then more, Argentinian troops clambered from their decimated positions and walked cautiously towards the waiting Paras. Through the smoke which rolled over the sodden field like choking clouds, Carter spotted more men running hell for leather, away from the trench.

'I don't believe it,' murmured Fisher. 'The bastards have chucked it in.' He smiled broadly.

Clavell watched them as they trudged forward, eyes scanning the waiting British anxiously as if they feared they would be fired upon.

'No shoot,' one of them called, his words faltering and uncertain. 'No shoot.'

Captain Palmer shouted something in Spanish and the approaching Argentinians seemed to look more at ease. They were murmuring something to one another, their hands now held in front of them to show that they carried no weapons.

'Tell them to line up over there,' Clavell told the captain who repeated the order in faultless Spanish. The enemy troops obeyed and stood in a line against the wall of a large green building which looked like a barn.

'Search them,' the Colonel said and he watched as Sergeant James and two other NCO's stepped forward, swiftly but expertly checking for hidden weapons. The Argentinians stood silently, their heads lowered as the search was carried out. The other Paras watched, feeling contempt for their beaten enemies. Only Anderson felt any sympathy for them. The captured soldiers were mere boys, the stress of the fighting and the weeks of sitting about in mud holes etched on their faces. One of them looked as if he were in tears, another was bleeding from a slight wound in the cheek. Anderson counted sixteen of them.

'They're clean, sir,' said James, turning to face Clavell.

The Colonel nodded then turned to Regan.

'Contact Bridgehead HQ,' he said. 'Tell them we have prisoners and wounded. I'll need a couple of choppers.'

Regan hastily relayed the message while the rest of the Paras followed Clavell towards the second trench. It was practically full of thick mud, the ground around it pock-marked with shell holes, the smoke still rising from some of them. There were packages of food in the trench, some split open, the contents lying wasted in the mud. There were a number of bodies lying in the remnants of the trench and a few scattered around the breastwork.

Moss saw two Argentinians lying close together, both had been killed by the same blast. One had been hit in the chest by a lump of shrapnel, the other burned to a crisp by the fireball. The stench of charred flesh and excrement was strong in the air, mingling with the pungent odour of cordite.

Turner jumped down into the trench and began rummaging around in one of the food boxes, digging out tins of corned beef and even a bar of chocolate. Delighted, he slipped them into his pack.

Sergeant James stood impatiently as a medic attended to the wound in his ear. It wasn't as bad as it looked, the bullet having just nicked the lobe, but that didn't prevent the sergeant from swearing in pain when the medic pressed antiseptic to it.

Harris knelt beside one of the bodies, a corporal who had been eviscerated by an explosion, and noticed that the man was wearing a wedding ring. Almost unconsciously Harris touched the ring finger of his left hand and a brief image of his wife flashed into his mind. He wondered what this Argentinian's spouse would say when she learned her husband had been killed.

Carter stood behind him, his gaze also falling on the dead man's wedding ring. He put out a hand and touched Harris's shoulder.

He nodded, got to his feet and followed the rest of the platoon as they made their way down the slight incline towards Darwin itself.

Moss noticed Major Fulton leading another platoon, his tunic spattered with blood. The paras kept in a ragged line as they approached the houses, splitting up at a signal from Clavell. The buildings were hurriedly searched, Moss and Fisher scurrying towards the closest one. They were met with no resistance. The house was empty. All they found were discarded rifles and yet more ammo, most of it still in magazines. Fisher, his rifle lowered, scanned the room in which they stood.

'What the fuck is that?' he muttered, motioning towards a bloodied heap which lay in one corner of the room. The stench coming from it was almost overpowering and, as Moss took a step closer, he felt the nausea sweep over him. There were bones, lumps of grey and red matter and a pool of rust coloured congealed blood around the gory heap and the youngster drew close enough to see that there were maggots writhing in the eye sockets and mouth.

'It's a dog,' he said, his voice a harsh whisper and then he turned away in disgust.

'Jesus Christ,' murmured Fisher. 'They must have eaten the bleedin' thing.'

The two men left the house and wandered out into the streets once more where many more Paras had now joined the advance. Men reported the same thing in every house. Arms, ammo, even medical supplies left behind.

The sky, by this time, was filled with the grey light of early morning and everything took on a new clarity, but the rain clouds still scudded menacingly over the settlement. The wind, ever present, whipped the drizzle into sleet and made visibility even more difficult. Clavell raised the binoculars to his eyes and squinted down the powerful lenses, turning the focus wheel until everything was clear. Before him, rising in the smoky, rain-filled morning, was the outline of The Hill of Gorse. Through the binoculars he could see several Argentine positions and he swept the powerful lenses back and forth. The hill could be outflanked but not completely bypassed. According to his calculations, it was another five miles to Goose Green and it was there that the Paras could expect to encounter real opposition. But first they had to take the damn hill.

The artillery were moved forward to the outskirts of Darwin, pulled through the quagmire by the heavy Scanias who found it difficult going in the terrible conditions, but soon the 105's were set up and the gunners were training their sights on the positions on the hill. Clavell could see that there were enemy guns on top of the hill and he realized that his men were going to come under shell fire as well as small arms' attack.

The men waited patiently while the Colonel and his officers ambled off into a nearby house to discuss the best way of taking the hill.

'The bastards haven't got much guts, have they?' said Robertson, scathingly.

'Did you see them?' said Anderson. 'Kids.'

'Kids my arse,' rasped Wallace. 'The cunts are old enough to hold guns, they're old enough to shoot at us.'

'We found a dead dog in one of the houses,' Fisher said. 'They'd eaten it.'

Sergeant James shook his head. 'I told you, they're animals, the lot of them.'

'Jesus,' murmured Jennings. 'Can you imagine that? Eating a bloody dog?' He winced.

'You'd eat shit if you were hungry enough,' said Carter.

Fisher nudged Turner in the ribs. 'Old "dustman" here would eat shit even if he wasn't hungry.'

The men laughed.

'You lot can fucking laugh,' said Turner. 'But I've used my head. I picked up some of the grub they left behind. So, when you lot are short of rations, don't come crying to me for some of this stuff.' He held up one of the corned beef cans he'd taken from the dead Argentinian.

'It might be poisoned,' said Brent, and the smile faded from Turner's lips. 'I mean, if they had all that food left, why were they eating dogs?'

Turner looked at the can for a second then tossed it aside.

The other men laughed as he unloaded his pack of captured grub. He dumped it in the muddy road beside him, kicking the cans away.

'I only said it might be,' Brent grinned.

Turner was about to say something when the men heard an all too familiar sound. The high-pitched whistle which signalled the arc of a shell. They threw themselves down, into the mud, hands clasped over their heads as the shell sped to earth. When it hit, the power of the explosion was stunning. It lifted a number of Paras twenty feet into the air and the house which they'd been sheltering behind collapsed as if it had been made of matchwood. Brent squirmed around to look up in the direction from which the shell had come. He saw the tell-tale puff of smoke wafting up from one of the massive cannons on the top of The Hill of Gorse.

'Shit,' he gasped. 'They're using 155's.'

The 155mm cannon to which Brent referred had been arranged in a battery of six on the hill top and, from there, could hit anything below them. The Argentinian gunners hastily shoved in another of the massive shells and there was another thunderous roar as the weapon spat out its lethal load.

'What the fuck do we do?' yelled Robertson, panic in his voice as another of the huge projectiles came hurtling towards them.

'Try praying,' said Carter and, next second, a plume of fire fully twenty feet high exploded into the air, mushrooming out into a cloud of black smoke. The earth shook beneath the impact and lumps of mud and stone rained down on the crouching Paras. Thankfully the second shell did no damage, apart from leaving a crater the size of a London bus in the main street. The men got to their feet, trying to find cover, not really knowing where to hide.

Their own artillery opened up in reply and Moss, hiding behind a house, saw the shells striking home on the slopes of the hill. Smoke began to fill the air as both sides let loose fusillade. Houses were flattened by the massive 155mm shells while the smaller British 105's pounded away at the waiting Argentinians dug in on the ridge.

Clavell and the other officers emerged from the house. Orders were shouted and the men found themselves moving forward towards the base of the hill. There was no cover at all, but, as yet, they were out of range of the enemy machine-guns and small arms. The artillery though, were a different matter.

The Argentinian gunners dropped their sights and sent more of the deadly missiles hurtling at the British who threw themselves to the ground in a vain attempt to avoid the murderous shells. Moss hugged the muddy soil as another one hit and he felt himself being rolled over by the after-shock. When he looked round there was a crater less than twenty feet from him. Beside it lay a Para corporal, a man he didn't recognise. The man's leg had been severed from the knee downward, the jagged lump of bone shining brightly amidst the pulped, raw mess of torn flesh and muscle. The corporal was screaming insanely and two men held him down while a medic desperately tried to apply a tourniquet to the leg. Blood jetted wildly from the torn veins and arteries splattering the three men.

Moss buried his head in the soil as another of the mighty shells screamed in, this time much further away from him. Yet still the impact made him shudder and the men nearby looked up angrily towards the blazing barrels of the 155's atop the hill. Clavell, first to his feet, gave the order to advance and, running in zig-zag patterns, the Paras continued up the hill. The British artillery by this time had got the correct range and were landing shells right on the top of the ridge.

An Argentinian gunner screamed in agony as a lump of shrapnel shaved off half his face, the scream bubbling away beneath a torrent of blood. He staggered around helplessly for a second, crimson spurting from his severed carotid artery, splattering those nearby, then with a final despairing moan, he collapsed. His body jerked convulsively as he underwent the familiar death-throes. The remaining gunners and, indeed, a number of troops on top of the hill, now found themselves the prey instead of the predators and the Paras racing up the hill were thankful that the mighty guns were finally silent.

The British gunners, sweating despite the cold, pushed in shells, ramming them into breeches which were becoming hot due to the incessant firing. Empty cases fell to the ground and hissed angrily on the mud but the fire was kept up, pummelling the hill, giving as much support as possible to the men racing up the slippery incline, drawing ever nearer to the first of the Argentinian machine-gun nests.

Led by Colonel Clavell, the men raced on, the enemy troops now in their sights. A second unit under the command of Major Fulton were moving around the westerly side of the hill where they set up mortars to cover the other platoon.

The 51mm weapons were hurriedly fixed together and, along with a few old two-inch mortars, the familiar plop of shells could soon be heard as the seven pound bombs began to fall on the Argentinians. Many were designed to explode before hitting the ground and the men on the slopes looked up to see air bursts filling the dirty grey sky. Like giant firecrackers, the bombs exploded about twenty feet off the ground showering everything beneath with lumps of red hot shrapnel.

An Argentinian sapper looked up as he heard the first of the air bursts, collapsing a second later as a chunk of burning metal the size of a ten pence piece tore into his eye, ripping its way from the back of his head. A greyish slop of brain exploded from the wound and the ruptured eye socket gushed blood and vitreous liquid in a violent fountain.

The gunners hurriedly hitched up their massive 155's to the back of trucks and, leaping into the back, were quickly driven down the hillside in the direction of Goose Green, the nine-ton guns bumping along behind.

Sergeant James, crouching in the high grass which covered the slope, saw the hasty departure and breathed an audible sigh of relief; then, sten gun held firmly in his grip, he clambered to his feet firing a short burst in the direction of an Argentinian dug-out which lay less than fifty yards away. Bullets ploughed up the earth heaped around it and, following his example, some of the other men began to bring their fire to bear on the dug-out which, as yet offered no reply. Then, suddenly, three Argentinians appeared and cut loose.

James and the others, hidden to a certain degree by the swirling smoke, dropped down again as bullets from the enemy PAM's blasted small geysers of dirt up around them.

The staccato rattle of small arms filled the air, chattering even more loudly, it seemed, than the bursts of artillery and mortar fire.

Led by Colonel Clavell, half a dozen Paras, Moss and Carter amongst them, crawled slowly towards the dug-out while the remaining men kept their enemy busy with a withering fusillade of automatic fire. Moss could feel his heart thumping as he crept through the wet grass and mud, drawing nearer to the dug-out. The defenders were crouched down for the moment, trying to avoid the furious hail of bullets being directed at their hiding place, but one of them suddenly spotted the approaching Paras and stood up. He shouted something and raked the crawling men with a concentrated burst of automatic fire. The private next to Moss shouted in pain as one of the bullets struck him in the shoulder and there was a strident snapping of bone as the slug shattered his clavicle. The Para rolled over and Moss fired blindly with his own rifle as the bullets continued to chew up the ground around him. Then he heard the powerful retort of the LSW and, on looking round, saw that Brent had drawn a bead on the troublesome Argentinian. His first shot hit the man in the arm, ripping away most of the bicep and making him drop the sub-gun. Then Brent fired again, his aim more accurate. The heavy grain bullet, moving in excess of 1,500 feet a second, hit the Argentinian squarely between the eyes. Moss watched in awe as the enemy private's head seemed to explode, the entire face and skull dissolving into crimson pulp under the impact of the shell. The bullet even blasted a hole in the back of his helmet as it powered through his head. The corpse toppled backwards into the dug-out and, as if it were some kind of warning, the other men seemed to hesitate. The enemy troops inside momentarily froze and it was at that point Clavell tossed the grenade. It landed perfectly. Right in the middle of the dug-out. The Paras heard shouts of fear from inside and then, a deafening explosion. Bodies were flung into the air by the blast and Clavell was up and on his feet before the last man had slumped to the ground. The Colonel raked the dug-out with a burst from his Sterling, then, satisfied that the half a dozen

Argentinians inside were dead, he waved the other Paras forward.

They swarmed up the hill, still keeping low to avoid the increasingly heavy firing from the machine-gun nests at the top of the hill. Mortar shells from Major Fulton's unit were still falling amongst them, but the Argentinians kept up a steady fire and, as the British neared the top of the hill, their own artillery were forced to cease fire for fear of hitting the Paras. Now only the rattle of sub-guns, the harsh crack of rifles and the occasional roar of a mortar bomb filled the air. The slopes were heavy with smoke and, in places, it was difficult to see more than a few yards ahead. Moss found himself creeping almost blindly through the fumes, the stench of cordite strong in his nostrils. He could see Carter, just to his left, and slightly ahead of him was Fisher. Then, suddenly, the smoke was blown aside and the men saw, to their horror, that they were less than ten yards from a machine-gun nest. Immediately, the gunners inside opened up, the sound much louder than usual as the gun pounded away. They dived to the ground as bullets sang over their heads, then, as Moss looked round, he saw that there was another outpost to their right. About a dozen Paras were caught in the cross-fire and Moss saw three go sprawling, one bleeding badly from a wound in his side. Carter shot out a hand and pulled the wounded man towards the shallow dip in the ground where he had managed to find cover. The Para was unconscious, his face pale, his eyes closed. Carter looked at the wound in the man's side and exhaled deeply. It was a bad one, the flesh torn away to reveal muscle and the hint of intestine.

'We're pinned down,' shouted Fisher, raising his voice to make himself heard above the thunderous roar of the machine-guns. He looked across the smoke-covered hillside and noticed that more of the Paras were sheltering in hollows as the Argentinians continued to spray them with fire. Fisher guessed that they could be no more than twenty feet from the top of the hill, but the enemy positions there were heavily fortified, the ramparts strengthened by wood and by sandbags. It was from behind two such constructions that the machine-guns were hammering away.

Brent, crouching in a hollow a little to their right, chanced a look at the guns which held them in check.

'Brownings,' he said, authoritatively. 'M2's.'

'Who gives a shit what they are?' rasped Turner, ducking low as another hail of bullets passed just above his head.

All along the hillside, the Paras were halted by the murderous fire being directed at them. Men tried to sink down into the mud to avoid the lethal concentrations of lead flying at them and many returned fire as best they could.

Moss was shaking as he jammed a fresh magazine into his rifle. Carter saw his nervousness and reached out a hand, touching the boy's shoulder. He gripped it tightly for a second and nodded. The youth swallowed hard, perspiration beaded on his forehead. Jesus Christ, he was scared.

'Where the fuck is our air support?' rasped Morris. He glanced up into the sky as if expecting to see Harriers streaking out of the cloud, coming to their rescue. He smiled momentarily when he *did* hear the loud roar of plane engines—but that joy was short-lived. A moment later there was a banshee wail of engines as six Pucaras screamed overhead, tracer fire drilling holes in the ground around the Paras.

Fisher saw them too.

'That's all we bleedin' well need,' he hissed, watching as the planes wheeled, swinging in for another pass.

Pinned down by the machine-guns on the crest of the hill, the Paras could only watch helplessly as the enemy planes swung in low, their machine guns firing, the bombs beneath them gleaming ominously in the half light.

'You fucking bastards,' roared Wallace, firing his sten gun in the direction of the attacking planes but, next second, he was diving for cover as the first aircraft sped in, dropping its bomb. There was a massive explosion and some of the men were showered with debris. This was followed by a second, then a third. Huge craters were blasted in the hillside and Moss closed his eyes as the ground shook beneath him. The whole hill seemed to be moving, threatening to crumble as more bombs hit it, each one sending geysers of flame spouting into the air.

Through the smoke, Carter could see a Scout helicopter hovering just above the remains of Darwin. It had dropped down to pick up the wounded and he could see it dipping about in the air above the settlement. It was towards the British chopper that one of the Pucaras now swung. It roared in at a staggering speed, machine-guns blazing and, as Carter watched, the helicopter swerved to try to avoid the darting tongues of fire. But it was no use. The tail was blasted off and, a second later, the entire vehicle exploded as the fuel tank was hit. The chopper disappeared beneath a cloud of red and black smoke, the rotar flying off as the stricken Scout plummeted earthward. A pall of smoke rose from its burnt out remains and the Pucara wheeled, screaming in for another attack on the Paras. Its companion aircraft were also coming in for what Moss had reckoned to be their third pass. But, as they were about to open fire, some of the men not only heard but saw what looked like giant fireworks hissing across the grey sky, heading inexorably for the attacking Pucaras. The projectiles had been fired from somewhere beyond Darwin and they bore in on their targets at a speed quicker than the eye could follow.

The first of the Blowpipe missiles struck its target and blasted it from the sky. The second was similarly lethal. Two massive balls of flame lit the morning as the decimated aircraft fell to earth. The remaining pilots suddenly seemed to have lost interest in the Paras and were more concerned with escaping the speeding missiles, another of which hit its appointed mark. The Pucaras swept past the British troops, fleeing for their lives, the last aircraft pursued by the speeding Blowpipe. It was like a snail trying to outrun a hare. The terrified pilot reached for the eject button on his control panel but he was too slow. The missile hit his plane and transformed it into a blazing ruin. His body, transformed into a human torch, was sent spinning through the air along with large chunks of burning debris, some of which landed amongst the crouching Paras. A piece of the powerful engine came hurtling out of the clouds and thudded into the soft mud less than ten feet from Carter, who threw himself down.

Moss looked up to see the two remaining Pucaras roaring away. That threat, at least, had been removed but, as if to remind him of the danger that lay ahead, a fresh burst from one of the entrenched Argentinian M2's caused him to duck down once more. The private next to him wasn't so lucky.

One of the bullets struck him in the chest, the impact lifting him off his feet and hurling him a couple of feet across the hollow. Fisher scrambled across to the man who'd been hit just above the breast-bone. The bullet had shattered a portion of his ribcage and ruptured a lung. Fisher could hear the air hissing in the wound as the man tried to breathe.

'Get a medic,' he shouted, but there were none to be found.

The Para was gasping for breath and blood was dribbling from his mouth. He held out a hand imploringly to Fisher who could only cradle the man's head helplessly in his lap, watching as his eyes rolled upward in their sockets exposing the whites.

'Oh Jesus,' rasped the lance-jack, lowering the Para's head gently to the ground. 'What the fuck are we going to do? We'll be stuck here all day if we don't get some support from somewhere.'

Colonel Clavell was thinking the same thing. Lying in a hollow about fifty yards away, he looked around at the men with him. There were nearly thirty, Anderson and Jennings amongst them. Captain Palmer crouched beside him, the Sterling gripped tightly in his fist.

'Get the men together,' said Clavell, calmly. 'We're going to have a go at those bloody machine-guns.' He checked the magazine in his weapon and peered up at the twin machine-gun nests about a hundred yards away, still thundering away at the pinned down British. Palmer nodded and scurried around the waiting men, giving out orders. Then he returned to the Colonel's side.

'We'll use smoke-bombs,' Clavell told him. 'It'll give us a little bit of cover. Hand-grenades at fifty yards and then open up on them with everything we've got.'

Palmer nodded and gave the order for the men to fix bayonets.

Anderson was sweating profusely as he did so, seeing the vicious steel gleaming on the end of his rifle. Jennings did likewise and then the men rose onto their haunches, ready for the order.

Clavell and Palmer primed the smoke-grenades then, at a signal from the Colonel, threw them. The small projectiles flew through the air, landing about thirty yards ahead of the machine gun nests. Immediately they crackled into life, thick grey clouds of smoke billowing from them. The other Paras were momentarily taken aback by the sight but then they saw Clavell and the others racing across the open ground towards the enemy positions. Unfortunately for the British, the powerful wind quickly blew the smoke away and the Argentinian machine-gunners found themselves with a clear field of fire and what looked like easy targets. But the Paras zig-zagged, drawing closer and closer.

Machine-gun fire swept back and forth as they charged and two men went down but the others charged on, now supported by rifle and sub-gun fire from the troops in the hollows. Carter saw Clavell and Palmer at the head of the unit as it charged, and he saw the Colonel tug a grenade from his belt and hurl it in the direction of one of the nests. It exploded short, throwing up a fountain of earth and stone but still the Paras charged on, into the murderous cross-fire.

Guns blazing, Clavell and Palmer sprinted across the mud and grass in their efforts to reach the enemy.

The same burst of fire caught them both.

Clavell was hit in the chest and shoulder, the first impact staggering him. He felt blood burst from the wound and his legs seemed to buckle under him. Beside him, Palmer pitched headlong into the thick grass as two bullets smashed into his stomach, knocking the wind from him. He grabbed at the wounds, trying to hold in his entrails now spilling from the jagged lacerations. He fell back, blood running freely from his nose and mouth. But Clavell staggered on, the men around him firing their weapons at the Argentinians, their initial fear now replaced by anger. Roaring vengeance, they dashed the last few yards towards the nests which opened up for the last time.

Clavell was hit again, the bullet tearing through his left lung, erupting from his back, smashing the scapula as it did so. Pieces of bone and lung tissue sprayed out as the bullet ripped through him and, finally, he fell, face down in the mud. But his men had reached the Argentinians by now and there was no question of waiting for a surrender. They hurdled the low parapet, taking the flabbergasted Argentinians by surprise.

Anderson drove his bayonet forward, skewering one man to a sandbag, twisting the deadly blade.

Jennings raised his rifle to his shoulder and fired twice, watching with something akin to satisfaction as his opponent was blown off his feet by the impact of the slugs. He spun round, looking for long seconds, into the eyes of a young Argentinian no more than seventeen. The youth had his rifle trained on Jennings but seemed too petrified to pull the trigger and, for what seemed like an eternity, the two faced each other. Then, with a snarl of contempt, Jennings stepped forward, driving his bayonet deep into the boy's chest. He kicked the body to one side.

In the other nest, the Paras were performing with similar fury, cutting down any enemy soldier who they came upon, and now those men who had been pinned down joined the advance. Moss scrambled to his feet, running across the open ground. He passed the fallen bodies of Clavell and Palmer and glanced at them briefly, then, before he knew it, he was inside the first machine-gun nest. The stench of cordite was strong as ever, but this time there was a more powerful odour. The coppery smell of blood, mingled with the pungent aroma of excrement. There were Argentinian bodies littered about the machine-gun nest, some slumped over the breastwork; others who had tried to run lay beyond on the rear slopes of the hill. Smoke drifted lazily across the hill top, blown by the wind. Moss looked around. Some of the enemy had surrendered and stood forlornly to one side with their hands behind their heads. Others had fled, leaving helmets, weapons, ammunition, even food behind. The equipment was strewn all the way down the rearward slope of the hill, scattered amongst the bodies which lay there.

Carter saw men gathered around the bodies of Clavell and Palmer. He saw Sergeant James there, his head lowered as he watched the bullet-riddled body of his CO being lifted by four other men. Two medics were there, crouching over Captain Palmer who still had his hands firmly clamped to his stomach wounds. His eyes were open and staring blankly into the sky. Carter watched as he too was lifted and carried away. The Para climbed the rampart and walked across to James who was watching the mournful little procession making its way down the hill.

'Dead?' asked Carter, swallowing hard.

James could only nod and Carter saw that he was trying to fight back the tears.

'I've fought with that man, been under his command for more than fifteen years,' said the sergeant, his voice cracking. 'There was no finer officer in the British Army.' He took a deep breath, as if ashamed of his emotion. 'God help the next fucking Argentinian I get my hands on,' he rasped and stalked off to rejoin the other men.

'Hey, Sarge,' Carter called.

James turned.

'If it's any consolation, he was my CO for eighteen years.'

James smiled thinly and motioned for Carter to join him. Together they walked across the bloodied ground towards the machine-gun nests. They passed one or two Paras who were herding more than two dozen Argentinian prisoners away down the hill. The enemy troops all had their hands behind their heads, the Paras SLR's trained on them.

'If one of them gets smart,' said James, 'shoot the bastard.'

He and Carter joined the rest of the troops in the dug-outs and the sergeant saw Captain Hansen of the first platoon peering through his binoculars, down the hill to the right.

'It looks as though Major Fulton and his men have bypassed us,' said the officer, watching the tiny dots of khaki through the powerful lenses. He lowered the binoculars and turned to Regan.

'Contact the artillery,' he said. 'Tell them we're moving on.'

Regan nodded and relayed the instructions. Hansen watched him, waiting until the message was complete, then he added:

'Major Fulton will have to be told of the Colonel's death.'

'Will the Major be taking command of the battalion, sir?' asked James.

Regan nodded, reaching for the map which he had in his pack. He spread it out before him on the shattered rampart of the machine-gun nest and traced a finger on it, jabbing at their present position. He read out a set of co-ordinates which Regan was to relay to Field HQ so that the wounded and the prisoners could be picked up. He scanned the map once more, gently pulling at one end of his thick moustache.

'We've got to reach Goose Green by nightfall,' he said.

The settlement lay just under five miles away and Hansen looked at his watch.

It was 9.40 am.

Five

As the day dragged on and morning became afternoon, there was no respite from the blustery wind and the incessant showers of icy rain.

The two sections of Paras joined up at the base of The Hill of Gorse and Major Fulton, after being told what happened to Clavell, took command of the battalion. The Paras still felt the anger seething through them at the death of their commander and they seemed to find extra strength in their tired legs as they drew nearer the outskirts of Goose Green. The countryside was still frighteningly bleak and bare, offering no cover at all except for the odd dip in the ground and there were no trees or bushes and no walls to hold in the sheep, some of which were roaming around on the hillsides on either side of the Paras. Robertson looked up at the animals, their herds depleted by pillaging Argentinians desperate for food. The sheep seemed to watch as the British troops marched on, in a wide column, towards their objective.

The clouds were still thick, hanging low over the island, but, in places, they were clearing. Patches of grey sky showed through. There was no hint of a change in the weather and the Paras found that their route was littered with abandoned ammo and weapons, the track churned into liquid mud by the comings and goings of their enemies.

Brent knelt quickly and picked up a discarded weapon. He held it before him, inspecting the piece of hardware.

'After souvenirs?' asked Jennings, smiling.

Brent shook his head, his mind on the weapon. It was about two feet in length, a short barrel protruding from a grooved grip. The butt was similarly grooved, a long thin magazine sticking out of it. There was no stock on the weapon. It looked relatively new from its sleek sheen. Brent hefted it before him.

'What is it?' asked Fisher, nodding in the direction of the weapon.

'It's an UZI,' Brent told him. 'Israeli manufacture. It's an SMG. Twenty-five, thirty-two or forty round magazine. 600 rounds a minute. Muzzle velocity about 1,280 feet per second. It'd cut a man in half from close range. Blowback action, four grooves in the barrel, right hand twist . . .'

Fisher cut him short. 'I only asked what it was,' he said. 'I didn't ask for a bleedin' lecture.'

Brent shook his head and dropped the weapon into the mud.

'America; France; Israel;' he said. 'I wonder if there's any country *not* supplying the Argies with weapons.' There was a note of cynicism in his voice.

'So what?' said Fisher. 'Our equipment is better anyway.'

'That's not the point,' said Brent. 'It's the principle.'

Fisher nodded, forced to agree.

'On your soap-box again, Brent?' said Turner.

'I suppose it doesn't matter to you that we're being shot at by weapons supplied to these bastards by countries that have publicly given support to our cause.'

'Look, all I care about is getting through this lot in one piece. If you get shot you get shot—who gives a shit which country the bullet was made in?'

'Less talking back there,' hissed Sergeant James who was trudging along just ahead of the men. In front of him were Captain Hansen and Major Fulton, both of them speaking as they picked their way through the mud. James could see Fulton motioning animatedly in the direction of Goose Green, still, as yet, hidden by the low hills and the ever present blanket of drizzle which made visibility bad.

'I wonder what my Mrs is doing now?' Harris pondered aloud.

'Probably entertaining the milkman,' said Jennings, grinning.

Harris raised one eyebrow. 'I doubt it, not unless he's fond of heights. She was eight months gone when I left home.'

'Climb every mountain . . .' sang Jennings, softly, and the men nearby laughed. Even Harris grinned broadly.

'You mean you're actually going to be a father?' Wallace said, wiping some mucus from his frozen nose.

Harris nodded.

The corporal exhaled deeply. 'Christ, as if there weren't enough like you already.'

'What do you want?' asked Anderson. 'A boy or a girl?'

'Well, actually,' Harris began, his lips beginning to crease up in a smile. 'I quite fancied a Ferrari.'

Once more, the men broke into a chorus of guffaws and, this time, Sergeant James turned and headed back towards them. He didn't look very happy.

'All right,' he rasped. 'Who's the fucking comic?'

'Sorry, Sarge,' Harris said, apologetically.

James looked daggers at him. 'Our CO and half a dozen other blokes are lying back there full of fucking holes and you've got something to laugh about.'

Harris coloured. 'I said I was sorry, Sarge,' he repeated.

'Well, when the Argies open up on us again, perhaps I can hear you laugh then. It might cheer us all up.' The NCO stalked off back to the head of the column.

Harris watched him go, feeling guilty.

'He was right, Bomber,' said Anderson. 'What with the Colonel getting hit and . . .'

Harris cut him short. 'I know all about that,' he said. 'Look, I liked the old boy too. He was a bloody good officer, and what's more one of my oldest mates copped it back there too. Did *you* see Ginger Baker?' he demanded. 'Well, I was standing beside him when an Argie's bullet took half his fucking head off,' he sucked in an angry breath. 'So don't talk to me about feeling sorry. What do you expect me to do? Moan and groan for the rest of my life? That's not what our boys would have wanted. They'd have wanted us to laugh, and they'd have wanted us to beat the fuck out of the Argies which is exactly what *I* intend to do.' He lowered his head. 'That's what we owe the blokes who've died so far. We owe them victory.'

A brooding silence descended on the column.

Moss had heard everything and now he looked at Carter as if expecting the older man to say something, but he merely smiled thinly.

'You all right?' he asked the youngster.

Moss nodded.

'Do you think it'll get worse?' he asked. 'The fighting I mean.'

'Yes,' said Carter, flatly.

As if to reinforce his fears, the men suddenly looked skyward as they heard the all too familiar roar of plane engines.

'Take cover,' roared Major Fulton as three Pucaras came screaming out of the east, skimming low over the hill tops. The Paras threw themselves down, trying to find one of the many dips in the ground—there was certainly nothing else to hide behind. They crouched in the mud as the enemy aircraft hurtled over them and Carter heard the familiar whistle as their bombs fell to earth; but, even with their heads down, the men could tell that the Pucaras were way off. The bombs fell to earth a full five hundred yards from the furthest man, all of them landing in a close pattern on a hillside. The Paras looked up to see huge tongues of flame burst from the bombs. They exploded almost simultaneously, but not with the usual roar and fountain of earth. This time huge spurts of blazing liquid erupted from the ruptured bombs and squirted into the air like some kind of fiery ejaculation. The blazing liquid flooded the hillside, immediately incinerating anything it touched. Robertson watched in awe as three or four sheep, stranded on the hillside, were turned to charred lumps in the blinking of an eye. Thick black smoke rose over the flames which continued to burn with a ferocity and power unseen by any of the Paras. The heat wave rolled over them like a blanket, even from such a distance, and a peculiar smell, something akin to the odour of marzipan, wafted in with the heat.

'Jesus Christ,' gasped Fisher, watching the inferno. 'Incendiary bombs?' He looked at Brent who was eyeing the blazing hillside anxiously.

He nodded, almost imperceptibly. 'I think so.'

'God help us if we'd have been caught under that lot,' Harris said, his face pale.

The men were still watching the blaze when the aircraft wheeled in the sky and came in again, this time from the west. Their bomb load used up, they resorted to strafing the Paras with their 20mm cannon and machine guns. The men ducked low once more as shell spattered the ground, each one exploding with a dull bang. Tracer sputtered over the mud and the roar of the high-powered engines seemed to grow to deafening proportions as the Pucaras finally sped away in the direction from which they'd originally come.

'I thought we were told no planes could get off the ground today,' said Brent, sarcastically.

'We were,' Wallace told him.

Brent grunted. 'Well, they seemed to be doing all right.'

Wallace was about to say something when the men were ordered to their feet. They hastily formed up into platoons again and, at an order from Fulton, moved on.

The ground was beginning to slope upwards once again and that, combined with the ever present mud, made the march all the more exhausting. The Paras had been on the move for well over nine hours already but they pressed on, almost eager to reach the next set of Argentinian defences, knowing that they were nearing Goose Green itself. Indeed, as they crested the hill, the men could see the buildings of the settlement ahead of them. Carter guessed that they must be less than a mile away.

Fulton peered through the binoculars, scanning the area of open ground in front of the settlement. It was dotted with dug-outs, each one connected by a hastily dug but fortified trench. Ramparts of sandbags had been built up around the sides of each dug-out and even as he watched he could see that there were several artillery and mortar positions amidst the swarms of infantry in the trenches.

Fulton split the battalion into three groups, each under command of a captain. The last group, with Moss and the others amongst its numbers, he led himself. The Paras had barely begun to move when the Argentinian artillery opened up on them but the British were fired with a determination their opponents lacked.

Moss found himself running towards the first of the dug-outs with Sergeant James and Carter close by him. The youth could hear the plop of mortar shells as they were fired and all around him the earth was ripped open as they fell. Many of the Paras leapt into the smoking craters, using them for cover.

Turner set up the GPMG on the lip of one such hole and squeezed the trigger, drilling the nearest dug-out full of holes, smiling when he saw a couple of Argentinians fall as they were hit. All around, the men threw themselves down, firing from prone positions, the officers and NCO's raking the enemy positions with sub-gun fire. James gritted his teeth and emptied his Sten gun, the shell cases flying into the air and raining down in a golden stream. He tore the empty magazine out and slammed in a fresh one, racing forward along with half a dozen of his men.

Moss saw Major Fulton hurl a grenade into a dug-out, watching as it exploded with a force powerful enough to send even the heavy sandbags several feet into the air. The dazed survivors staggered from the remnants of the bunker only to be cut down by rifle and machine-gun fire. The Paras charged on, through the first line of defence, many of the enemy troops simply hurling down their weapons, eager to surrender. Moss saw a dozen being held at gun point by a couple of paras, then the youth was ordered forward and he began zig-zagging across the desolate open ground, running the gauntlet of Argentinian bullets. Carter was beside him again, the rifle held across his chest as he ran, the gleaming tip of the bayonet winking at Moss.

A grenade was fired from one of the Argentinian PA 3's, landing away to Moss's left. He turned to see it explode. The blast caught two other Paras as they were running and both went sprawling, one rolling over and over in pain, clutching at a wound in his chest. The other lay very still, face down in the mud, a stream of blood seeping out from beneath him until it had formed a dark puddle around his body.

Turner was still blasting away with the machine-gun, effectively pinning the Argentinians down, enabling the Paras nearby to reach the dug-out relatively unharassed. Led by Carter, they hauled themselves up over the parapet, guns blazing and bayonets flashing. Taken by surprise, the young Argentinian soldiers were helpless. One or two immediately threw up their hands in surrender but the others fought back. Carter ducked beneath a blow and struck upwards, using the butt of his rifle as a club. It smacked into the Argentinian's jaw and the Para heard the sharp crack as the lower mandible was broken by the impact. The man staggered, blood spilling over his lips and Carter took his chance, driving the bayonet deep into his opponent's stomach.

From point-blank range, Sergeant James let loose with his Sten gun, the impact of the bullets nearly cutting those Argentinians unfortunate enough to be in his way in half. The screams of wounded and dying men began to fill the air, competing with the roar of explosions and the staccato rattle of small arms. Moss heard all the sounds but to him, loudest of all seemed to be the pounding of his own heart as he found himself confronted by two Argentinians no older than himself. The first was slow to move and Moss shot him down, but the second ran at the boy, a look of frenzied despair on his face. As quickly as he could, Moss raised his rifle again and squeezed the trigger.

The hammer slammed down on an empty chamber.

Moss had no time to react. His opponent launched himself and crashed into the boy, both of them sprawling on the ground. But the Argentinian had the advantage, he straddled Moss, pinning his arms and locked his hands firmly around the boy's throat. The young Para saw lights dancing before his eyes and his breath was little more than a wheezing sound as the Argentinian pressed harder. With his last ounce of strength, Moss brought his knee up in the small of his attacker's back. The grip loosened slightly and he repeated his action, slamming his knee repeatedly into the other man's back until finally, he toppled over. Moss scrambled to his feet and lashed out at his fallen opponent, the kick catching him in the temple. The steel-shod boot split open the Argentinian's skin, and blood burst from the cut, running down his face. But still he staggered up and, with mounting desperation, Moss saw that his enemy had managed to pick up a rifle. He swayed drunkenly, trying to sight the weapon and, in that split second, Moss saw a small pickaxe lying beside him. It had obviously been used for entrenching purposes. In one movement, the youth snatched it up and, with a blow combining demonic force with pure desperation, buried it in the top of his opponent's skull. There was a sickening crunch as the rusty point split the head open like an overripe peach. A sticky flux of blood and brain burst from the gaping rent and splashed Moss who fought back the hot bile he felt rising in his throat. He bent quickly, retrieved his rifle and, slamming in a new magazine, ran on. The Argentinian's blood was splattered thickly on his clothes and he could smell it, but he managed to find Carter who was in the process of shooting down an enemy officer. The older man spun round and saw the blood.

'You hit?' he asked, anxiously.

'It's not my blood,' Moss croaked.

Both of them ducked low as a mortar shell hit the parapet of the dug-out, sending a funnel of earth and steel into the air. A Para nearby was thrown off his feet by the blast, a piece of shrapnel the size of a tennis ball ripping through his left shoulder, almost severing the entire arm.

Medics were scurrying back and forth all over the field. Moss could see men being dragged away to safer positions. In some places Argentinian troops were throwing down their weapons and dashing forward, arms raised in surrender. There were shell craters all over the battlefield, some still smoking, others housing Paras. Machine-guns rattled, bullets sang around their heads and lumps of earth rained down around them. The stench of smoke and cordite hung thickly in the air and millions of tiny cinders floated about. Spent cartridge cases littered the ground, steel helmets (one of which had a large hole in it) lay discarded, weapons smashed and useless gave the entire landscape the look of a vast rubbish tip. But, most striking of all were the bodies. Corpses twisted into unearthly positions, some limbless, even one or two decapitated. Moss turned away when he saw a severed head lying less than two feet from him. And the blood. Staining the dark mud in crimson puddles, mingling with the dirty water. Above them, the sky was dark with rain, the thick cloud mingling with the streams of smoke from numerous explosions. The stench of blood and excrement, the pungent odour of burnt flesh.

This was war, thought Moss, his face pale. He fought back the nausea as he scanned the scene of destruction, something which he'd seen in films, read about but had never dreamed he would one day be part of. In films it was all make believe. The men got up and walked away when it was over. But not so here. No pretence. No sham. Real death and real pain were the only things this war had to offer. Moss saw a corporal being carried away by two of his companions, one half of his face little more than a lump of crimson porridge. He was moaning quietly as they carried him over the rough ground towards a medic who was busily attending to a wounded Argentinian who had been shot in the knee. His leg was twisted at an impossible angle, the knee cap itself hanging off to expose a network of muscles and sinews beneath. The enemy soldier was no more than nineteen and tears were pouring down his cheeks as he rocked backwards and forwards, holding the shattered limb out before him.

But still the shells and grenades fell, still the machine-guns and rifles chattered and the Paras pushed further on towards their ultimate objective. But, as they drew nearer to the settlement of Goose Green, Carter noted that the enemy were not so eager to surrender, but were fighting for every piece of ground. Officers screamed at them and the men stayed at their posts, blasting away at the attacking British who were steadily drawing nearer.

Captain Hansen and his men, away to the right, came under heavy artillery fire and were pinned down. Helpless beneath the barrage, they could only crouch in the hollows and pray as the huge shells came hurtling at them, blasting massive craters in the bog-like ground.

Carter could see many different coloured buildings which marked the settlement and he guessed that they could be no more than half a mile from it by now. He crouched on the edge of a shell crater, flanked by Moss and Fisher and fired at the next dug-out which confronted them. Brent, meantime, had managed to find a relatively sheltered position behind a rampart of sandbags and he was cheerfully, and efficiently, picking off anything within range with the LSW. The Argentinians in the trench ahead of him had only to show their heads and Brent would fire, taking careful aim, seemingly oblivious to the shells falling around him. It was like target practice for him, little more than a shooting gallery.

Harris watched as he despatched yet another enemy soldier.

'Anything off the top shelf,' he said, wryly.

Both of them smiled.

However, their brief interlude was rudely interrupted by an enemy mortar shell which landed only feet from them. It exploded noisily, blasting open the rampart, showering both men with mud and lumps of stone. Brent was knocked off his feet and dropped the LSW. Harris yelped in pain as a needle thin sliver of shrapnel sliced open the back of his hand, the wound burning for a second.

'Shit,' he rasped, looking down at the vicious cut which was bleeding freely. 'Medic,' he called and one of the men nearby scuttled over, hastily bandaging the wound. Brent picked himself up and inspected the LSW, relieved to find it hadn't been damaged. And, apart from a ringing in his ears, neither had he.

The clouds had cleared to a certain degree by late afternoon and Carter glanced at his watch to see that it was 3.30 pm. The Paras were still held in check by determined enemy resistance, but no sooner had Carter lowered his arm than he heard, for the third time that day, the roar of jet engines. But this time from behind him.

A number of men looked up, at first fearing that the enemy aircraft had circled them. But looks of relief spread across their faces as they recognised the unmistakeable outlines of the attacking planes.

They were Harriers.

The gleaming jets roared in low, hurtling towards the ground at a speed which seemed to indicate that they intended crashing into the Argentinian positions intact but, at the last moment, they opened fire with their 30mm cannons and veered away. For long seconds the ground was torn open by dozens of large eruptions and the entrenched Argentinian troops dived for cover. One dug-out was hit, men thrown into the air by the force of the multiple blasts, and half a dozen troops running for shelter were cut down as the Harriers roared overhead, wheeling round and coming back for a second strike. This time, the three of them came in parallel and simultaneously released their missiles. Those Paras who were able, watched as the rockets hissed from their firing points bleeding trails of red and white flame from their tails. There was a high-pitched scream as they sped earthward and, seconds later, three enormous explosions, each one flinging mud, rock and troops many feet into the air. Vast palls of black smoke rose from the craters and the shattered bodies of numerous Argentinian soldiers lay scattered around, some wounded begging for help from their comrades, many of whom had simply dropped their weapons and were fleeing for their lives over the empty ground between them and Goose Green itself.

Moss watched as they began to pull out, at first unit by unit in a relatively orderly fashion and then in a flood tide as panic and terror swept through them. But still, amidst all the chaos, one machine-gun nest kept up a withering fire against the Paras and Moss found himself caught up in the half a dozen or so men who had taken it upon themselves to silence this last outpost of Argentinian defiance. Led by Sergeant James, the Paras crept forward, using the abandoned enemy positions, and even a dead body, for cover. Carter crouched beside two dead Argentinians, ducked low beneath their bodies. One had been shot in the eye and the Para found himself gazing into the man's remaining socket, the orb seeming to fix him in a reproachful stare. The overpowering stench of excrement filled his nostrils but he ignored it as best he could, using the bodies as a leaning post as he fired away with his SLR. He saw James scurrying forward, the Sten gun spitting flame as he raked the machine-gun nest. The enemy troops inside replied and the thunderous roar of the Browning M2 momentarily drowned out the rattle of the British sub-guns. A Para who Carter didn't recognise went down in the furious fusillade, his body jerking uncontrollably as the heavy slugs tore into it. The multiple impact lifted him off his feet and he fell into the mud, less than a foot from the rampart of the dug-out. James threw himself down, simultaneously lobbing a grenade towards the troublesome enemy nest. It exploded with a dull boom and there were screams from inside. The Paras took that as their cue and dashed forward.

Moss was amongst the first there. He used the rampart as a kind of spring-board and leapt into the dug-out, rifle lowered. Carter joined him, his bayonet looking rusty because of the dried blood on it. Both men scanned the remains of the dug-out. Of the four Argentinians who had been inside, three were already dead. The fourth was screaming madly, trying to staunch the fountain of blood spouting from his severed jugular vein. Gradually his screams gurgled away and the body went into spasm, the sickening sound of anal discharge reaching Moss's ears as the enemy soldiers' sphincter muscle gave out, signalling his death. The youth paled and turned away, but Carter slapped him on the arm, standing beside his young friend until the youth had regained his composure.

All enemy fire seemed to have ceased and James saw Major Fulton scurrying across the smoke shrouded battlefield towards the remnants of the dug-out. The Major ran a cursory eye over the carnage before him and Moss could see that he himself was bleeding from a small cut just above the eye. With his eyes bulging whitely amidst his blood and smoke stained face, the Major looked like some kind of African warrior.

'They've pulled back to Goose Green itself,' he told the men. 'Captain Hansen reports that the troops facing him have withdrawn too.'

The Major raised his binoculars and scanned the area before him. Beyond the settlement he could still make out the shape of the Argentinian 155mm guns, but they too were silent.

'What now, sir?' asked James.

Fulton lowered the field glasses and looked at his watch.

The hands had crawled on to 6.15 pm, and the sky was already becoming dark. The officer gave orders that the Paras should dig in for the night, using the empty enemy positions for cover. Then he scuttled off to inform the other NCO's and platoon commanders of his plans. The Paras were to wait until morning before actually launching an attack on the settlement itself.

'All right,' bellowed Sergeant James. 'Let's get this bloody place cleaned up, shall we?' He jabbed a finger towards the dead enemy troops who were lying in the dug-out and the Paras set about the unsavoury task of removing them. Carter and Moss lifted one of the bodies. A youth no older than sixteen who had been killed in the grenade blast. His chest was little more than a crimson pulp, the gleaming white of shattered ribs showing through the bloodied mess of his upper torso. The two Paras carefully lifted the body over the parapet of the dug-out and dropped it down into the mud. As Moss looked up he saw a wounded Para being carried away by two of his companions and, a little closer to the machine-gun nest, a blanket was being draped over another man who had been hit by the bullets from the M2. Brent meantime was examining the machine-gun itself, musing over its parts, toying with the ammo belt which still dangled from the now useless weapon.

'All right, Einstein,' shouted James. 'Leave the fucking gun alone and help clear this lot up.'

Brent slung the LSW over his shoulder and helped Harris to remove the corpse of an Argentinian sapper. They carried the corpse, trailing blood and urine, to the edge of the dug-out and dumped it with the rest. All over the battlefield, a similar cleaning up operation was taking place as the Paras removed bodies from trenches and machine-gun nests so that they could use them as shelter for the night. The sky was growing darker and, with the darkness came more rain, whipped into the faces of the men by winds which threatened to reach gale force proportions. But, finally, the task was completed. There was no counting of casualties; that would be done in the cold light of day when the fighting finally came to an end. Moss slumped down in one corner of the dug-out and wondered when that would be. Would there ever be an end to it? Or would the war simply drag on and on? He closed his eyes for a moment, massaging the bridge of his nose between thumb and forefinger. His hands were covered in blood and he could smell its familiar odour strong in his nostrils as he sat there in the mud. Someone was lighting a fire, using pieces of broken-up ammunition boxes, and soon a kettle was boiling merrily away on top of the fire. The flames twisted and turned in the wind but the parapet of the dug-out at least gave the Paras some protection from the savage weather.

Mugs were soon filled with drinking chocolate and the men sat around, warming their hands around the cups and at the yellow flames. Turner decided to make himself a pot noodle and sat there eating happily inside the blood-spattered hole, seemingly oblivious to the smells all around him. He ate hungrily and even Carter managed a few mouthfuls of thin soup which he made up from a packet.

Anderson paled as he saw the two men eating.

'How the hell can you eat after what's happened today?' he said, feeling sick. It was all *he* could do to finish his mug of hot chocolate.

'A man's got to keep his strength up,' said Turner, shovelling another spoonful of noodles into his mouth.

'How many of the bastards do you think we killed?' said Wallace, his remark addressed to no one in particular.

'Does it really matter?' said Carter. 'We drove them out of their positions, that's the most important thing.'

'I wonder how many of our boys are dead,' said Harris, quietly.

No one spoke.

The silence seemed to descend like a cloud for long moments as the Paras thought about those who had fallen during the day's fighting. Then, finally, Harris broke the silence.

'I bet my old lady's worried about me,' he said.

Jennings grunted. 'She's probably having the time of her life without you around.'

Moss didn't speak. He wondered how his mother was feeling now? What would she be thinking? Had he been killed, wounded, taken prisoner? If only he could get word to her somehow, but all mail had been temporarily halted during the advance. Still, he reasoned, if he'd been killed she would have been told quickly enough. He wondered what the mothers and wives of those who had fallen during the fighting would feel like when they learned that their loved ones had died? He pushed the thought to one side, taking a sip from his mug.

'They're a windy load of sods aren't they, these Argies?' said Fisher, scornfully.

Anderson shook his head. 'Like I said before, they are only kids.'

'Don't give me that again,' the lance-jack rasped. 'They dropped enough of our boys today. Do *you* want to go back and count the bodies?' He pointed an accusing finger at Anderson.

'I still can't help feeling a bit sorry for them,' he persisted. 'I mean, they probably didn't want this war any more than we did.'

'Then why did they invade the fucking islands?' snapped Fisher. 'These are ours. They belong to England.'

'Strictly speaking, they don't,' Anderson countered. 'The United Nations recognises us as the administering power, but the Argies had landed men here in the eighteenth century, the same as we had.'

'To hell with the history lesson,' rasped Wallace. 'They're our fucking islands.'

Anderson continued. 'When I said the Argentinian troops didn't want this war I meant it was their government who sent them here. They didn't ask to come. They're conscripts.'

'Yeah,' said Fisher, spitting into a puddle. 'You've told us once.' He looked at Anderson, their eyes locked even in the darkness. 'Well I couldn't give a toss if they're conscripts or not. They're Argies. They're the enemy.'

'And now we've captured some of them, we're going to have to feed the bastards and look after them until they can go home,' said Harris, irritably.

'It'd be simpler to shoot them,' Wallace snapped.

One or two of the others murmured their approval at the suggestion.

Anderson shook his head. 'They should be allowed a certain amount of dignity. There's still some honour in war, even in defeat.'

It was Carter who spoke next.

'Do you honestly believe that, Anderson?' he said, mockingly.

'Yes I do.'

Carter exhaled deeply. 'There's no honour in war. There never has been. Kill or be killed that's all it is. Do you think for one second those fucking Argies holed up in Goose Green, or anywhere else on this island for that matter, would know the meaning of honour? War's about death; not heroics, not honour. It's about winning. You don't win a war by dying for your country, you win it by making the other silly bastard die for *his* country.'

'Nice speech,' said Anderson, acidly. 'But I still stick with my views.'

'Fine,' said Carter. 'But just remember your views on honour next time you turn your back on one of those fucking Argies. Me, I wouldn't trust any of them as far as I could chuck them. You can keep honour. I'll stick to victory and I couldn't give a damn how many of the bastards I have to kill.' He paused. 'Even if they are only kids.'

Moss listened to the exchange with interest, sipping slowly at his hot chocolate, the wind whistling around him. Another heavy silence descended over the men, some of whom were trying to catch a few hours sleep. Carter merely sat cleaning his rifle with an oily rag he'd taken from his pack. Watched by Moss he removed all traces of dried blood from his bayonet. The older man could sense his young companion's eyes on him and looked round.

'Something on your mind?' hc asked him.

Moss shook his head. 'Not really, I was just thinking about what you said.'

Carter smiled. 'About what?'

'About there being no honour in war.'

'Do *you* think there is, Ronnie?'

Moss gazed into his mug of hot chocolate as if seeking an answer in the brown liquid. 'My dad always said that it was an honour to die for your country.'

'Tell that to the blokes' relatives who we lost today,' Carter said, sarcastically.

'No but I mean, what Anderson said about the Argies being conscripts, not really wanting the war, it's true isn't it?' It came out more as a statement than a question.

'All I can see on these battlefields,' began Carter, 'is men in grey uniforms shooting at us. I don't want to see any further than a uniform and once you start thinking otherwise, you might as well go home.'

Moss nodded. 'It was a pity about Colonel Clavell,' he said.

'Remember that next time you have any doubts about this war. It was one of those *kids* who killed him.'

Moss nodded and pulled the collar of his greatcoat up around his ears, trying to shield them from the biting wind. He was shivering and he could feel the dampness of the mud seeping through the material of his uniform. The rain still lashed down, driven by the powerful wind which snaked across the silent field like a whiplash. Tents which had been erected, some to house the wounded until choppers could drop in to ferry them out, were buffeted mercilessly by the strong gales and one was even torn up by the powerful wind. Medics and those Paras nearby struggled to replace it, battling constantly against the howling typhoon-like conditions. Snow even covered the bloodied mud lightly and the Paras felt it stinging their faces as it blew over them. Moss tried to sleep, hands tucked in his pockets, knees drawn up to his chest. He dozed for a few minutes, then was awoken by a fresh onslaught of freezing rain or snow. He lay down in the mud, using a piece of cardboard from one of the ration boxes to cover himself. It afforded just that little extra warmth needed and, eventually, he drifted off to sleep.

Major Fulton stood patiently by as Private Regan fiddled with the controls of the radio. The set crackled, hissed loudly with static then seemed to settle into a steady hum.

'I've got no idea what frequency they're using,' said Regan, still fiddling with the set.

'Just keep trying,' Fulton told him. He cupped a hand around the match, struggling to light his cigarette in the gusting wind, which threatened at one moment to blow him right off his feet. The match went out and Fulton cursed. Captain Hansen offered his lighter and finally the Major managed to light his cigarette. He thanked the captain and sucked hard on the fag, his eyes still on Regan.

'I think I've got it,' said the wireless operator, smiling. He twisted a dial a couple of times then nodded. 'Yeah, that's it.'

Fulton took the handset from him and, in faltering Spanish, asked if there was anyone who could understand what he was saying.

A slightly puzzled Argentinian voice assured him that there was and, for a few moments some aimless chit-chat went back and forth over the air-waves, then finally Fulton asked to speak to whoever was in charge. The voice at the other end went silent for a moment, a note of hesitancy entering it when it returned. Fulton repeated his request to speak to whoever was in charge, identifying himself as the commander of the British forces around Goose Green.

Another silence, then the Argentinian told him to wait a minute.

'What the hell are they playing at?' asked Hansen, irritably.

'I just hope they're not trying to pin-point our positions,' said Fulton, anxiously. Then he heard a new voice on the handset. A deep, almost hoarse voice came back to him. The man identified himself as the commander of the Argentinian troops, surprisingly, thought Fulton, speaking in rough English.

'My name is Fulton,' said the Major, speaking slowly so that his opposite number could understand.

'Yes.' The voice crackled over the set again.

'Can you understand what I am saying?'

'Yes.'

Fulton looked up at Hansen and shrugged.

'My men are in strong positions around the settlement,' he explained. 'I can call on air and artillery support if necessary.'

'Yes,' the voice croaked.

'Do you understand me?'

'Yes.'

'In order to avoid further bloodshed, on both sides, I am offering you the chance to lay down your arms. We will talk tomorrow.'

Silence.

'Do you understand what I am saying?'

'Yes.'

'Great conversationalist isn't he?' said Hansen, smiling.

Fulton raised an eyebrow in exasperation.

'My men, not fight,' the voice said.

'That is correct. You will lay down your arms. You will not fire on my men. Any of your troops who hold a white flag will be given safe passage. Do you understand?'

'White flag. No shoot.'

'That's correct. Are we agreed that you will lay down your arms?'

'Yes. No shoot.'

'No shoot,' Fulton echoed, smiling thinly. He exhaled deeply. There was a vicious hiss of static and then the set seemed to go dead.

'I think we just negotiated a surrender,' said the Major, smiling broadly.

'You and I know that, I hope our Argentinian friend does,' said Hansen.

Fulton gave orders that there was to be no attack the following morning—merely, he hoped, a leisurely advance to liberate Goose Green. Hansen and the other officers present hurried off to spread the word amongst the men.

The surrender was but hours away.

Six

As dawn broke the next morning, the Paras were already moving forward towards Goosc Green. They moved slowly and cautiously across the last half mile which separated them from the settlement itself and the men could now clearly see the buildings which made up this tiny village, although it was so small it scarcely even qualified for that description. A platoon of engineers, spread out in a wide line ahead of them, scanned the pock-marked ground for mines, one of them pausing every so often to check on some suspicious-looking lump of turf, but the advance continued unchecked—through the mud which was littered with discarded helmets and equipment.

The order had been passed during the night that the enemy were surrendering but it was still with a feeling of anxiety that the Paras moved forward, eyes constantly scanning the area ahead of them. There were still some machine-gun nests and trenches on the outskirts of the settlement and the Paras could see Argentinian troops standing about in these. Moss swallowed hard, his eyes fixed on one of the heavy machine-guns which was tilted towards the British. He could feel his heart hammering against his ribs. Carter and Harris advanced on either side of him. They too were aware of the danger they were in should the enemy troops decide to take it into their heads to fire.

'I hope someone told *them* they were surrendering,' murmured Fisher, nervously.

The men were less than fifty yards from the first trench when a white flag fluttered into view. It flapped in the strong breeze and an almost audible sigh of relief swept the Paras ranks. They quickened their pace, half a dozen of them moving towards the trench where the white flag fluttered.

Moss watched as the Paras approached the trench, the officer leading them pointing first to his own sub-gun and then to the floor, indicating that the Argentinians should lay down their weapons.

He was actually on the lip of the trench when one of the enemy soldiers opened up on him.

The strident rattle of a PAM 1 broke the stillness of the morning and the horrified Paras watched as the officer was hurled off his feet by the high velocity impact of the bullets. He sprawled on his back in the mud and, with the white flag still fluttering above them, the Argentinians in the trench opened fire on the paras nearby. The men threw themselves down, shocked into immobility by the act of treachery. They could only lie still as a hail of hot lead whizzed over their heads.

'Those dirty fucking bastards,' roared James, dashing towards the trench. He fired a burst from his Sten-gun and ran on, surprised to find Anderson at his side. The private had pulled the SLR from his shoulder and was aiming it at the nearest Argentinian.

'You scum,' he roared and shot the man in the face. 'Scum.' He fired again, not even stopping when the enemy troops finally threw their guns down. He leapt down into the trench and drove his bayonet deep into the side of his nearest enemy. 'Animals,' he roared, tears in his eyes. Then he felt strong arms grabbing him and turned to see Carter and Wallace trying to restrain him.

'Fucking animals,' roared Anderson again.

Carter and Wallace held him against the wall of the trench, the corporal taking his gun from him.

'Come on,' shouted Wallace. 'Cool it.'

'They had a white flag up,' Anderson blabbered. 'A white flag.' The tears were rolling down his cheeks. 'Bloody scum.'

He watched as the prisoners were led away by the furious paras, many of who had to be restrained by their officers. One recalcitrant Argentinian sergeant was dragged from the trench by his hair when he wouldn't co-operate. Captain Hansen ran across to the Para and stepped between him and the sergeant. The captain held up a hand, pushing the barrel of the private's SLR away from his captive.

'They shot at our men, sir,' rasped the private. 'They were supposed to be surrendering and they shot at our men.'

Hansen gripped the private by the shoulders.

'I know but we mustn't take reprisals.' He raised his voice, trying to make all the men hear. 'No reprisals.'

The Paras were fuming as they dragged their enemies from trenches and dug-outs, nudging them just that bit too hard with the muzzles of their rifles when they wouldn't move fast enough.

'How could they do it?' murmured Anderson, watching as the bullet-riddled body of the Para's officer was carried away. 'They were showing a white flag. They were giving up. How could they?'

He looked at Carter, his eyes bulging, the blood vessels standing out like routes on a road map.

'That's what honour in war is?' The question hung in the air. 'Do you still believe in it? Now, after what you've just seen?' asked the older man.

Anderson had no answer for him. He simply lowered his head, taking back his rifle when Wallace handed it to him.

Moss stood nearby, watching, flabbergasted as the beaten Argentinians filed past him in a long grey line, hands clasped behind their heads. They had dropped their weapons in the mud, there was even half-eaten food and boxes of mortar shells lying around in the ooze. Those who had been wounded in the previous day's fighting were helped along by their comrades, those not able to walk were carried. The paras stood vigilantly as the forlorn column was herded away from the strongholds on the edge of the settlement. There was a strong look of triumph on the faces of the British troops, but it was mixed with anger and something which looked distinctly like hatred. Moss saw two engineers counting each Argentinian as he passed by and now, as he turned, he saw them filing out from the buildings of Goose Green itself.

Major Fulton, accompanied by a handful of Paras, advanced up what must once have been the main road, now nothing more than a rutted quagmire. From one green painted house a group of Argentinian officers, also waving a white flag, emerged. Moss and Carter, along with the remainder of their platoon, also began to trek up the narrow muddy street, glancing around them as they did so. The windows in many houses had been broken, in one or two places, the front doors had even been torn off to build fires.

Argentinian troops were spilling from the ruined dwellings, marching forlornly out of the settlement to join their captive comrades who were already on the way back towards Darwin, guarded by a mere handful of Paras. It was all that was needed. The grey-clad troops were beaten men. Some even smiled as they threw down their weapons, eager to be taken from the hell-hole which had been their home for many weeks.

'Search the houses,' snapped James and the men split up into twos, entering each dwelling cautiously, ever alert to the danger of booby traps. Moss found himself paired with Turner and the two of them moved carefully through the first house they came to. The door had been smashed in, part of it hanging from its hinges. It led into a hallway which was littered with pieces of broken furniture and Turner shook his head as he pushed open the door which led into the sitting-room. The carpet had been torn up, rolled into one side of the room. A sideboard had been smashed, the little ornaments which used to stand on it now lying in a hundred pieces beside it. The drawers had been pulled out and their contents rifled. Upstairs the same had been done to bedroom furniture, clothes taken from wardrobes and cupboards and torn up. The destruction was sickening, but the thing which made the two Paras shake their heads in disbelief was the piles of rotting faeces which dotted the floor. The stench was almost palpable in its intensity and both men momentarily recoiled.

'My God,' murmured Turner, angrily.

When they returned to the street they found that the tale was the same in many of the residents' dwellings. Homes ransacked, belongings smashed, excrement on the floors. Scarcely a window remained unbroken in any of the houses. Carter found a Union Jack which had been spat upon and the words:

'Malvinas Argentina' scrawled upon it.

In one of the houses Wallace and Jennings found tins of food, most of it mouldering. The store itself had been totally ransacked, every window smashed. A sign proclaiming, 'Special Offers' flapped in the wind. There was more excrement in the store, some smeared on the walls.

'These aren't men,' snarled Sergeant James. 'How can we be expected to treat the bastards like human beings when they behave like fucking animals.'

He cast a look of disgust in the direction of a column of enemy prisoners.

Major Fulton strode across to the men who had gathered outside the store.

'The islanders are locked up in there,' he said, pointing towards a large white-washed building about fifty yards away. It was, he informed them, the Community Hall. Moss and the others, led by Fulton, made their way to the hall and broke open the doors.

The building was about half the size of a small supermarket and it was crammed full of people, all of whom turned expectantly when the doors were opened. Fulton stood before them and announced that the settlement was now back in British hands. An enormous cheer went up and the people flooded forward, almost knocking the Major over. Delighted islanders hugged the smiling Paras, men embraced them, women kissed them. Moss found himself amongst a group of five women, all of who seemed anxious to hold him.

'Thank God you've come,' said one of them, kissing him.

'Now this is what I call a welcome,' said Jennings, grinning as a young girl threw her arms around his neck.

Children ran about seemingly oblivious to the mud which was ankle deep in places. Carter watched them jumping about joyfully, half a dozen or so making for the small playground nearby. Then he found himself surrounded by islanders. A tall man embraced him, following the gesture with a bone-crushing handshake.

Fisher had his beret knocked off by an over-zealous woman who plastered him with kisses. The lance-jack smiled broadly.

But, through the joyous celebration, Moss could still see Captain Hansen and another officer talking animatedly with the Argentinian commanders. Next second, Hansen came sprinting across to his CO and Moss saw them exchange brief words.

Fulton immediately tried to make himself heard above the joyful pandemonium, his voice containing an unmistakeable note of foreboding. The troops at any rate heard him and, soon, the entire gathering had grown silent.

'I have just discovered,' Fulton began, 'that the Argentinians have laid mines in several places in and around the settlement.'

'Oh Christ,' someone muttered.

'Please could everyone remain where they are until my men have discovered the location of these mines.'

No one moved. The Paras looked swiftly around, ensuring that all the islanders were in one place, then they fanned out cautiously. Argentinian sappers were dragged from the passing column of prisoners and ordered to point out the exact whereabouts of the lethal devices. Carter held one by the lapel and pushed him up against the wall of a house.

'Mine,' he rasped and the terrified Argentinian motioned frenziedly over his shoulder.

'Mine,' he repeated, turning and pointing towards the spot about twenty yards from the community hall.

'Oh my God,' murmured Carter.

The Argentinian was pointing to the children's playground.

There were about half a dozen kids in there all happily playing on the swings and slide, oblivious to the fact that they were in the middle of a minefield.

'There's some in the kid's playground,' said Carter, anxiously, walking towards Major Fulton. 'Sir,' he said. 'The kids' playground is mined.'

For long seconds, Fulton was dumbstruck, all he could hear was the gleeful shouts of the children. Shouts which might any second be drowned out by the roar of an explosion should one of them unwittingly step on a mine.

'We've got to get them out of there,' he said to Carter.

The Para nodded.

Watched by the rest of the troops, the two men walked slowly to the white wood fence which surrounded the playground.

'Jenny's in there,' a woman gasped, clutching her husband's arm, watching helplessly as her little girl swung happily back and forth on the set of swings in the playground.

'Kids,' called Carter. 'Listen to me.'

The children turned their heads and looked at the two Paras who stood on the other side of the fence.

'Is everyone listening?' Carter called, trying to keep his voice even.

There was a chorus of giggles and shouts of yes.

'We're going to play a new game,' Carter called. 'You have to stand still for as long as you can. Those of you on the swings, you just sit there for as long as you can without moving.' He felt a bead of perspiration pop onto his forehead. 'Now we're going to carry you out of the playground but you've got to keep still all the time. If anyone moves, they lose the game.' (Once and for all, thought Carter. Fuck this game up and you don't have to worry about starting another).

He glanced at Fulton who was easing himself slowly over the fence, his eyes scanning the muddy ground for the telltale marks to show where a mine had been laid.

'Is everybody ready?' Carter called.

The kids assured him that they were.

'All right, here we come and remember, just keep as still as you can.'

Fulton crouched, waiting as Carter clambered over the fence, cautiously putting his heavy boots down where he was sure there were no mines. He guessed that there must be about ten yards between himself and the kids, all of who were frozen like statues, smiles on some of their faces as they watched these two men edging slowly towards them, joining them in this new game. Carter swallowed hard; none of the kids could have been much older than ten. Beside him, the Major crept along, close to the ground, eyes ever open for even the slightest hint of a mine.

'Wait,' he suddenly hissed and Carter looked down to see his superior pointing to something nearby.

Jutting out of the earth about an eighth of an inch above the surface were two thin metal prongs, forming a small 'V'.

'Anti-personnel mines,' said Fulton.

Carter exhaled deeply. That particular type of mine was perhaps, in the circumstances, even more lethal than the conventional type. At least if one of them were unfortunate enough to step on an ordinary mine, most of the blast would be funnelled upward, but the AP's were a different matter. Should the metal prongs be touched, the movement would activate the device which was attached to a powerful spring. After two seconds, the mine would be propelled into the air by this spring to roughly waist height where it would explode, spraying ball-bearings and shrapnel in all directions. Carter looked down at the prongs for a second longer then began edging forward again, Fulton at his side. The two men separated, the Major heading towards the two children who were perched on the rickety wooden roundabout. He stopped in his tracks momentarily and turned to face the group of Paras who stood helplessly by as their companions picked their way through the maze of death.

'Fisher,' the Major called. 'Give us a hand and be careful, they're AP's.'

The lance-jack handed his rifle to Moss and clambered over the fence, following in the footsteps of his colleagues, his eyes alternately scanning the muddy ground and the waiting children. He saw two of the prongs to his left, two more a little further on, but he kept going.

Carter spotted two of the mines set close together near the slide. There was a small boy perched atop the slide, ready to hurtle down. It was towards him that the Para moved first. The boy looked restless and was tapping on the metal frame of the slide as if he had tired of the game.

'Don't forget,' Carter told him. 'Keep as still as you can.' He edged closer towards the slide, the mines seemingly more dense in this particular part of the playground. He spotted another as he reached the metal steps. There was a metallic clang as he put his heavy boot on the first step.

'I want you to climb down to me,' he told the boy who looked puzzled.

'But you said I shouldn't move,' the child countered with the kind of devastating logic children are prone to produce at the wrong moment.

Carter was momentarily stuck for an answer then he said:

'You only have to keep still once you reach the ground.'

This seemed to satisfy the boy and he scrambled down into the Para's arms. Carter steadied himself and turned towards a little girl who was sitting motionless on one end of a sea-saw. Moving as slowly as he could, the boy hanging round his neck, the Para edged towards the little girl, trying to smile as he did so. He could feel the perspiration on his forehead and back, despite the freezing wind which buffeted him, but he stepped tentatively onward towards the child on the see-saw.

It was only as he got to within three feet that he noticed another of the mines.

It was laid directly beneath the spot where the see-saw would come to ground should the child's weight be removed. The second Carter picked her up, the wooden bar would swing over, activating the mine. He froze again. Thoughts whirled in his mind. Maybe the see-saw would just balance out flat when he took the little girl off? Perhaps he could hold it level with his hand? What if . . .? To hell with it, what was he kidding himself for? The moment he picked the girl up the see-saw would tilt over onto the mine and everyone in the playground would be pelted with lumps of metal. What the fuck was he going to do? He glanced behind him. Fulton had already reached the two kids on the roundabout and was carrying them, one under each arm, back towards the safety of the fence, retracing his steps in the mud. Fisher too had reached the kids on the swings and was lifting them into his arms. He paused momentarily then also began making his way back.

Carter took a deep, almost painful breath, moving just that little bit closer to the see-saw. The little girl looked up at him, her big blue eyes fixing him in a captivating stare.

'I'm not moving,' she said proudly.

'I know you're not, sweetheart,' said Carter, smiling. 'Just stay still for a little bit longer.'

The boy who Carter held was becoming restless again.

'I want to get down,' he protested.

'No,' said the Para, through clenched teeth. 'You've got to be carried, that's all part of the game.'

'I'm fed up with this game,' the boy told him. 'Let me down.'

It was the last thing Carter needed. As if his problems with the mine weren't bad enough, now this little brat wanted to walk back himself. (All right, off you go kid, but be careful not to step on one of those silly mines in case it flies up and tears your head off.)

Fisher passed close by, his two wards held under each arm. As the lance-jack drew closer Carter turned his head.

'The see-saw,' he whispered. 'Look under the other side.'

Fisher did so.

'Bleedin' hell,' he gasped. 'Don't pick her up for Christ's sake.'

'I'm not going to,' snapped Carter. 'Just get me something to counter balance it will you?'

Fisher hurried off as best he could, eyes still scanning the ground for the tell-tale prongs, chancing a look back at Carter every so often. When he finally reached the fence he handed the kids over to the other paras standing nearby. Mothers immediately raced forward to snatch up their children. Fulton too returned safely, turning to see Carter standing motionless beside the see-saw.

'What the hell is he doing?' asked Fulton.

'There's an AP under the see-saw,' Fisher explained. Then he turned to Anderson. 'Get me an ammo box, anything heavy. Hurry.' Anderson scuttled off to find something and returned a second later with a wooden box. It was full of bullets and he handed it to Fisher who set off into the minefield once more.

'What's that?' asked the boy Carter held, pointing towards the metal prongs jutting up from the mud.

'It's nothing,' Carter said, seeing Fisher approach cautiously, the ammo box in his hand. He picked his way through the mud until he was standing beside his companion.

'As you lift her,' said the lance-jack, 'I'll put the box on the seat.'

Carter nodded.

'All right, sweetheart,' he said. 'I want you to stand up but don't take your feet off the seat,' he added, quickly.

Still smiling, the little girl did as she was told and Carter watched as Fisher knelt down beside her, pushing the box onto the seat just behind her. He looked up and nodded and the other Para quickly snatched her up into his arms.

The see-saw didn't move.

'Let's get out of here,' said Carter, breathing an audible sigh of relief.

The two of them finally reached the safety of the fence and Carter deposited the kids on the other side. Fisher patted him on the back, Fulton smiled.

'Good work, lads,' he said.

'Did I win?' said the little girl, beaming up at Carter.

He bent down and kissed her. 'Yes, sweetheart,' he said. 'You won.'

Chuckling gleefully to herself, she ran off to rejoin her parents.

The stream of Argentinian prisoners who had stopped to watch the goings-on in the playground were now herded on once more but, as they passed the group of islanders, a woman ran out from the crowd and suddenly lashed out at one of the grey-clad troops. Her nails raked his face, drawing blood, and the stunned Argentinian put up his hands in defence as the woman rained blows on him. Two Paras and a civilian, who Carter took to be her husband, moved forward. The civilian managed to drag her away but the woman was screaming at the passing prisoners. Carter saw that one of the kids in the playground belonged to her. Other islanders also shouted insults at the Argentinians as they passed. To see these men who had been their captors for so long, now turned into captives must have been poetic justice indeed for the people of Goose Green. The sappers were taken from the column and, leading groups of three or four Paras, were ordered to point out where the other minefields lay. Other prisoners were given the job of cleaning up the town itself, gathering the hundreds of discarded helmets, ammo boxes, even water bottles from the streets, and trying to help the islanders put their wrecked homes back in some semblance of order.

People returned to their houses to find what the Paras had found earlier and Moss saw a man and his wife sitting on their front step, the woman weeping hysterically when she saw the state of their home. Elsewhere, he saw a man shovelling rubbish out of his front room into the street, another man hosing down the inside of his house in an effort to remove the traces of excrement from the floor and walls. A dog ran about unheeded, barking at the prisoners as if even *it* knew what they had done. Moss watched the long procession leave the settlement, heading out on the dirt track in the direction of Darwin.

Messages had already been sent by radio for helicopters and soon Wessex and Sea King choppers would be flying in to ferry out the dead and wounded. The prisoners, on the other hand, would have to walk all the way back to the San Carlos bridgehead. Moss watched them go, a couple of Paras searching them as they reached the outskirts of the town. He saw one take a grenade from an Argentinian. The enemy soldier had kept the weapon concealed in his coat; quite when and where he intended to use it, Moss could only guess. The man was checked over again then pushed back into line. The column moved forlornly onward.

Just outside the settlement, British engineers were constructing make-shift barbed wire enclosures for the prisoners until an inventory of their numbers could be made. The Paras watched with a mixture of triumph and hatred as their enemies were pushed into these enclosures like so many grey-clad sheep. They sat down dejectedly on the mud, looking around with a trace of bewilderment on their faces. Moss noticed just how many of them were youngsters like himself. One was crying, nursing a slight wound in his shoulder and, just for a second, Moss felt a twinge of sympathy for his beaten enemy. They did indeed look pathetic. Their war was over. *His* had only just begun.

He turned suddenly when he felt a hand on his shoulder and when he spun round to face this intrusion into his thoughts he saw that it was a woman. He guessed that she was in her fifties, her greying hair mostly hidden beneath a scarf, her eyes framed by large glasses. She wore a grubby patterned dress and large wellington boots and looked like a farmer's wifc. She smiled broadly at the youth and handed him a steaming mug of tea. Moss grinned and took it.

'Thank you,' he said gratefully, and sipped at the tea.

All around him now he noticed that other men of his platoon were standing around drinking mugs of tea which the islanders had brewed for them. Even Major Fulton, deep in conversation with two civilians, was drinking from a large china mug. Moss looked at his own mug and saw that it bore the legend:

'The marriage of The Prince of Wales and Lady Diana Spencer; Wednesday 29th July, 1981'

It suddenly made him think of home. Of how, while on leave, he and his family had sat around the TV set, along with millions of other people all over the country, watching the wedding. He sipped from the mug and felt suddenly very homesick.

'You're all very young lads,' said the lady who'd given him the tea. She was looking at the rest of the platoon, some of them leaning on the fences of the islanders' homes, others even standing in the doorways of their houses. 'It must have been hard for you.'

'It was sometimes,' Moss confessed. 'The Argies put up quite a fight yesterday.'

The lady touched his cheek gently.

'You remind me of my son,' she said, softly.

Moss coloured slightly.

'He was in the army. He was killed in Korea.'

'I'm sorry,' said Moss.

The lady just smiled. 'Drink your tea,' she told him, then scuttled back into the house, returning a moment later with a tin of broken biscuits which she pushed towards the youth. Moss took one and thanked her. She urged him to take some more, wrapping a dozen or so in a handkerchief which she retrieved from her apron. 'Take these,' she told him and he did, gratefully.

Carter and Fisher were drinking tea as well, the two Paras standing nearby chatting to a man and his wife. The man introduced himself as Paul Nash; his wife, Harriet, stood close by him.

'I never dreamt they'd do anything like this,' said Nash, motioning to the shell of his house, wrecked and ransacked by the Argentinians. 'It'll take us weeks to get it right.'

'How long had they kept you locked up?' asked Fisher.

Nash shrugged. 'Nearly a month. It felt like a year.'

'Bastards,' muttered Fisher then turned to Mrs Nash and apologised for his bad language.

She merely smiled and dismissed it but Fisher apologised again all the same. He sipped at his tea.

'What will you do with all the prisoners?' Nash wanted to know.

'That's up to our CO.' Carter told him. 'They've got to be searched and counted, their wounded have got to be attended to. After that I suppose they'll just be sent back home.'

Nash shook his head. 'After what they did here, I don't know how you can bother with their wounded. I mean, what would they do to any of our wounded if they caught them? They'd probably shoot them.'

'Did you lose many men in the battle?' asked Mrs Nash.

Carter lowered his head slightly. 'Our battalion commander was killed on The Hill of Gorse, we lost a few wounded and dead as well.' He sipped at his tea.

'By the time we've finished with them,' Fisher began. 'The bleedin' . . .' He apologised to Mrs Nash again. 'The blasted Argies will be sorry they ever landed here.'

'You're a cockney aren't you?' asked Nash, smiling.

Fisher nodded.

'Which part of London?'

'Bethnal Green.'

'It must seem strange to you, to all of you having to come this far to fight for a piece of rock that's not much bigger than London,' said Nash.

'It does belong to us,' said Carter. 'I mean, you're as British as we are, aren't you?'

Nash smiled. 'And proud of it too.'

The two Paras raised their mugs in salute and the little group laughed merrily.

Brent was busy inspecting a captured Argentinian rifle. He turned it over in his hand, watched by half a dozen children. The rifle was a Belgian FN, not unlike those the British themselves carried. Brent checked the firing mechanism then removed the magazine which, to his surprise, he found was full. As he looked up he saw the children watching him. One of them, a little girl with her hair in pony tails, approached him and offered him a large bag which contained a sticky mess of sweets. Brent smiled and took one out. He popped it into his mouth and thanked the little girl.

'You can have these if you want,' the little girl told him. 'My daddy says you're all very brave men.'

Brent smiled down at her. 'What's your name?' he asked.

'Joanne,' she told him.

He ruffled her hair with one hand. 'You keep your sweets, Joanne,' he told her. But then he paused a moment and dug his hand into the bag once more. 'But, I tell you what, I'll take one for later on.' The little girl smiled broadly at him as he walked away.

'Jesus Christ, look at that,' muttered Jennings, motioning towards a girl in her twenties who was chatting to Morris. He nudged Harris in the side nearly making him spill his tea.

'What is it?' said Harris, irritably.

'That bird over there,' Jennings told him.

'Just drink your tea,' Harris told him—then he too chanced a sly look at the girl. She was indeed very attractive, her short blonde hair reminding him a little of his wife. She finished her conversation with Morris and turned towards them. 'Here,' whispered Harris, 'she's coming this way.'

'Would you like some more tea?' she asked them both.

Harris declined but Jennings drained what was left in his mug and nodded.

'What's your name, love?' he asked.

'Marion,' she told him, sweeping a hand through her hair.

'Vince Jennings,' he said. 'Pleased to meet you. This is Tom Harris, we call him Bomber.'

Harris too smiled.

'We're all very grateful to you for what you've done,' she said, then skipped off to get the tea.

'I wonder *how* grateful,' said Jennings, watching the smooth curve of her buttocks as she walked away.

Harris looked at him.

'What do you mean?' he wanted to know.

Jennings raised one eyebrow suggestively.

'You've got a one track mind, you have,' Harris told him.

'So you're telling me you'd refuse her if she was willing?'

Harris sighed. 'I'm a married man for Christ's sake, I'm shortly to become a father and you're . . .'

Jennings cut him short.

'Would you refuse?'

Harris grinned. 'No, I bloody wouldn't.'

Both men cracked out laughing.

As it happened, Jennings never got his second cup of tea. All attention was suddenly diverted towards a group of Paras led by Captain Hansen who had been checking the area just beyond the community hall.

'Major Fulton,' the captain called. 'We've found something, I think you should have a look.'

Fulton called a dozen men around him, Moss and the others amongst them, and scurried off to where Hansen waited. The captain led them down a narrow alleyway to an open field about fifty yards from the hall itself. The Paras froze at the sight which confronted them.

The field behind the hall was perhaps twice the size of a football pitch and, dotted all over it, some in piles as tall as a man, were long cylindrical objects. They glinted ominously in the dull light, looking like beached torpedos. The men moved closer, a smell wafting in on the breeze. Moss recognized it as the marzipan-like smell which they'd experienced when the Pucaras had attacked them on their way to Goose Green. The realization seemed to strike him like a blow to the face. These bombs had been the ones dropped from the enemy aircraft. There was a clear liquid oozing slowly, thickly, from the nose of one of the projectiles and the grass all around it was black and burned, a smell of charred earth reached the men as they moved cautiously towards the shapes. They reminded Harris of pea pods, except these were steel grey in colour. To Carter, they looked like cylindrical coffins.

'What are they?' asked Wallace, standing close by one of the things, his eyes drawn to the viscous liquid dribbling from one of them. It hissed as it hit the grass and he saw a thin plume of smoke rising from the blackened spot.

'What is that stuff?' the corporal demanded, stepping closer.

'Keep back,' Hansen shouted, ushering the men away.

'Brent,' said Wallace, whispering to the weapons expert. 'What *is* it?'

Brent sniffed the air, his suspicions of earlier on now fully confirmed.

'It's napalm,' he said. 'Those bloody things are full of it.'

Major Fulton moved forward, kneeling beside one of the leaking bombs. He too watched in horrified fascination as the sticky fluid oozed from the detonator seal. He swallowed hard and looked round at Hansen.

'How many bombs are there?' he asked.

'Eighty-nine, sir, we counted them.'

'Dear God,' murmured the Major. 'If a stray shell or a bomb from a Harrier had hit this lot . . .' He allowed the sentence to trail off, the thought too horrible to contemplate. But it was there in his mind nonetheless. The resulting explosion would have set off the napalm and Goose Green would have been obliterated in a welter of screaming fire.

'We thought they were dropping incendiary bombs,' said Fisher. 'But it was really that stuff?' He swallowed hard.

'Thank God they were off target with it,' echoed Harris.

'Napalm,' said Wallace. 'Didn't the Yanks use that in Vietnam?'

Brent nodded.

'At the height of the war they were dropping 1,500 tons of it a month.'

'Jesus,' murmured the corporal, his eyes, like those of his comrades, still fixed firmly on the bombs and their leaking cargo of fiery death.

'It's a mixture of kerosene and gelatine,' Brent explained. 'It's designed to stick to whatever it touches. It burns at over 1,000 degrees.' His voice had become a hoarse whisper.

'And they stuck it right next to the place where they were holding the islanders,' rasped Carter. He looked at Anderson. 'There's another illustration of your "honourable" war.' There was a harsh note of cynicism in his voice.

Moss watched as British artillerymen and engineers inspected the bombs, checking each one for booby-traps, careful that they didn't get in the way of the dripping liquid. One of the gunners came hurrying across clutching something in his hand. It looked like a booklet of some kind and he handed it to the Major who read;

'La Bomba Napalm; 1978'

He passed it to Hansen who flicked through the booklet.

'Jesus Christ,' he muttered. 'It's a bloody instruction manual. How to put the damn things together, how to arm them.'

'Nationality?' the CO wanted to know.

Hansen shrugged, wrinkled his brow.

'It's in Spanish, it could be from any of the South American countries.' He flipped through the booklet once more, finally turning to the back page where he ready something about the printing. It proclaimed proudly;

'Brasilia'

'The bastards got it from Brazil,' he said.

Fulton nodded. Barely able to contain his rage he ordered Hansen to fetch two dozen Argentinian prisoners from the hastily-built stockades to help in the pin-pointing of any more mines or booby-traps which might be littering the settlement and the area around it. Hansen took some men and hurried off to obey the order.

'I think making prisoners clear their own mine-fields is against the Geneva convention,' said Anderson.

'And what about that fucking stuff?' rasped Carter, pointing to the napalm. 'Is that in the rule book?' He stormed off, followed by the rest of the platoon. Anderson was left alone momentarily to gaze at the lethal cigar-shaped bombs, then he too hurried off to join the rest of the men.

All round Goose Green, the field was littered with spent shell cases, cartridges, empty and full magazines, and discarded equipment, which the Argentinians were clearing up. Moss watched in awe as a seemingly endless supply of unwanted rifles, small arms and ammunition were piled up in one part of the settlement. The ground around Goose Green was pock-marked by shell craters, but moving amongst them he could see Paras and Argentinians, the enemy troops pointing out the location of mines and then digging them up with their entrenching tools. The same implements which they'd used to plant them with in the first place. There was a savage irony about it all.

The airstrip itself, the reason for the attack, was intact and usable and some of the Paras watched as a couple of Sea Kings dropped down to let off supplies and fresh rations. On the runway there was a wrecked Pucara, hit by a stray British shell. It stood motionless, the pilot still in his cockpit, the same blast which had torn the wing from his plane having ripped away most of his head. He sat stiffly at the controls, his sightless eyes gazing ahead, out over the desolate, bloodied ground which made up the approaches to the settlement. A thin film of drizzle drifted over the battlefield and Moss shivered, wiping his nose with the back of his hand.

As he watched, on top of the schoolhouse a Union Jack was raised slowly. It gradually reached the top of the pole where it fluttered defiantly in the strong wind. Moss heard some cheers from a group of islanders who watched the little ceremony and the Paras who had raised the flag saluted proudly. The little group of islanders suddenly struck up with a faltering chorus of 'Rule Britannia' and Moss smiled to himself. Once again he felt that swell of pride as he looked at the flag. It waved brightly against the dark grey backdrop of Falklands sky, a message of hope for the islanders.

A warning for the Argentinians.

SEVEN

Moss and the other men of the platoon stood around the large hole in which lay the blanket-covered bodies of thirteen dead Paras. The wind was still blowing furiously, whipping fine particles of snow into the faces of the waiting men. They stood erect, gazing straight ahead of them, across to the other side of the hole where the padre and the officers stood. Moss could hardly hear the words the padre spoke because the wind was blowing so wildly, howling in his ears like a maddened wolf while he and his comrades stood ankle deep in the mud. They held shovels before them, given to them by the islanders, and it was with these that they had dug the mass grave which housed their dead comrades. One of the blankets covering a corpse flapped mournfully in the wind, its corner rising and falling with each fresh gust to reveal the waxed, pale countenance of the dead Para beneath. Moss looked down. The bodies looked so small lying there in that large grave.

The padre, Father Driscoll, continued with the service, struggling to keep his feet in the gusts of gale force wind. The officers had their berets off and their hair was being blown about. Moss thought how dirty everyone looked. None of the Paras had been able to shave for three days and some hadn't even been able to wash. There was a peculiar odour hanging around the graveside. A combination of death and dirty bodies. The pungent stink of body odour was powerful in his nostrils as was the sickly-sweet aroma of rotting flesh. Smells which even the strongest wind couldn't seem to blow away.

Moss looked up again, chancing a sideways look at Carter who stood beside him. The older man had his eyes closed and Moss had the curious feeling that he could hear what Father Driscoll was saying. Indeed Carter could, in a manner of speaking, *hear* what was being said for, although the wind carried the padre's words away, the older Para had seen and heard enough military funerals in his time to know what was being said. He'd been a pallbearer more times than he could remember—but not this time. It had just been a matter of lifting the blanket-covered bodies and placing them gently in their final resting place. No pomp, no finery, no cortège of flower-filled cars for accompaniment this time. Just the harsh weather of the Falklands, the grey sky hanging over the scene like the blankets which covered the bodies in the grave. And yet the funeral's simplicity only increased its poignancy and, when Father Driscoll finished speaking (a fact which the troops were aware of only because he closed his Prayer Book), Carter watched as a solitary bugler blew the last post. His notes were faltering, so cold were his lips and at times it didn't seem as if he were going to be able to complete the lament. The wind rose, carrying the swelling notes away with it as easily as the lives of the thirteen men in the grave had been taken. Carter gritted his teeth and once again closed his eyes.

Harris fought back tears as did Moss, the younger of the two in particular thinking how easily it could have been *his* body lying there in the mud.

In the settlement itself, Argentinian soldiers were ordered to remove their hats as the mournful wail of the bugle sounded the death-knell for that baker's dozen of Paras who had died for something which few people ever really stop to think about.

The right to be free.

Then, finally, it was over. The buglar lowered his instrument and stood stiffly to attention. The men stood silently for long moments, each lost in his own thoughts, then at a given order they replaced their berets and those with shovels set about the task of burying their dead comrades while the remaining Paras filed off to complete the cleaning up operation in the settlement itself.

The time was 2.19 pm.

By 3.00 the hole was filled in. Harris and Carter fashioned rough crosses from pieces of broken wood which lay littered about the field and fastened the two pieces together with string. Then they drove them into the soft mud.

The men once more stood by, looking at the flat ground with its two rough markers.

'It all seems so simple doesn't it?' said Anderson.

'Too simple,' echoed Fisher.

'Thank God they didn't get the chance to use that napalm or there could have been a lot more of us in that bloody hole,' said Wallace.

'Thirteen's enough isn't it?' said Anderson, bitterly. 'You know they always refer to casualties as "light" in the papers. Have you ever noticed that? "Light casualties were sustained", that sort of thing.' He shook his head. 'I wonder what the families of those poor sods will think when they read about it in the papers. How many have to die before it becomes important enough for people to start worrying?' He picked up his shovel and propped it over his shoulder like a makeshift rifle, then, followed by the rest of the platoon, he walked back across the battlefield. Over the bloodied mud, littered with helmets and shell cases, torn apart by craters.

Only Sergeant James remained by the graveside, his eyes fixed on the twin crosses. Carter hesitated, waiting for him to follow.

'You all right, Sarge?' he asked, taking a step towards the NCO, forced to raise his voice to make himself heard above the wind.

'Does it still get to *you* after all these years?' asked James, enigmatically. 'I mean how many men have we seen killed between us during our years in the army do you reckon?'

Carter shrugged.

'Dozens,' he said.

'And yet it still doesn't harden you does it?' said James, the remark aimed at himself. 'When you see them lowering those coffins into the holes, or picking up the pieces of blokes who've been blown to pieces, you don't think, "well, there goes another one".' He paused. 'I loved that Colonel. He was the finest officer I ever served under.'

'It's how he would have wanted it, Sarge,' said Carter, reassuringly. 'To die in combat.'

'You know Carter, you're probably right,' said James. 'How come you never made it to Sergeant?' He smiled.

The Para grinned. 'They must have thought I had too much brain.'

Both of them laughed, walking slowly away from the grave to rejoin the rest of the platoon.

Captain Hansen saw the platoon as the men trudged wearily towards him. The officer was standing on the edge of the airstrip watching as groups of Paras and Argentinian prisoners carried the boxes of discarded ammo to a place where it could be picked up by the next group of Sea Kings that arrived. There were vast stores of it and, at the far end of the airstrip, piles of artillery shells had been stacked in uneven piles. Moss and the others watched as enemy troops, watched over by a Para sergeant, began moving the 155mm shells, picking each heavy projectile up one at a time and carrying it to a nearby ditch where two or three engineers went over it, checking its armament. They were performing a similar task with the huge pile of weapons and ammunition. One of the engineers suddenly stood up and waved a handful of slugs in the direction of Hansen.

'Sir,' he shouted. 'These are bloody dumdums.' He brandished the shells almost accusingly, looking angrily at an Argentinian who was carefully laying down one of the huge cannon shells.

'Dumdums,' repeated the engineer, examining the bullets which had deep crosses scored in their heads. Outlawed by the Geneva Convention, the dumdum bullet was designed to explode on contact with bone. All it took to make one of the murderous things was a moment or two of diligent cutting with a bayonet, scoring deep grooves in the top of the bullet in question. That simple action created what amounted to a tiny bomb.

Carter had heard the engineer's shout and he looked across at Anderson.

'You know your ideas about honour in war must be even more ridiculous than I first thought,' he sucked in an angry breath. 'Napalm, mines in kids' playgrounds and now dumdum bullets. You ask us to feel sorry for these bastards,' he pointed to an Argentinian who was struggling with the weight of a shell. 'After all we've seen in the last couple of days, you still think we owe them their self-respect?'

Anderson didn't get a chance to answer.

There was an explosion of almost seismic proportions, the air suddenly filled with a blistering heat. The Paras found themselves flung into the mud by the blast, the after-shock and heat wave rolling over them like a floodtide. Moss looked up and saw that the blast had come from the pile of artillery shells on the airstrip. There were several bodies lying around, most of them grey-clad Argentinians. One was trying to drag himself away from the scene of the explosion, trailing the shattered remains of one leg behind him. His comrades lay still, their bodies torn apart by the ferocity of the detonation. The Para sergeant was staggering about with a hand clapped to his forehead and Moss could see blood running through his fingers. Medics rushed forward to tend to the wounded, casting anxious glances at the remnants of the ammo dump for fear of further explosions. Moss and the rest of the platoon hauled themselves up out of the mud, watching as a pall of black smoke rose into the air. The youngster saw Captain Hansen and an artillery sergeant walking over to the shells. The captain was gesturing animatedly towards them.

'Fucking things must have been booby-trapped,' said Wallace, brushing some mud from his uniform.

The men passed close by, glancing at the scene of devastation before them. Fortunately, the prisoners seemed to have taken the brunt of it and Carter saw that one of them had been decapitated by the blast, his severed head rolling around like some kind of macabre football, buffeted by the strong wind. Medics and other men hurriedly dragged the corpses from the airstrip, trailing blood behind them as they did so. A Para private was sitting in the mud supporting an injured arm, waiting for a medic to attend to him. Moss could see the shining white of bone sticking through his ripped uniform and the pulped flesh of his lower arm. The man was finally helped to his feet and, supported by two of his companions, guided away.

Moss and the others walked slowly past, Fisher shaking his head in disbelief as he studied the pieces of wreckage and human debris which littered the runway. An arm lay nearby, the fingers still twitching spasmodically.

'I suppose that's what you call poetic justice.'

The men were surprised to see that the words came from Anderson who was watching, almost mesmerised as an eviscerated Argentinian was carried away, his intestines hanging like thick bloodied spaghetti from the gaping maw which was his lower abdomen. 'They booby-trapped the shells and they died because of them.'

Carter thought about saying something but didn't.He knew now that Anderson realized honour was something reserved for fiction. It didn't exist in 'real' war. There were no rules, no respect between enemies. Only the single, overriding factor which he had discovered many years before. Kill or be killed. It was as simple as that.

As simple as dying.

Eight

As night wrapped its black fingers around East Falkland, the temperatures dropped to below freezing.

Moss, Carter and the rest of the platoon were dug in about half a mile east of Goose Green. The subzero climate had turned the steady drizzle of the day into a stinging snow, hurled at the slit trenches and tents by the ever present wind. Harris and Carter had used broken-up ammo boxes to shore up the worst rifts in the walls of the trenches but, even so, the sticky mud continued to ooze amongst the men and they sat on pieces of cardboard to prevent the dampness reaching them. Wallace was smoking a roll-up, the bluish smoke drifting through the air like diesel fumes. He took a few drags then handed it on to Fisher who was playing cards with a couple of the others.

Bundled up in their overcoats, the men were huddled around an upturned wooden crate which had been used to hold rifles. They were using it as a table, and as they played cards, the kitty lay in the middle for all to see.

'Who's in for another hand?' asked Fisher, shuffling the cards with frozen fingers. He dropped a couple of cards but fished them out of the ankle deep mud at the bottom of the slit trench and, after brushing them off on his tunic, slid them back into the pack. 'Come on, let's see your money,' he said.

'Money?' snorted Wallace. 'You've got to be joking.'

Fisher smiled. 'Place your bets, gents,' he said.

The Corporal bet two fags, upping it to three when he saw the hand he'd been dealt. Jennings offered his copy of 'Men Only' as a stake.

'Are you sure about that?' Fisher asked him.

Jennings nodded. 'I've looked at the fucking thing so many times, I know every hair on those tarts' fannies personally.'

The other men laughed.

'Come on, guts.' said Fisher, looking at Turner who was in the process of shoving two biscuits into his cavernous mouth. 'What are you putting in?'

Turner shrugged.

'What about some of that grub you're hoarding in your pack?' said Harris, pushing a few coppers into the kitty.

Turner looked shocked.

'What do you mean, hoarding?' he said, indignantly.

Harris touched his temple knowingly.

'I saw you stuffing those bars of chocolate into your pack when we were in Goose Green, that old girl gave you a handful of the bloody things.'

Muttering irritably, Turner finally relented and added a bar of chocolate to the kitty as his stake. The men considered the cards they'd been dealt.

'I didn't realize it was so bleedin' cold out here,' said Fisher, shivering.

'We're not that far from Antarctica,' Brent told him. 'That's why.'

Brent, like Carter, was busy cleaning his equipment and they, like the rest, could hear the mournful wail of the wind as it buffeted the tent, flinging particles of snow against its canvas sides. Moss was crouched beside them, a pencil held in his gloved hand. He had a piece of paper before him, having just finished writing a letter home. The lad held the letter, sipping at his mug of soup with the other hand.

'To your girlfriend?' asked Brent, nodding in the direction of the letter.

'Parents,' Moss told him.

He quickly scanned what he'd written:

Dear Mum and Dad,

Just a few words to tell you that I'm fit and well. We're ashore now and have been for about six or seven days, it might be longer. You seem to lose track of time out here. It always seems so dark, it's difficult to tell whether it's day or night. We've seen a lot of action and, no doubt, you'll read about it in the papers. I am all right though so you needn't worry. We lost thirteen men in the fighting at Goose Green. We are near there now. Colonel Clavell was killed, so we are all a bit upset about that. The weather is terrible, it is snowing now and the mud is up to our ankles all the time, as soon as we dig a trench it fills up with mud again. It's so cold too. I was very scared during the fighting, I think all of us were really. The other blokes are tired and none of us have been able to have a wash for days. It is really miserable out here but we are in good spirits. I wish it was all over though. Tomorrow we are marching to Fitzroy.

I hope you are both well, and also all the family. I will write again when I get the chance.

Love from Ronnie.

Moss folded the letter and slipped it into an envelope, hurriedly sealing it. He would give it to one of the chopper pilots next time the rations arrived. The lad wasn't sure if any mail was even leaving the islands, or coming in for that matter. He didn't know if his parents would ever get to read the letter.

'I will write again when I get the chance.' The phrase seemed to reverberate back and forth inside his mind. Perhaps it should have read 'I will write again *if* I get the chance'. He tried to drive the thought from his mind but it refused to go. He closed his eyes but the thought was replaced by images. The infernal imagery of war: the explosions, the blasted corpses, the pock-marked fields, the shattered limbs, the faces of dying men frozen with that particular look which was a mixture of surprise and pain. But, for Ronnie Moss, the image which burned most brightly in that mantle of hell glittering with bleeding stars was the one of the Argentinian. The one he had killed in close combat, the one with the pickaxe in his head, the one whose brains had spilled out like grey porridge.

And the bodies of his comrades, laid out beneath their grey blankets in that grave which he had helped to dig. He could not help but wonder whether or not he himself would end up beneath one of those blankets.

'Full House,' called Harris, proudly, reaching out to grab the kitty. His shout startled Moss who snapped open his eyes, the images fading quickly.

'Just a bleedin' minute,' Fisher said, turning his cards over. 'Four Aces and a King. Get your sodding hands off that kitty.'

'You're cheating,' said Turner, looking at his own cards and then at the lance-jack.

'That,' said the cockney in an officious-sounding voice, 'is a very serious allegation. Where is your evidence, you gutsy sod?'

Turner flipped over his cards. 'Because *I've* got two bloody Aces.'

'Well, four beats two doesn't it?' said Fisher, unimpressed.

'You twisting sod,' said Wallace. 'No wonder you've been winning every bloody hand.'

The other men threw in their cards and moved away, muttering mutinously.

'If there's one thing I can't stand,' said Fisher, 'It's bad losers.' He grinned and began sorting through the kitty. 'Come on, anyone for another round?'

'I wouldn't play fucking tiddly-winks with you,' Wallace told him.

'Now, now, Knocker,' the lance-jack chided. 'It's only sour grapes because you lost.'

'I bet all those bloody cards came off the bottom of the pack anyway,' protested Harris.

'Look, it doesn't matter *how* you win as long as you win,' Fisher told them. 'That's what my old man always used to say. It don't matter if you have to bend the rules a bit, he used to say, the ends justify the means.'

'Is your dad dead?' Harris wanted to know.

'No,' said Fisher. 'He's in the Scrubs. Six years for fraud.'

The rest of the men cracked out laughing.

Even Moss managed a smile. He was chewing thoughtfully on a dry biscuit, taking mouthfuls after each sip of his steaming soup.

'What are you thinking about?' Carter asked him.

Moss shrugged.

'Not much,' he said. 'I was just remembering what I felt like when we attacked Goose Green. *How* I felt.'

'I know how *I* felt,' said Morris. 'Bloody scared and I don't mind admitting it either.'

'I think we all did if we tell the truth,' said Carter.

'I'm surprised to hear *you* say that, Alan,' Brent exclaimed.

Carter looked puzzled.

'Why?' he asked.

Brent elaborated.

'Well, you've been in the army for Christ knows how many years, I would have thought . . .' He hesitated. 'Well, I just didn't think it affected you any more.'

'Just because I happen to have seen my fair share of death doesn't mean I'm not scared of it,' he said. He told them about his brief cxchange with Sergeant James that afternoon and the men of the platoon sat in almost stunned silence as he related the tale. The older Para smiled thinly. 'Someone once said that war is 95% boredom and 5% sheer bloody fear. I think it's the other way around.' He returned to cleaning his rifle.

'I'm just thankful they didn't get a chance to use that fucking nalpam,' said Wallace.

'Napalm,' Brent corrected him.

'Whatever,' snapped the Corporal. 'I'm just pleased they missed us. We wouldn't have had a fucking chance.'

'Did you see those sheep caught in it?' asked Robertson.

'There's bloody blokes getting shot and blasted about left right and centre and you're worried about a few poxy sheep?' said Fisher.

'Nature always seems to suffer badly in a war,' the little Scotsman continued. 'I mean, look at the livestock that have been killed since the Argies first invaded.'

'Yeah, well the bastards have been eating them haven't they?' Fisher said, sharply. 'I mean they even ate that fucking dog we found.'

'The country's been ruined by the war,' Robertson said.

'It'd take more than a war to ruin this place,' Harris said.

'It's the bleakest bit of land I've seen in my life.'

'But it's still a piece of England,' Carter interjected and his remark seemed fitting conclusion to the conversation. A silence fell over the men and each seemed content to continue with the task of cleaning his rifle, checking his equipment or simply trying to get comfortable in the quagmire which was the slit trench. The wind continued to howl madly around the canvas which covered it and more than one of the men felt the first icy barbs of frost jabbing fingers at them through the chill night. Even through his gloves, Moss could feel just how numbingly cold the metal of his rifle had become and he, like the other men, rubbed grease into the firing mechanisms to ensure that the weapons didn't seize up completely. Brent, in particular, had field-stripped the LSW and was almost lovingly oiling and greasing each moving part of the complex firing mechanism. Finally satisfied, he rapidly reassembled the weapon, raising it to his shoulder and squinting down the sight. He wrapped it in its protective cloth and laid it against the wall of the trench.

Harris wrinkled his nose and looked around.

'What's the matter with you?' asked Morris, catching the look of disdain on his companion's face.

'What's that bloody smell?' Harris wanted to know.

And now the other men began to notice it, a cloying, rank odour which seemed to hang thickly in the air like invisible fog.

'Have you dropped your guts again, Turner?' said Fisher and the men laughed, all eyes turning towards Turner who was chewing on one of his bars of chocolate.

'Fuck off,' he grunted. 'It's not me.'

Wallace smiled, impishly and looked at Harris.

'Are you sure it's not you,' he said. 'They say a monkey always smells its own shit first.'

The other men broke up into a chorus of guffaws.

'It's not Turner,' said Carter, finally detecting the smell himself. 'It's all of us.' He lifted one arm and sniffed. 'Look at us, we're filthy. We haven't had a bloody wash since we landed. We all stink.'

The men began to realize that he was right and the smell suddenly didn't seem quite so important. They laughed about it.

'I shouldn't think the Argies will need radar or planes to spot us,' chuckled Fisher. 'If we're upwind of them, the bastards will be able to smell us.'

'You know, I heard that being dirty can be a good thing,' Brent said. He clarified. 'Natural body oil, like sweat, combined with dirt is supposed to keep you waterproof.'

Fisher reached back, his hand accidentally slipping into one of the pools of muddy water at the bottom of the trench. He held up the dripping limb.

'Waterproof eh?'

The men laughed.

'I hope you're wrong about the Argies smelling us coming,' said Anderson. 'If they're waiting for us again . . .' He let the sentence trail off.

'They can't run forever,' Carter said. 'Port Stanley's only about thirty miles from here. They've got their backs to the sea. In the end there won't be anywhere else for them to go.'

'How long do you reckon it'll take us to reach Fitzroy?' Harris wanted to know, his remark addressed to no one in particular.

'It depends what they've got lined up for us on the way.' said Carter, ominously.

Moss looked at him. He swallowed hard. Just what would be waiting for them the following day when they set off towards Fitzroy? The men knew that the ground between there and Goose Green was just as open and exposed as the rest of the island and, the youngster thought, the Argentinians would most certainly have had time to make better preparations than they had at Goose Green. He shuddered. The previous two days' fighting had been bad enough; a bout of combat even more savage than that was a daunting prospect indeed. He lay down on a piece of cardboard, listening to the wind, trying to blot out the thoughts from his mind. All around him, his companions were settling down in the foul conditions. Wallace extinguished the hurricane lamp and the place was suddenly flooded with thick impenetrable darkness. Moss drew his knees up to his chest and lay curled in a foetal position, waiting for the welcome oblivion of sleep, but it seemed that he was to be denied that respite. Thoughts tumbled over and over in his mind and, the more he tried to block them out, the more they surged back into him consciousness. A vision of home surfaced and he clung to it. Christ, what he wouldn't give to be home. Maybe if he was wounded . . .

He remembered the sight of the wounded men of the last couple of days. Legs shattered by explosions, faces dissolved into bloody pulp, limbs hanging off after the effect of close-range bullet wounds. Those men were going home, if they lived, but they would carry with them forever the memory of the living hell that was East Falkland. And yet Moss knew that he too, if he lived, would always carry a scar. A wound which had been slashed across his consciousness by the horrors he had seen. The dead and dying, the blood, the smell of death, the horror of artillery bombardment and, most striking of all, the image of that young Argentinian with the pickaxe still embedded in his skull. Moss feared that it would be something which resurfaced in his nightmares for the rest of his life. However long that was to be. He clamped his eyes tight shut, the sound of the wind now mingling with Turner's loud snores.

Fisher, also unable to sleep, prodded the big man with the toe of his boot and the noise ceased. The lance-jack pulled his greatcoat tighter around him, blowing on his gloved hands, but it was useless. The icy cold seemed to penetrate the very bones of the men. Many lay awake, just listening to the unceasing assault of the elements on their flimsy quarters, aware only of the screeching wind and the dreadful wetness which surrounded them, seeping through their uniforms. It was the first night that they'd really been able to rest for more than two days, but, despite their exhaustion, they found it difficult to sleep—some, like Moss, plagued by thoughts of what was to happen the next day, but most just unable to sleep in the revolting conditions.

Harris thought about his wife. It seemed like an eternity since he'd seen her, held her close to him. For all he knew his child could have been born by now. He hoped that he would live to see it. What would she do if he was killed, he wondered? He couldn't, wouldn't, expect her to remain alone with the child. Paula was only twenty-three, a year younger than he was. If anything happened to him, surely she would find someone else. Maybe in time even forget all about him. Harris swallowed hard. The thought of his child running about calling some other bloke 'daddy' was practically unbearable. He whispered his wife's name in the darkness.

Jennings was thinking about a woman too but he didn't know her name. Indeed, it didn't even matter if she had a name. She was blonde. Some nights she was a red-head, others a brunette. But, tonight, she was blonde. Long, flowing blonde hair which curled over her shoulders, spilling between the valley of her breasts which were firm and bared for him to see. She wore only a pair of white, high-heeled ankle straps and Jennings could see himself at her feet, his hands groping slowly up the inside of her thighs towards that patch of tightly curled golden hair. He slipped into the dream without even realizing it, the welcome approach of sleep intensifying the vision. Now he was kissing that soft mound and she was gasping in pleasure, urging him on, pushing her pelvis against his face. He stood up, her own moisture still on his lips as they kissed fiercely. He stepped back to look at her. It was as he did so that her head seemed to explode, the blonde hair suddenly becoming thickly matted with blood and pieces of brain, her eyes bursting from their sockets. And Jennings saw the smoke from some invisible rifle barrel in the distance as she fell forward, her blood splashing him.

Vince Jennings sat up, his body bathed in perspiration.

'Shit,' he gasped, blinking hard in the blackness, trying to make out shapes in the almost palpable gloom.

'What's wrong?' muttered Wallace, his voice sounding like gravel.

'I had a dream,' said Jennings.

'I bet I know what about eh?' said the Corporal, grinning.

Jennings nodded. It was a long time before the vision faded and he lay down once more in an effort to sleep. The wind still screamed around the tent and snow was filtering in through the flap in the canvas. Jennings lay awake listening to the sounds, his mind unsettled by the brief dream. Finally he slept, this time dreamlessly.

Carter, too, slept without the irritation of dreams. Crouched against the trench wall, he dozed uneasily, hands tucked into his pockets.

The Paras slept as best they could, those who were able. Other lay in the mud, their thoughts focused on many different things. Home, wives, girlfriends, victory.

Survival.

Men who weren't religious whispered little prayers to themselves.

Above them, the clouds continued to hurl down their snow, whipped into a frenzy by the incessant blustery wind. Particles of frost sparkled in the half-light and the filthy water which lay in the puddles was crusted over with ice. Over this freezing hell hung something much darker than the blackness of the night.

It was the spectre of death.

Nine

The farmstead was atop a slight rise, about two hundred yards from where Moss and the rest of the platoon crouched. The youngster peered over the hedge behind which they sheltered and squinted through the early morning mist at the clutch of white-washed buildings which made up the farmstead. He glanced to his left and saw Major Fulton studying the place through his binoculars. Then, suddenly both men ducked low as they heard the arc of a mortar shell. It fell to earth a little way behind them, the impact of the blast sending a fountain of earth and stones flying into the air. Away to the right, a group of British 51mm mortars replied and the shells were soon flying back and forth with alarming rapidity. Plumes of smoke rose into the morning sky and the men checked their weapons, preparing for the imminent assault.

The ground which led up to the buildings was open but criss-crossed by countless shallow gulleys. They at least would provide some cover. The ground sloped upwards sharply, levelling out as the farmstead was reached and then rising once more beyond it. Over that last hill lay Fitzroy.

It had taken the Paras nearly eight days to reach their next objective. The march across land had been slow, made more difficult by a rain storm which had yet to cease. The ground was practically impassable for vehicles and the big Scanias which dragged the artillery were still several miles behind, their cursing crews trying to dig them out of the oozing quagmire. The Paras themselves had been forced to help their comrades in the artillery on a number of occasions during the march on Fitzroy, heaving guns from deep puddles, pushing the massive bulk of lorries when they became bogged down in the sticky ooze. Even now, as the men awaited the order to attack, many found themselves sinking up to their calves in the mud. Moss amongst them. He shifted uncomfortably in the reeking slime, clutching the SLR tight across his chest, his heart thudding against his ribs.

Fulton peered myopically through the lenses of the binoculars, picking out a number of enemy troops moving freely amongst the buildings. He scanned the position closely. The farmhouse itself had been fortified, as had the fences which surrounded it. To the left of the buildings lay a dug-out which housed several mortars and, just ahead of that, two machine-gun nests. It was impossible to tell how many enemy troops were holed up in the farmhouse and its adjacent fortifications but, nevertheless, they were in a commanding position and Fulton sucked in an anxious breath as he considered the prospect of attack.

Another clutch of mortar shells hurtled from the sky, exploding almost simultaneously around the Paras. One man shrieked and toppled forward, propelled by the force of the explosions. A medic scuttled over to him, hurriedly fastening a tourniquet around his thigh. A lump of shrapnel the size of a ping-pong ball had hit him in the back of the leg, blasting off his kneecap, twisting the shattered limb into an impossible position. The Para groaned in agony as the medic worked over him. Moss turned away, his eyes tightly closed for a second.

There were more explosions, the sky now filled with grey smoke. The lad found it difficult to hear and he wondered if the continual bombardment had made him deaf but he was suddenly shocked back to reality by Carter's hand on his shoulder, shaking him.

'You all right?' the older man asked.

Moss swallowed hard and nodded.

'What the hell are we waiting for?' murmured Wallace, anxiously. He hefted the Sten gun before him and glanced up the hillside. There was a single dead sheep lying there.

'What's your fucking hurry, Knocker?' rasped Sergeant James.

There was an explosion nearby and both men ducked low, covering their heads as the debris rained down. Wallace felt a piece of stone bounce off his helmet and he cursed. Close to him, Carter was checking his rifle, ensuring that the magazine was full. He continued with his task, seemingly oblivious to the loud explosions going on all around. He fixed his bayonet.

Major Fulton took one last look through the binoculars then ducked down behind the hedge once more.

'There's a gulley there,' he said to Captain Hansen, indicating a deep cleft in the hillside which ran as far as the farmstead itself. 'Take a platoon and a few mortars. Cover us.'

Hansen nodded, rounded up the required amount of men and, dodging the swiftly falling bombs, they scuttled off in the direction of the depression pointed out by Fulton. The Major himself slammed in a fresh magazine, pulling back the bolt on his Sterling. He passed quickly along the lines of waiting Paras giving orders to the NCO's then, at a given signal, the men rose as one man, clambered over the hedge and charged up the hill towards the fortified farmstead. Bullets tore up the muddy ground around them, and for brief seconds, as they struggled over the covering hedge onto the hillside itself. Moss felt the breath catch in his throat and he threw himself down as one of the machine-gun nests opened up. Dozens of small geysers erupted only feet ahead of him, spattering across the front of the attacking Paras. The lad was sweating and his legs felt like jelly but he ran on, slipping once on the slimy slope, falling into the glutinous muck. But powerful hands shot out and pulled him to his feet and the youth found himself running alongside Carter and Brent. They were approaching the first of the hollows which pitted the hillside when the mortar bomb exploded behind them. The shock-wave lifted the three men off their feet, hurling them into the mud as if they'd been tossed by some huge invisible hand. Moss groaned and rolled over. Brent, hands pressed to his temples, was up on his knees, a thin trickle of blood running from his nose. Carter shook himself, let out a painful breath and clambered to his feet. His two companions were grateful to find that they were unharmed. A Para close by had not been so lucky. The blast had sent stones and shrapnel in all directions and a lump of it had hit him in the shoulder, smashing the clavicle. He lay still in the mud, shells exploding all around him, while a medic struggled to drag him back to the relative safety of the hedge.

Moss, Brent and Carter slithered into the hollow, bringing their weapons to bear on the farmstead. Brent chose his targets carefully, bringing down a couple of Argentinian troops.

A little to their right, Turner opened up with the GPMG, its heavy-grain slugs ripping across the rampart at the outskirts of the clutch of buildings. Pieces of wood flew into the air, blasted away by the impact of the bullets. Turner raked the enemy positions, covering Major Fulton and a small group of men as they drew nearer the first of the machine-gun nests.

Ducked low to avoid the withering fusillade of fire which dug up the ground around them, the men advanced and, at a signal from the officer, tossed grenades at the emplacement. They threw themselves down, covering their heads as four thunderous explosions rocked the very hillside itself. The machine-gun nest disappeared beneath a blanket of smoke and flame, the funnels of fire from the multiple blasts rising like shrieking geysers into the chill morning air. Bodies, pieces of equipment and lumps of earth were all lifted high by the impact and Fulton, first on his feet, swung the Sterling on the remains of the nest and cut down the one Argentinian that remained. Spurred on by this momentary triumph, the rest of the Paras charged forward once more.

Quite how many enemy troops were ensconced in the small farmstead was difficult to say, but the British found themselves racing into a withering salvo of small arms fire and three or four of them went down.

Robertson shouted in pain as a bullet caught him in the hip, the loud and sickening crack sounding almost deafening to Moss who was beside him. The hip-bone was splintered by the shot and the little Scotsman pitched backward, his rifle falling from his grip. Moss hesitated for a second, looking down at his fallen companion but Carter dragged the boy down just as a machine-gun opened up, spattering the ground before them with 7.62mm bullets. Carter grabbed the youth by the lapel and looked angrily at him.

'Don't ever stand around like that,' he rasped, the bullets singing over their heads.

'But he was wounded,' Moss protested.

'Then leave him to the medics,' hissed the older man. 'Next time you might lose your fucking head.' He released the youth who looked shocked. He glanced behind him to see Robertson being dragged into a hollow half way down the hill, trailing blood behind him. Moss felt dazed, as ifsomeone had beaten him about the head with a heavy stick. He was sweating profusely, his nostrils were filled with the stench of smoke and cordite and he was deafened by the constant explosions and rattle of small arms fire. But, even through the confusion, he could see that the fortified fence which ran around the farm was now little more than fifty yards away and, even as he watched, shells began falling in the very heart of the buildings, fired by the mortar battery supporting Captain Hansen's men on the left. Buildings simply collapsed under the force of the blasts, the flimsy structures collapsing in on those Argentinian troops sheltering inside. Men ran out into the yard to escape the falling roof, only to become victims of the shells which dropped wide of their targets.

And now, with the diversion complete, the Paras on the forward slope raced forward, those in the lead hurdling the ramparts in an effort to reach their foe. The Argentinian machine-gunners swing the M2 around, raking the men fighting over the fence, seemingly oblivious to the fact that they were bringing many of their own troops down in the random fusillade. Taking advantage of the temporary respite, Fulton and his group attacked the remaining nest.

The Major sprayed those inside with fire from his Sterling, watching as three of them went sprawling, one clutching at his throat. Blood was jetting madly through his fingers and he was writhing like an eel on a hot skillet, but Fulton paid his enemy no heed. He ducked beneath the swing of a rifle butt, aiming the sub-gun upward and firing a short-range blast which catapulted his attacker several feet across the nest. Another Argentinian put up his hands to surrender, screaming in shocked surprise when a stray bullet sliced off his middle finger. The severed digit dropped at his feet and the man fainted. Those still alive were quick to throw down their weapons and, leaving two men to watch the captives, Fulton dashed on to join the other Paras who, by now, had fought their way into the very centre of the yard itself.

Wallace was the first there. He looked around, trying to find cover as the Argentinians holed up in the buildings opened up on the exposed Paras. Two went down in the hail of bullets and, cursing, Wallace plucked a grenade from his belt and hurled it into the nearby barn. It exploded with a dull bang and a body was thrown out into the yard. The Corporal, now with Moss and Carter at his side, dashed towards the entrance, pausing in the clouds of thick smoke which billowed from the building. There must have been straw in there because they could see the orange light flickering from tongues of flame. Wallace opened fire with his Sten gun and the noise of the sub-gun seemed deafening in the close confines of the barn. Someone screamed, and Moss saw bodies moving through the smoke like ghosts in fog. Above them, in the loft, an Argentinian soldier fired down with his PAM 1 and the three paras drew back as the ground around them was raked with fire. The flames danced madly, the smell of burning mingling with the heady aroma of wet straw and mud. And there was something else which Moss noticed. A sweet, sickly smell which reminded him of burnt toast. It was the stench of charred flesh. As he watched, a figure staggered through the smoke and he could see that it was an enemy soldier. The man's hair and clothes were on fire and so were his hands. He held them out before him, stumbling towards Moss like an immolated sleep-walker. His eyes were bulging madly in their sockets, his mouth open and speaking soundless words of agony. Wallace shot him down.

Carter drew a bead on the Argentinian overhead and fired. The bullet hit him in the chest and he rolled over, losing his grip on the rafters. The body fell to the ground with a thud.

On the other side of the yard, Fulton and some other men were attacking the farmhouse itself but they found that the grey-clad troops had a machine-gun set up in the upper bedroom. Fulton found cover behind a rusty old tractor, the bullets singing off the hull, blasting away pieces of rust as if it were leprous flesh. He kept down, clinging to the side of the tractor. Two men joined him, one of them Fisher. The lance-jack chanced a quick look up at the offending machine-gun and nearly paid with his life. A bullet skimmed his cheek, drawing an angry red line across the flesh. It looked as though someone had marked him with a red biro. He yelped in pain and ducked down again, surprised that the wound wasn't bleeding. It felt as if it was burning. He dabbed a tentative finger at his cheek and winced. Major Fulton threw him a cursory glance, saw that he was not hurt and returned his attention to the farmhouse. Bullets were still hammering from the M2 and the Paras all over the yard were trying to find cover in the other buildings, two of which were ablaze. Smoke was rising in a huge cloud over the farmstead, dissipated to some extent by the ever present rain and strong winds, but still the barn and an outhouse flamed, spluttering dismally. The men inside coughed and wiped tears from their eyes. Moss was finding it difficult to breathe and his throat felt raw. He could almost taste the thick smoke in his mouth and millions of tiny cinders drifted through the air before him. He knelt just inside the door of the barn, firing at the farmhouse, ducking back out of sight when the Argentinian machine-gunners turned their weapon on the barn. Lumps of wood were blasted from the flimsy wall as the slugs thudded into it and Moss covered his face as splinters flew into the air.

Fulton, still crouching behind the tractor, suddenly snapped his fingers. Fisher turned to see his commander smiling.

'Rocket launchers,' said Fulton. 'Who's carrying them?'

Fisher hesitated a second.

'Morris, Briggs, Farmer . . .' He got no further. The Major scrambled to his feet and, catching sight of Ossie Morris nearby, sprinted across a few feet of open yard and flung himself down beside three or four Paras amongst whom was Morris. The men were using the wall of a pig-pen as cover, two of them even having climbed inside. Up to their knees in mud and pig shit, they kept up a concentrated fire against the house.

'Morris, your M72,' said Fulton, slapping the Para's pack. 'Use it against that house.'

Morris nodded, laid his rifle against the wall of the pigsty and fumbled in his pack for the rocket launcher, keeping his head down as best he could. He eventually withdrew the compact weapon and set about priming it. The 66mm anti-tank rocket launcher was less than arm's length when retracted but, as Fulton watched, Morris flicked a switch and pulled both ends of the thing, telescoping them out until he had a weapon as tall as a man. He pushed a shell in and raised the weapon to his shoulder, squinting down the sight.

'Now,' roared Fulton and Morris let fly.

The barrel flamed at both ends and a searing burst of fire roared from the mouth of the M72. Like ball lightning, the half-pound rocket sped from the gaping maw and powered into the farmhouse. There was an almighty explosion which sent pieces of masonry and lumps of metal flying in all directions. The roof of the house seemed to lift for a second before crashing back into position, immediately collapsing in on itself. A shower of sparks and smoke ballooned upward and the house momentarily disappeared beneath a choking blanket of grey smoke. The windows were blasted outward, showering the yard with shards of gleaming crystal, the high-pitched explosion of glass filling the air. The smoke rolled away to reveal the damage.

'Bleedin' hell,' muttered Fisher.

The roof and most of the upper floor had been blasted away and what remained of the farmhouse had been reduced to flaming ruin. Yet still, amidst the smoke and leaping tongues of fire, Argentinian troops were firing back at the bewildered British. The machine-gun, however, had been silenced. Now only the chatter of small arms could be heard.

Wallace, leaning against the entrance to the barn, shook his head in dismay.

'Fuck me,' he grunted. 'I thought that bloody rocket would have taken care of all those bastards.'

He was still pondering the question when Moss turned to see a savagely wounded Argentinian staggering towards them, his rifle lowered and pointed at the Corporal's back. For long seconds, Moss was frozen, unable to yell the warning which he knew would save his companion's life, then finally:

'Look out,' he shouted and Wallace spun round.

The enemy soldier, bleeding from countless wounds, tried in vain to drive his bayonet into the Corporal but Wallace merely side-stepped and shot the man down. He fell beside Moss who found himself pinned in the gaze of the dying man. Then the Argentinian rolled onto his back and the youngster once more was aware of the pungent stench of excrement, emanating slowly from the body. He remained there for long seconds, seemingly transfixed by the sight of the corpse, then suddenly he heard shouts from the yard and turned to see what was happening.

Four or five Argentinians, one of them supported by a comrade, were walking out of the smouldering ruin of the farmhouse, hands held high above their heads. Paras nearby, weapons still levelled at their foes, moved forward cautiously. The Argentinians still held their rifles and, with the memory of the Goose Green incident still fresh in their minds, the Paras were taking no chances.

In faltering Spanish, Major Fulton told them to drop their weapons which they immediately did. A British medic scurried over to attend to the wounded captive who had sustained a deep cut just below his right eye and was also bleeding from a wound in his thigh. The damaged leg hung limply beneath him and whatever had done the harm had obviously shattered the femur, a portion of which was protruding through the flesh. The Argentinian was in his teens and there were tears coursing down his cheeks as the medic guided him across to a second, smaller, barn where half a dozen Paras also lay wounded. Robertson was amongst them. He lay unconscious next to a corporal with a bullet wound in his right hand which had almost torn off the thumb. Another medic was hastily bandaging the limb. Father Driscoll was also moving amongst the wounded of both sides, helping where he could, speaking quietly to the men. The barn was thick with the smell of blood and sweat, mingling with the more powerful odour of wet straw and what appeared to be sheep dung. The remains of a sheep lay in one corner of the barn, the grisly reminder of the fact that the Argentinians were short of food. Its sightless eyes watched the comings-and-goings of the wounded impassively and, despite the cold weather, flies buzzed indolently around it and already a seething white mass of maggots were busy devouring what was left of the carcass.

In the courtyard, Major Fulton and Captain Hansen were discussing losses and what to do with the wounded. A radio message had already come through to say that, because of the weather, no helicopters would be able to reach the battle zone that day. The prisoners stood silently in the teeming rain, watching as the British officers discussed the situation. Moss scanned the mournful group of captives, not one of them older than himself. They stared back at him with a look of despair and bewilderment.

'Just kids,' said Anderson, appearing at his side.

All of them looked pallid and drawn, as pale as death. Their uniforms were worn and dirty and one of them, Moss noted, had a bloodied bandage wrapped around his hand. The knees and elbows of their uniforms were threadbare. One of the prisoners, the youngest, was tentatively touching at one of the boils which covered his face. Moss lowered his eyes, the sight sickening him. When he looked up again, the prisoners were being shepherded away by a couple of other Paras. The captives stumbled blindly down the hill, passing the blood-spattered, shell-torn slopes and the twisted corpses of their countrymen.

'We're going to have to set up shop here,' said Major Fulton to a medic. 'At least until the choppers can get through to take the wounded out.' He left Captain Hansen to select twelve men to stay behind and guard the makeshift field hospital. The other Paras formed up in a loose column and gathered behind their officers, ready to climb the steep slope which would lead them on toward Fitzroy.

Moss glanced over his shoulder as the battalion began its march up the hillside, his eyes moving swiftly over the remnants of the farmstead; the barn and outhouse still smouldering; the cratered yard and the bodies of the enemy troops being dragged away by the Paras who had remained behind. A pall of grey smoke hung over the battlefield like a dark shadow, that swirled and eddied as the wind and rain buffeted it. The icy droplets were still falling fast and Moss wiped his face as he walked, finding, as were his companions, that the wind was blowing in their faces. It flung the rain at them, reducing visibility, the stinging particles bouncing off their skin and uniforms. It bounced off their helmets, dripping from the rims. Moss felt a steady stream of it dripping down his back. He shivered and licked his lips. They felt numb and when he spoke his voice was slurred as if he couldn't form the words properly.

'Jesus,' he gasped. 'It's cold.'

'I can put up with the cold,' said Fisher. 'It's this bleedin' rain that gets on my wick.'

'Did you see those Argies that surrendered?' said the youth. 'They looked as if they were starving to death.'

Carter grunted. 'Yeah, and our bloody supplies will be feeding the bastards.'

'We ought to let them starve,' added Wallace.

'Quiet back there.'

The shout came from Sergeant James, slowing his pace as Major Fulton paused at the top of the hill. The officer raised the binoculars and squinted through them, pausing once to wipe rain from the lenses.

Below him, barely visible through the curtain of rain, was the settlement of Fitzroy.

It looked so small, even when the Major lowered his field glasses. The ground sloped away before them, dipping into a quagmire and then rising again as the outskirts of Fitzroy clung to the hillside. There were a number of Argentinian positions on the farther slope, just ahead of the settlement but Fulton could see no sign of troop movement. He sucked in an anxious breath and peered through the binoculars once more.

'What the hell's he waiting for?' Morris wanted to know. He wiped his nose on his sleeve.

The Major was crouching on the brow of the hill, Captain Hansen at his side. The men behind could see the two officers motioning towards the enemy positions. Whatever they were saying was drowned out by the ever present roaring of the wind and the whiplash of the rain. Indeed, at one point, Moss saw Fulton topple over, such was the power of the wind. The officer went sprawling in the mud for a second then, smiling, he clambered upright once more. The young private saw him pointing at something and, a second later, there was a loud explosion just to the left of the waiting Paras.

'Jesus Christ,' hissed Fisher and spun round to see the last of the blast fragments falling to earth.

Its high-pitched whistle hidden by the roaring wind, another shell landed close by and the Paras threw themselves down. The explosion left a large crater in the thick mud and smoke drifted mournfully from it. Carter looked up into the grey sky, almost expecting to see a flight of Pucaras or Skyhawks diving in on them. All he saw in the end was the brief, blinding flash of fire as another shell hit the ground. Lumps of mud showered the Paras who were trying to dig in as best they could, taken by surprise by the sudden bombardment.

Moss looked up and saw Fulton and Hansen scurrying back from the crest. Orders were shouted and men dashed into their appointed positions.

'What the hell is going on?' demanded Morris.

'The fucking Argies,' Sergeant James roared. 'They're attacking.'

Morris was momentarily stunned by this revelation but, as he slithered up to the crest of the ridge with the rest of the platoon, he saw that a large group of enemy troops were crossing the shallow valley, leaving the relative safety of Fitzroy itself to attack the oncoming British. They splashed through the swamp at the base of the valley, sinking up to their knees in the mud, weapons held above their heads and, as he watched, Moss was suddenly reminded of the landing at Port San Carlos. Of how he and his companions had come ashore in just such a manner. He could imagine the terror which his enemies must now be feeling as they struggled to keep their feet in the appalling conditions. Forced on by their officers, the Argentinians finally reached the slope which led up to the British positions. As they did so, a mortar battery opened fire and shells began to fall amongst them. Moss saw men hurled into the air. Others went down as if pole-axed and, as he glanced to one side he saw Carter shaking his head.

Turner dropped the legs of the bipod and squinted down the sight of the GPMG, waiting until the order was given before opening up. Brent was looking through the scope on the LSW, trying to pick out officers amongst the bunched Argentinian infantry. He spotted one and kept the weapon trained on his target.

The enemy troops were now less than fifty yards away.

Moss covered his head as another shell exploded, this time ahead of him. The smoke billowed up for brief seconds before being swept away by the furious rain which was still driving into the faces of the British. Men tried to shield their eyes from the onslaught. Moss was shivering, his entire body quaking, but he wasn't sure if it was all caused by the freezing conditions. His heart was thudding madly against his ribs as the Argentinians drew nearer, and he tried to control his breathing. He glanced across at Carter who had his own SLR pressed tight to his shoulder. The older man was watching the enemy advance with narrowed eyes, his forehead wrinkled.

'They must be fucking mad,' said Wallace as the enemy drew closer. He slid back the bolt on the sub-gun and pressed the cold metal stock to his shoulder.

The Argentinians were finding it hard going and they had slowed their pace despite the fanatical urgings of their officers. They struggled up the hillside, panting for breath, fearful of what they would run into when they finally reached the waiting Paras. They didn't have long to wait until they found out.

With the leading enemy troops a mere twenty yards away, Fulton raised his Sterling.

'That's close enough,' he whispered to himself and opened fire.

It was the signal for the entire contingent of Paras to do likewise and, in a split second, the air was suddenly filled with the chatter of small arms. The wave of lead hit the leading Argentinians and brought them down in heaps. They hesitated but were pushed onward by their officers to meet the full fury of the British guns.

Turner tightened his finger around the trigger of the machine-gun, raking the oncoming grey men, the empty cartridge cases spraying upward in a brass cascade. Teeth gritted, he kept up a sustained fire, the butt of the weapon pounding against his shoulder.

Brent chose his moment carefully and watched as the bullet from the LSW sent an Argentinian officer sprawling in the mud, his lower jaw torn off by the impact.

The Sten gun jerked in Wallace's grip as he fired short bursts.

'Come and get it, you bastards,' he growled, watching as more and more of the grey-clad Argentinians fell beneath the concentrated fire. All along the line rifle and sub-gun barrels flamed and the Paras watched as their enemies first hesitated, then began to turn and run. However, officers quickly stepped in to rally their terrified men and now the Paras found that bullets were singing over *their* heads. Moss kept low, firing at all before him, watching as the Argentinians stood almost motionless on the forward slope firing at the British. But, in their exposed position, they were sitting ducks and the Paras' deluge of bullets was horrifyingly accurate. More enemy troops went down, the wounded trying to crawl away in the mud, those not able to helped to their feet by comrades.

Turner saw one Argentinian with his leg blasted in two places by slugs being supported by two of his companions. The Para turned the machine-gun on them and brought the whole trio down in a bloodied heap. Yet still the officers continued to scream at them and once more they rallied, firing back at the British.

A private near to Moss was hit in the face, the bullet shattering his cheekbone as it ploughed into him. The man's face dissolved into a crimson ruin and he rolled over onto his back.

'Shoot the officers,' bellowed Fulton, spraying the enemy troops with his Sterling.

Brent heard the order and swung the LSW onto an Argentinian captain who was physically pushing two men back towards the British lines. Brent drew a bead on his victim then, with unerring accuracy, sent a heavy-grain bullet powering into the officer. It hit him in the throat, the impact shattering his larynx, almost tearing his head off. The body toppled backwards spouting blood into the air and, immediately, the two Argentinians fled, hurdling the corpse in their hurry to escape. Brent peered through the scope, looking for more officers. He spotted a young Lieutenant who had succeeded in gathering half a dozen men around him. The little group were firing into some Paras away to the left and Brent saw at least one of his companions hit in the furious exchange of fire. He sucked in an angry breath and aimed carefully at the Lieutenant, waiting until the man's head came squarely between the cross-threads of the sight. He squeezed the trigger, watching as the bullet found its mark.

It caught the unfortunate officer just above the right eye, the power of the impact ripping away a large chunk of his skull. The bullet tore through his head and burst from the other side, the exit hole gushing blood and sticky grey matter thickly into the air. His helmet was sent spinning several yards, the chinstrap torn by the incredible velocity of the bullet.

The six or seven men who had been with him dropped their weapons and just stood still. Others were fleeing down the corpse-strewn hillside, knocking officers aside in their efforts to get away. Anderson watched in horror as an Argentinian Major shot two of his own men down as they fled past him. He stood over the bodies for a moment, as if to approve their punishment for running. He confronted another fleeing man and pointed his pistol at the terrified private who merely dropped his rifle and tried to push past the officer. Anderson saw the Major pointing up at the hilltop then, as the private tried to get away, the Major shot him in the back.

'They're shooting their own men,' gasped the Para incredulously. His face was white, his lips fluttering soundlessly for a second. He grabbed Carter by the arm. 'They're shooting their own men,' he babbled once more but Carter was unimpressed.

Anderson exhaled deeply, the breath coming out almost as a dejected sob. He could barely believe what he had seen. Was this what war was really all about? Was this the fanaticism of which men spoke? He felt sick, disgusted by the horrific scenario which he had witnessed. He lay prone, the rifle still gripped firmly in his fists, his head touching the reeking mud.

'You hit?'

He looked up to see Carter staring at him.

Anderson shook his head. He gazed ahead of him, seeking out the officer and he felt an odd kind of satisfaction when he saw the Major lying face down in the oozing mud at the bottom of the valley. Of the other Argentinians there was no sign. The slopes on both sides of the depression were littered with helmets and discarded weapons. There were about forty or fifty bodies scattered about, some wounded. But their cries for help were carried away on the wind and all the Paras were aware of was the pelting rain. It continued to lash into their faces. Moss felt as though his head had been immersed in freezing water for a week. His eyes were red-rimmed and he coughed harshly. The smell of damp and wet clothes was powerful enough even to cover the odour of cordite and blood. Smoke wafted lazily over the slopes, like the gossamer shreds of some torn shroud. Medics were already scurrying around from man to man, checking that everyone was o.k., attending to wounds as best they could.

Major Fulton went from unit to unit, getting reports from the platoon commanders on the state of their men. Moss saw him talking to Sergeant James, the NCO nodding as he listened. Then, a moment later, the officer scuttled off and

James hauled himself through the mud towards the waiting platoon.

'We're moving on,' the Sergeant bellowed, cupping both hands to his mouth to make himself heard.

Carter saw half a dozen men, a couple dressed in sappers' uniforms, cross the crest of the hill. They were carrying long metal poles with flat steel planchettes attached to the bottom.

'The approaches must be mined,' Carter said, watching as the six men moved cautiously down the slope to the valley floor and then tentatively up the other side, coming close to the dug-outs and slit trenches which the Paras had first noticed when they reached the top of the hill. The mine detectors were supported on either side by twelve men, all heavily armed. The bulk of the battalion followed at a safe distance, headed by Fulton and Hansen.

There was no sign of movement from the bunkers or the settlement itself, but the Paras kept their eyes open just the same. If this war had taught them one thing it was to expect the unexpected. Moss and his companions trudged on, discovering just how bad conditions on the valley floor really were. The mud clung defiantly to their boots, threatening to tug them off. In places knee deep, it made vile sucking sounds as the men struggled through it. There was a pungent odour in the air which reminded Moss of rotting vegetation.

'What's that bleedin' smell?' said Fisher, wrinkling his nose. 'Has someone blown off?'

'It's methane,' Brent told him. 'Marsh gas. This must be some sort of bog.'

'Well, it certainly smells like a shit house,' added Harris, almost slipping over in the slimy ooze.

Carter didn't join in the conversation. His gaze was riveted to the six men ahead with the mine detectors. He put up a hand to shield his face from the rain, watching as one of the men swept his device back and forth, motioning to a patch of ground just ahead of him. One of the Paras just behind him stepped forward, sliding his bayonet from its scabbard. He dropped to his knees in the muck and began probing around with the blade, looking up at the sapper when both of them finally heard the chink of metal on metal. The Para set about digging the mine out while his companion moved on, trying to find more of the lethal devices. Over a wide area a number of the mines were discovered, each dug out in the same laborious manner.

The sappers and their escorts were about two hundred yards from the first house (itself flanked by two machine-gun nests) when they saw the Argentinians rising from behind the ramparts of sandbags and wood.

Fulton held up a hand as he noticed a tatty white flag fluttering in the breeze. He walked forward slowly, his arm still raised, his men holding their weapons at the ready. Once more the vision of the Goose Green incident flashed into their minds. Rifle barrels were brought to bear on the enemy troops who stood shivering in the rain as Fulton and a handful of men approached. The Major, his arm still raised, seemed to be moving in slow motion and Moss swallowed hard as he watched the Officer approaching the enemy positions. The white flag continued to wave.

Fulton shouted something in Spanish and one of the Argentinians replied. A second later they threw down their weapons and clambered over the rampart. Hands held high above their heads, they began walking slowly towards the waiting Paras. Moss guessed that there must be about fifty of them; most bore wounds of some description and, once again, he was amazed by their youthfulness although the rigours of the weather and the combat were etched upon them. They were soaking wet and shivering and they moved forward with a haste which testified to their relief that the war, for them at least, was over.

The leading Argentinian was about thirty feet from Fulton when he stepped on one of the mines.

There was a thunderous roar, a geyser of fire and earth and the grey-clad man disappeared.

'Shit,' murmured Anderson, ducking as the last of the debris rained down. A severed ear landed close by and the Para looked away. Nothing remained of the Argentinian; only the smoking crater showed that he'd been there at all. His companions froze, not daring to put their feet down should the same fate befall them, but Major Fulton motioned them forward, indicating a route cleared by the sappers. Cautiously, the enemy troops walked towards their waiting captors, arms still held high above their heads. Led by a young corporal, they were escorted to the rear, leaving the Paras to move on, unmolested, towards the settlement itself.

What they found was a familiar sight. Discarded weapons and ammo, helmets and packs thrown away and, most disturbing of all, the mindless destruction which had been committed against the homes of the islanders. The Paras passed through Fitzroy discovering that there were no civilians to be found. Houses were searched but it was obvious to all of them that the inhabitants must have fled before the Argentinians arrived.

'Probably buggered off into the hills,' said Harris, looking up at the desolate ridges which surrounded the settlement.'

'There must be little farmsteads all over the island,' Anderson added, wiping his nose with the back of his hand.

The battalion moved through Fitzroy, relieved to find that the bridge was still intact. They crossed it, their boots beating out a loud tattoo on the metal surface. The inlet beneath them frothed and foamed and the smell of salt water wafted over them.

'Just like being at the seaside,' said Harris, smiling. Moss looked down at the choppy water and it made him feel sick. He'd been plagued by seasickness during the entire voyage from England and now, the sight of the wind-whipped water beneath him brought those memories flooding back. The rain had eased slightly and the men found that they had only the wind to contend with. It buffeted them mercilessly as they crossed the bridge and Moss had visions of being blown over the side into the choppy water beneath.

'I wonder why the Argies didn't blow the bridge?' Fisher asked. 'Or at least booby-trap it.'

'Maybe they were in too much of a bloody hurry,' said Carter.

Fisher stroked his chin thougthfully. 'You know, I didn't expect them to attack us, the way they did back there. I mean they've been running for most of the time. Why change tactics now?'

'How far are we from Port Stanley?' asked Brent.

Fisher shrugged.

'Ten, maybe twelve miles,' he said.

'There's your answer then,' Brent said. 'There isn't much further they *can* run.'

Moss shivered and looked up at the sky, relieved to find that the rain had stopped altogether. However, banks of grey cloud still scudded menacingly across the heavens, a warning of more to come. The wind plunged icy fingers into him and he narrowed his eyes against the onslaught. The hills rose sharply again beyond the bridge and the men found themselves walking, once more, in the sucking mud which clung defiantly to their boots. They fought their way up the slippery slope, spread out in a wide line as they approached the crest of the hill.

Fulton raised a hand for them to halt. He raised his binoculars once more and peered down at the small settlement before them. It seemed to be resting on the very edge of the foaming water, only a narrow strip of beach separating the houses from the sea. The mud round about looked almost red, dotted here and there with clumps of stunted grass.

'Bluff Cove,' said Fulton, quietly.

Hansen heard him but his attention was riveted to something which was moving just beyond the village. The Captain touched his superior's arm and motioned towards the scenes of activity. Fulton trained the field glasses on the position indicated by Hansen, adjusting the focus dial until everything swam into crystal clarity.

'Troops?' said Hansen, flatly.

Fulton nodded.

'I don't think they've seen us,' he said, Then, lowering the binoculars:

'Have the men dig in, I'm not risking another frontal attack. We'll wait until morning.'

Hansen nodded and scuttled off to relay the orders. Fulton ducked down, squinting once more through the powerful lenses, scanning the men below him. They were moving around quite freely on the far side of the settlement, quite oblivious to the Paras on the hill above them. The drifting banks of drizzle acted like a mist, effectively masking the troops. All Fulton could make out was their dark outlines as they went about their business. He guessed that there were about five hundred of them, maybe more. They were spread over a wide area and he could see the shape of heavy guns through the swirling clouds of fine rain. The Major exhaled deeply. It was going to be a difficult job dislodging *that* lot.

Ten

Moss sat huddled on a piece of cardboard, a mug of steaming soup held in his hands. The ground at the bottom of the slit trench was pockmarked, the holes filled with water. Outside, beyond the relative shelter of the canvas which covered the trench, the wind was whipping up light flurries of snow and those men on guard duty moved about constantly for fear that they might succumb to exposure. There had already been two cases that night. The temperature, Brent informed them, was ten below freezing.

Moss looked around at his companions: they too were drinking from battered mugs and the steam which rose from their beverages seemed to glide around the dug-out like a white fog. Carter was chewing on a stale biscuit, dipping it into his hot chocolate to soften it.

'I wonder how old Robbo is?' said Fisher, gazing down into his mug as if hoping to find the answer there.

'He might be wounded,' said Harris, 'but at least he's got his ticket out of here.'

'That's a hell of a fucking way to get home,' said Carter, acidly. 'He'll probably be on crutches for the rest of his life.'

'I reckon we underestimated the Argies,' said Morris.

'How do you mean?' Wallace wanted to know.

'Well, that business today. Did you expect *them* to attack *us*?'

The Corporal shook his head.

'I told you,' Carter interjected. 'They're getting desperate.'

'I heard that there's quite a few men gathered around Bluff Cove,' said Moss. 'Perhaps they're going to make a stand there.'

Carter shook his head.

'It's too open, they'll wait until they get to the heights around Stanley.'

Turner exhaled deeply.

'I couldn't give a shit where they decide to fight,' he grunted. 'I just wish to Christ that we could get all this over with.'

'Amen to that,' echoed Anderson.

There was a moment's silence finally broken by Fisher.

'I wonder what'll happen to the islands when the war's over,' he pondered.

'It all depends who wins,' said Brent, cryptically.

Wallace turned on him angrily.

'What the fuck is that supposed to mean?' he snarled.

'I didn't mean that they'd beat us,' Brent said, quickly qualifying his statement.

Anderson swallowed a mouthful of soup and bit his bottom lip contemplatively.

'You know, that's something none of us have considered, is it? I mean, what will happen if they beat us?'

'But they won't,' rasped Wallace.

'No, leave off, Anderson,' added Fisher. 'We've already seen that they ain't got no bottle. I mean just look at what happened at Goose Green, at that farm-house, even today. The Argies haven't got the guts for a long fight.'

'Even if we win though,' Anderson persisted. 'We chuck them off the island, right? What's to stop them invading again?'

A silence fell over the men, as if each were waiting for someone to answer the question. It was something none of them had thought about up until now.

'This could turn into another Northern Ireland,' Anderson persisted. 'We'll have to have troops stationed here all the time, just in case the Argies try it again.'

Fisher waved the suggestion away.

'No chance,' said the lance-jack. 'After the way we've kicked the bastards about, they'll be only too pleased to get off and leave the bloody place alone.'

'Never mind the islands,' said Morris. 'What's going to happen to us after the war?'

‘Do you reckon we’ll get medals?’ Harris wanted to know.

Some of the others laughed.

‘Sitting around in this bloody mud, all we’re likely to get is bleedin’ piles,’ said Fisher.

‘I think I’ll buy myself out when it’s all over,’ said Turner.

‘What for?’ Wallace wanted to know.

‘Well, I’ve been in the army for seven years, ever since I was nineteen. I fancy being a civilian.’

‘What would *you* do in civvie street?’ Fisher demanded. ‘You’d have to get a job. There’s three million other poor sods out of work; who the hell would emplo you?’

‘I’d go and work with my brother, he’s got a garage in Manchester.’

Civilian. The word reverberated around inside Carter’s mind.

Civilian.

Christ, it was almost frightening when he thought about it. His twenty-one years would be up next July. What the hell was he going to do then? The prospect of life without the army frightened him. He sipped his hot chocolate thoughtfully. The army provided, it gave a man something to support him. It gave him friends. Not the shallow friendships which grew from day to day contact or chance meeting, but the comradeship which was forged between men who underwent the same joys and hardships together year in year out. It was a shelter. A convenient khaki-coloured wing which sheltered its fledgelings and its veterans. If you needed a new pair of trousers, the army gave them to you. If you felt rough, the army looked after you. Carter knew that there was none of that in civilian life. No one gave a fuck about anyone else. When you left the army you were on your own, no one to fall back on, no one to support you. It was you against the world, The older man exhaled deeply, the thoughts troubling him. He looked across at Moss. The youngster still had plenty of time ahead of him. He had only signed up for three years, and, if he made it through, he would be able to leave the forces in better shape than he’d joined. He would be able to adjust to that new world where everyone wore their own private uniform, fought their own private wars. But Carter knew that he himself would go down. Forced from the confines of an environment he knew and loved, thrown into the kind of conflict where success was judged by material possessions. Into a world where the fighting never stopped and there was always someone ready to cut your throat or stab you in the back. He shuddered a little and sipped at his drink.

'Well, I reckon they'll chicken out,' said Fisher.

'I hope you're right,' echoed Brent.

'I just hope no one gets hurt,' said Anderson. 'There's been enough killing already.'

The flap over the trench was raised and Sergeant James slipped in, joining the men, taking a cup of hot tea when it was offered to him.

'What's doing, Sarge?' Wallace wanted to know.

'Nothing at the moment,' James told them, cupping his hands around the steaming mug. 'The bastards aren't moving yet.'

'What's the drill for tomorrow?' asked Fisher.

'Well, there's about six hundred Argies down in Bluff Cove,' the sergeant told them. 'Major Fulton reckons that we should attack before dawn. The ground leading to the settlement is too open.'

'Everywhere on this bloody island is open,' said Turner.

James ignored his comment.

'Captain Hansen will take half the battalion around the northern flank, the Major will take the rest straight at them.'

'But what about mines?' Anderson wanted to know. 'What if the approaches are mined like they were this morning?'

James took a sip of his tea.

'Then you'll be the first to know about it.'

Harris smiled.

'Only six hundred of them eh? It should be a doddle. I mean, there were 1,500 at Goose Green weren't there?'

He looked around as if expecting the other men to share his optimism but an uneasy silence remained upon them. Harris sighed.

'What time is it now?' Fisher wanted to know. He glanced at his own watch which had been smashed by a lump of shrapnel the day before.

'Going on for ten,' said James. 'You lot better get some shut-eye. We move out at 0.400 in the morning.' He scrambled to his feet and clambered out of the trench, scuttling off to complete his check of the other platoons. The men settled down as best they could, huddling closer together for warmth. The flap of the canvas whipped back and forth noisily in the wind. It reminded Moss of someone clapping, the disembodied applause finally carried away on the banshee-like howl of the wind. The youth curled up into a ball and blew on his hands, trying to restore some of the circulation to his frozen limbs. Even enclosed in the cocoon of his sleeping-bag he found it difficult to find any warmth.

The hurricane lamp had been extinguished, and the men lay in darkness. Wallace was smoking a roll-up; Carter had his eyes closed but no sleep would come. Turner shifted uncomfortably in his sleeping-bag, the dampness seeping slowly through the material. Then, through the blackness, a voice drifted. A voice which sang as beautifully as any of the men had ever heard.

'I hear the drizzle of the rain, like a memory it falls. Soft and warm, continuing, tapping on my roof and walls.'

The men listened, stunned when they realized that the voice belonged to Harris.

'And from the shelter of my mind, through the window of my eye,

I gaze beyond the rain-drenched streets, to England where my heart lies.'

It ceased abruptly.

'That song was playing on a juke-box when I first met my old lady,' said Harris, quietly.

'It's beautiful,' Anderson told him.

Harris smiled. 'You know how you always think of different things when you hear a song, how some songs can bring back memories. Well, that's what I always think of when I hear that.' His voice was cracking slightly. 'Christ, I wish I could be with her. Just once more,' he whispered and he spoke her name softly.

Moss was weeping soundlessly.

The wind and snow kept up their ceaseless barrage against the trench and its canvas covering. The wailing wind reminding Moss of a man in pain.

He wondered how many times he would hear that cry the following day.

Moss yawned and rubbed his eyes. It didn't seem more than five minutes since he'd drifted into an uneasy sleep and now, he lay crouched in the windswept grass which covered a bank about two hundred yards from Bluff Cove. Once again, the youth could smell the strong odour of salt water, the wind bringing it in from the nearby inlet. In the twilight of dawn the houses of the settlement were just black outlines against the grey sky. Small drifts of snow had piled up in several places during the night, dotted about the grassy slopes like ruptured pillows. It reminded Moss of the Yorkshire Moors. He'd been there once with his parents when he was twelve. The memory resurfaced briefly but he drove it away. The snow and rain had stopped but the ever-present wind still gusted strongly into the faces of the waiting Paras. Some lowered their heads, shielding themselves from the icy blast. Moss could feel his eyes stinging and he shivered uncomfortably as he waited for the order to move forward.

There were no fortifications around the outskirts of the settlement. Curious, thought Carter. The Argentinians would certainly have been expecting an attack in this area sooner or later and they would have had plenty of time for putting up defences, but the place seemed relatively unguarded. That in itself was ominous and Carter wondered if the approaches to the settlement *were* mined as they'd all feared.

Fulton checked his watch, squinting in the darkness, looking closely as the second hand crept around to the appointed mark. He waved his arm forward and the Paras began their slow, cautious advance.

At exactly the same time, on the northern side of the settlement, Captain Hansen was leading the other half of the battalion in.

Moss gripped his SLR tightly and, despite the cold, found that beads of perspiration were glistening on his forehead. He swallowed hard and crept forward, sticking close by Carter and Harris. Away to his left, he could see Major Fulton, the Sterling gripped tightly in his fist as they drew nearer to the first of the buildings. Moss wasn't sure where to look. He glanced down at the ground every few yards, conscious of the fact that they could be crawling through a minefield but he was also aware that enemy troops might appear at any moment ahead of him and begin firing.

Fisher sneezed and received an angry glance from Sergeant James.

The lance-jack shrugged and crawled on.

The Paras were now less than twenty yards from the first building and still they could see no movement ahead of them. The silence was almost deafening, broken only by the rushing of the wind in their ears.

Then, they heard it. The rattle of weapons and half a dozen dark shapes appeared ahead of them.

'Halt,' called a voice in broad Scots. 'Who goes there?'

The Paras froze.

'Advance and be recognised,' the voice told them.

Fulton got cautiously to his feet, the Sterling still gripped tightly in his hand.

'Major Fulton. Two Para.' He paused. 'Who the hell are you?'

'Private McLeish, First Platoon, Scots Guards.'

Fulton smiled and walked forward towards the waiting men, the other Paras joyfully getting to their feet along with him.

The Scot saluted and Fulton returned the gesture.

'We thought you were bloody Argies,' said the Major, smiling.

'They fucked off . . .' The private apologised. 'They *cleared* out before we arrived, sir.' he said.

'Who is your commanding officer?'

'Colonel Narey, sir. He's in that building there, sir,' the private said, pointing towards a white-washed building about fifty yards away.

Fulton asked how long the men had been in Bluff Cove.

'We were landed yesterday, sir,' the private explained. 'There's a full battalion here at the moment and some artillery. A battalion of Welsh Guards are being landed later today.'

The Major nodded and walked on past the Scotsmen, towards the place where he had been told Colonel Narey was.

The other Paras by now had reached the settlement and the two sets of troops were greeting each other warmly.

'You lot took your fucking time getting here, didn't you?' said one the the Guards, grinning. He fumbled in his pocket and took out a pack of cigarettes, offering them to those troops nearby.

'Why did they send a bunch of bloody jocks in?' Fisher wanted to know. 'We were doing all right by ourselves.'

'They knew you British could never manage the Argies alone so they thought they'd let us have a go,' another of the Guards told him. The Scots round about laughed.

'Are you linking up with us?' Carter wanted to know.

'Not yet,' the private told him. 'We've got to wait until the Welsh Guards are landed.'

Fisher grinned. 'Scottish, Welsh, all we need is the bleedin' Irish and it'll be like the home Internationals out here.'

Moss stood somewhat bewildered as Paras and guardsmen milled around him, more of the Scots appearing from the darkened buildings like khaki-clad ghosts. Soon the entire settlement was buzzing with a pleasing chorus of chatter, laughter and jeers as the two units greeted one another with a warmth usually reserved for long lost friends.

They talked about football, they talked about women, they talked about the weather. But no one mentioned the war. It was almost as if, by common acknowledgment, neither battalion wanted to discuss the conflict. They ate, smoked and drank together while their officers gathered in that single white-washed building and discussed what was to happen next.

Harris spotted two men dressed in heavy overcoats and forage caps, one of whom was wearing glasses and carrying a large black box.

'Who the hell are they?' he asked one of the Scots.

'Newsmen,' the Guard explained. 'They've been with us ever since we left Portsmouth.'

'Doing what, for Christ's sake?' Harris continued.

'Taking pictures, talking to us. One of them interviewed me, asked me what I thought about the war.'

'They're probably waiting for someone to get killed,' rasped Turner. 'So they can get some really good pictures to send back home.'

'They're only doing their jobs,' Anderson said. 'The people back home have a right to know what's going on out here.'

'So, how would you feel if you turned on your telly and saw a picture of your son with his head blown off?' Turner continued. 'I don't think they should be allowed to take pictures of things like that.'

The Scot shrugged.

'They're not so bad. I mean, they've had to live like we have,' he explained. 'They haven't had any special privileges and they've got just as much chance of getting killed as any of us.'

Turner grunted disdainfully and watched as the two reporters trudged through the mud and disappeared amongst the buildings.

'Have you heard any news?' asked McLeish. 'About the other blokes on the island?'

Carter shook his head.

'The marines have reached Mount Kent and I heard that there's some Ghurkas being landed soon.' The Scot laughed. 'I tell you, we'll wipe these fucking Argies out in a week.'

Another Guardsman joined in. 'The only thing I can't stand about this bloody place is the weather.'

'I'd have thought you lot would have been used to it, I mean, it's like this in bleedin' Scotland ten months of the year isn't it?' said Fisher.

'It's not as cold as this,' said the Scot, shivering. 'If I was a brass monkey, I'd be looking for a welder.'

The men nearby laughed. The talking continued, cigarettes were passed back and forth and mugs of hot chocolate were drunk. Moss felt more comfortable, a little less vulnerable amongst these big brash Scots who laughed and joked. They didn't seem to feel the fear which he himself had come to know only too well. Still, he reasoned, they had yet to go into battle. Perhaps then . . .

The men continued talking, hardly noticing the early morning fog which had drifted in off the inlet. It covered the settlement like a floating shroud, wrapping ethereal fingers around the soldiers as they stood and spoke. Moss shivered again and looked up at the watery sun which had managed to break through the cover of low cloud. It was the first time any of them had seen the sun since they had landed. It seemed to hang there almost precariously, looking as if the powerful wind might blow it from its position in the morning sky. Clouds swirled around it and it gave off no heat but it was still a welcome sight and its appearance produced a kind of galvanising effect on the troops. Men suddenly seemed to brighten up, capable of ignoring even the blustery wind which still whipped across the grassy slopes.

The officers, led by Fulton and Narey, finally emerged from the white building after about an hour. They stood around in a tight bunch—about eight of them, Moss counted. Then he watched as the Major and Narey shook hands and saluted. The Para CO then made his way over to the waiting men. They extricated themselves from the crush of guardsmen and formed up into a column behind Fulton.

Brief goodbyes were exchanged although the men had no doubt that they would be seeing each other again. At least they hoped so. Moss felt strong hands slapping him on the back and he smiled up at the mountainous Scots who surrounded him. Then, orders were barked and the guardsmen scuttled away to get on with their own work, preparing the settlement for the landing of the Welsh troops later that day.

The Paras moved off and, within ten minutes, Bluff Cove was just a distant memory. But it was one which was to resurface all too quickly and for reasons which no one could have foreseen.

The sun, which had appeared so briefly, was once more hidden by dark clouds and the rain returned, bringing that fine drizzle which clung to the men's clothes like another skin, like dew on a spider's web. The sky became dark once more, almost premonitory of the horrors to come.

Moss couldn't be sure how far they marched that day. Each footstep was an effort as the Paras struggled through the endless stretches of mud which led from Bluff Cove towards their next objective. As they marched he could see it in the distance. The towering outline of Mount Challenger. As they reached the foothills of the plateau it was approaching 6.00 pm and the night was drawing in, darkness inexorably flooding the sky, bringing with it that almost inevitable flurry of snow. The Paras dug in amongst the craggy rocks which littered the foothills, finding to their surprise that the ground was hard in places. In others it was the familiar story of sodden mud which oozed around their feet as they struggled to dig slit trenches in the quagmire.

'You know that's what I can't figure out,' said Harris, driving his spade into the soft mud. 'If it's so fucking cold out here, how come the ground's always like shit?'

'In case you hadn't noticed,' Brent said. 'It has been raining nearly non-stop since we landed.'

'Yeah I know, but bits of ground are harder than others. Why?'

Brent exhaled deeply and looked at Harris.

'Look, I'm not a bloody geologist,' he said, irritably. 'How the hell do I know why it's soft in some places and hard in others?'

'I thought you were an expert on everything, Brent?' said Fisher, smiling.

'Just most things,' Brent countered.

There was a sudden high-pitched whistle which the men recognised as the arc of a shell. Instinctively, they threw themselves down and, a second later, there was an ear-splitting roar as an explosion rocked the ground. Lumps of earth and stone flew up into the sky and smoke billowed up from the crater. The shell was followed, a second later, by another. Then another. The Paras hugged the ground, trying to find shelter in half-dug slit trenches as the hail of artillery shells rained down. Moss closed his eyes and crouched beneath a piece of rock nearby. Lumps of stone and metal clattered down around him and he curled up into a ball as the debris hurtled out of the sky.

Carter saw a completed trench hit by a shell, bodies hurled several feet into the air by the blast. Screams of wounded men were blown away on the wind, drowned out by the sudden cacophony of noise as the shells erupted. There were men running about trying to find cover. Carter saw two Paras throw themselves into a crater, which, a second later, blazed again as another round landed in it. The men inside were obliterated and the older man swallowed hard as he saw a severed leg spinning into the dark sky, spraying blood all around.

Then, as suddenly as it had begun, the bombardment ended. The Paras remained still for almost fifteen minutes as if fearing that any movement on their part would provoke the Argentinian gunners into unleashing a fresh salvo but, finally, Carter clambered to his feet and looked around him. All over the foothills, the other men of the battalion were clambering upright, some dragging themselves from the reeking muck of their slit trenches. But there were those who did not get up.

He saw medics running back and forth, men being carried away. In some cases dragged. A corporal with a stomach wound was carried past by two of his companions and Carter glimpsed the jellied pulp of his intestines through the man's clawed hands. He gripped the ragged edges of the wound as if trying to retain his vital organs. Blood was running freely from both his nostrils and Carter could hear the man moaning softly as he was carried past. The older Para watched for a second and then stuck out a hand to help Moss up.

'You all right?' he asked and the youth nodded, his face pale beneath the grime.

'I'd like to know where our fucking air support is,' rasped Wallace. 'I reckon old Woodward's scared of losing his fucking Harriers. Never mind us, the Argies can blow the shit out of us.' The Corporal threw down his pick angrily.

' "Windy Woodward" ', said Fisher, softly. 'That's what I heard someone call him you know,' he exhaled. 'I'm beginning to think they're right.'

The men returned to their task of digging the trench and, twenty minutes later, the task was completed. The tarpaulin was spread across the top and the men crawled inside.

'Do you reckon they'll open up again tonight?' asked Moss, anxiously.

'Who can say?' The answer was hardly reassuring but it was all Carter could think of.

Anderson and Turner were hastily setting up the tiny stove. It was a piece of metal which folded into three pieces and it burned fuel which came in blocks about one inch square. Once ignited with a match, these blocks would burn for about half an hour each. Every Para had three or four boxes containing about forty of the fuel blocks. The men took turns to boil water in their tiny kettles, using it to make up the packet soup, hot chocolate or tea which they had all become so used to over the past weeks. Turner eagerly devoured his rations, complaining when he found he'd got nothing left.

'The rations should be through any day now,' said Fisher.

'Thank Christ for that,' Turner said.

'They'd better bring ammo too,' Brent added, checking the magazine of the LSW. 'I'm down to about thirty rounds.'

The other men also checked their weapons, alarmed to find that they too were short of ammunition.

'We'll have to fight them with our bare hands,' said Wallace.

'What's wrong with these?' Carter wanted to know. He waved his bayonet in front of him before slotting it onto the barrel of his rifle.

'There's something almost barbaric about hand-to-hand fighting,' said Anderson, 'It's like going back to the Middle Ages.'

Fisher grunted.

'Well, I don't know about you lot but *I'd* rather see the bastard I'm fighting. It's better than getting your head blown off from two hundred yards away or getting hit by a bleedin' artillery shell. You've got more chance when it's one on one.'

Wallace finished rolling his cigarette and lit it. He'd used the last of his filters and none of the others had any, so when he inhaled, the sharp taste of the smoke made him cough.

'Jesus,' he gasped, spitting pieces of tobacco out.

'I wonder when we're going to get some mail,' Harris asked.

No one could give him an answer.

Moss was pondering over the same question. He couldn't remember the last time he'd heard from his parents. The youth didn't know if they had been getting his letters either. For all they knew he could be wounded, missing or dead. He shuddered and sipped at his cup of hot chocolate.

Jennings stroked a hand across his chin, the bristles rasping beneath his fingers as he did so. He wrinkled his nose, aware that the smell he could detect was from his muddied, sweat-stained clothes.

'What I wouldn't give for a hot bath,' he said, wistfully,

'I'd just settle for a good feed,' Turner added.

'I reckon you must have hollow legs,' said Fisher. 'I mean, you stuff your bleedin' face from morning till night and you're still fucking hungry.'

'Like I said before, a man's got to keep his strength up.'

A silence fell over the men once more, each content to mull over his own private thoughts. It was Moss who finally broke the silence.

'How far are we from Port Stanley?' he asked

'About ten miles,' Wallace told him. 'Probably less.'

'The Argies will stand and fight here,' said Carter, authoritatively. 'I reckon it'll be hard going from now on.'

His words hung ominously in the air.

'It hasn't exactly been a fucking picnic up until now has it?' said Fisher.

Moss listened to the exchange with trepidation.

'You know,' began Morris. 'I really thought this would be over in a couple of days. I thought the Argies would chuck it in as soon as we landed.

Carter shrugged.

'It's just a matter of time.'

The men looked up as they saw someone clambering in through the flap in the canvas which covered the trench. The Paras watched as two men slipped down into the mud. They were wearing combat jackets and helmets but carried no weapons. The first was tall, wisps of blonde hair curling from beneath his helmet. His companion was slightly shorter with glasses and dark hair. Both were in need of a shave.

'Come in,' said Wallace. 'The door's open.' He ran an appraising eye over the two men noticing that neither of them wore insignia of any kind.

'I hope we're not disturbing you,' said the taller of the two.

'Well, we were just about to go down the pub but we'll let you off this once,' said Fisher and the other men laughed.

'I'm Peter Granger,' said the taller man. He motioned to his companion. 'And this is my colleague, Norman Crane.' The other man nodded a greeting and Moss noticed the strange black box which hung around his neck. He realized that it was a camera. 'We're both with the *Mail*,' Granger announced.

'You're journalists,' said Wallace.

Granger nodded.

'May we sit down?' He looked around hopefully.

'Pull up a chair,' said Fisher, pushing a piece of broken wood towards the men. They squatted on it, protecting their backsides from the worst of the wet. Moss watched as Granger took a notepad from his pocket, fumbling around for a pen at the same time.

'Drink?' asked Wallace, offering him a mug of soup.

Both men gratefully accepted the offer.

'It's bloody cold out there,' Crane told them.

'It's bloody cold in here,' echoed Morris.

The two newsmen drank their soup watched by the Paras.

'So, how are you finding things out here?' asked Granger. 'The conditions, the fighting?'

'At first the Paras seemed reluctant to speak.

'It's tough,' said Wallace. 'But we thought it would be.'

Granger scribbled something down while Crane took the camera from its case and started fiddling around with it.

'What do you feel about the Argentinians?' asked the newsman.

'What do you mean?' asked Turner, suspiciously.

'How do you feel about them as troops, does it bother you that most of them are just kids?'

'Yes, it bothers me,' said Anderson.

Granger scrawled something down.

'I bet they don't print that bit,' Brent said. 'Showing concern for your enemy, that would never wash would it?'

'What are you talking about?' Granger wanted to know.

'Your editor is only interested in the death and glory isn't he? He couldn't give a fuck *why* we're fighting. All he's bothered about is getting some nice juicy stories and a few pictures of dead bodies so that people can cry and moan over their breakfasts.'

'Look, mate, I'm doing a job the same as you lot. I only report what I hear and see. At least we've got reporters out here.' The newsman's voice had taken on a hard edge. 'There's a bloody rag like *The Sun* getting all its info second hand. Their editors fight their wars from Fleet Street pubs.' He glared at Brent. 'You know what their catch-line is at the moment? "The paper that supports our boys". They have to decide whether they can afford to leave out the tart with the big knockers on page three at the cost of including news about what's happening out here. So don't lecture me about the morals of the press.'

Fisher clapped and smiled.

'Good for you, chief,' he said. 'It's about time someone shut old Brent up isn't it, brains?' He looked at his colleague. But Brent merely shook his head and began cleaning the LSW.

'How long do you think the war will go on?' Granger asked.

'Not much longer,' said Carter.

'No, the Argies will blow it out,' added Fisher. 'They've got no bleedin' bottle when it comes to the rough stuff.'

'How are you managing in these conditions?'

'With difficulty,' said Jennings, and the newsman smiled.

There was a pause, Granger chewing thoughtfully on the end of his pen.

'Don't you ever, truthfully, wonder just why the hell you're here?' he asked. 'Off the record. Haven't any of you *really* thought sod it, let the Argies have the bloody island?'

Carter broke the long silence.

'It's a piece of England. It belongs to us,' he said.

'Yeah,' added Fisher. 'It'd be like giving up Bermondsey to the Argies. They don't belong here anymore than they would in London.'

'That's what you *really* think?' Granger persisted.

'Yes,' Carter proclaimed.

'Why, what do you think?' Wallace wanted to know.

Granger sighed.

'When I first heard that I was being sent out here I thought that we should have just left the Argentinians to it. I mean, the bloody islands are 8,000 miles away for God's sake. But then, on the way out here, when I was talking to other troops, like yourselves, I started to realize that what you've just said was right. The Argies *didn't* have any right to be here.'

'A convert eh?' said Carter, smiling.

'I suppose you could say that,' said Granger.

'More soup?' asked Morris.

Granger shook his head. He was tapping his pen gently against his pad.

'I suppose you heard what happened in Bluff Cove this afternoon?'

The Paras looked blank.

Granger swallowed hard.

'The *Sir Galahad* and the *Sir Tristram* were unloading troops, Welsh Guards if I remember correctly. Both of them were hit by bombs. We don't know how many men were killed yet.'

'The Argies bombed our ships?' said Fisher, his voice low.

Granger nodded.

'The radar stations on Sapper Hill and Two Sisters must have picked them up. It was them who called in the bombers.

Our blokes didn't have a chance. There were four enemy planes,' he paused. 'I'm not sure what sort.'

'Oh My God,' murmured Carter. 'We were only talking to the Scots Guards there this morning. They said they were waiting for the ships to bring in reinforcements.'

'They never had a chance,' Granger repeated.

'Did you get plenty of pictures?' rasped Brent, acidly.

'Shut up, Brent,' growled Wallace.

'That's what they were there for,' Brent persisted, pointing at the newsmen.

'Shut up,' the corporal roared and Brent complied.

'I can't believe it,' said Fisher, quietly. 'How many did you say were killed?'

We don't know,' said Granger. 'Somebody thought about thirty, but it's probably more.'

Moss lowered his head, the breath catching in his throat. He had heard but he didn't want to believe. He tried to imagine what it must have been like for the men aboard the ships, caught in a floating inferno. His mind drifted back to the sinking of the *Sheffield* and he closed his eyes. How much longer was this going to go on? How many more men were going to die?

'I realize how you must feel,' said Granger. 'It hit us hard too and it wasn't a pretty sight.' He paused. 'I'd never seen a dead man before.'

'How did the fucking Argies get through our air cover?' Wallace wanted to know.

'There was no air cover,' the newsman told him.

Wallace banged the side of the trench.

'I told you, it's that fucking Woodward. He doesn't give a toss about anything but his precious bloody aircraft carrier and his poxy little planes.' The Corporal threw down the butt of his cigarette. It hissed angrily on the damp mud.

The two newsmen got to their feet.

'We'll leave you now, I'm sorry it had to be me who broke the news,' said Granger.

No one spoke as the reporter and photographer clambered up out of the trench. The flap fluttered in the wind but none of the men paid it any heed. In fact, it was long moments before anyone even realized that their guests had left.

'I knew one of the cooks on the *Galahad*,' said Turner.

'No air support,' Wallace rasped. 'There's never any fucking air support.'

'Our pilots are outnumbered ten to one by the Argies,' said Anderson. 'They can't be everywhere at once.'

'Then why the fuck weren't there GTA's set up at the landing sight?' the Corporal demanded.

'We attack tomorrow, don't we?' said Carter.

Wallace nodded.

'Well, God help those fucking Argies.'

A murmur of approval rippled around the trench as the men began cleaning their weapons, a kind of grim resolution etched on their faces.

Dawn was barely six hours away by the time they finished, and the determination which they had nurtured for so long had slowly but surely become hatred.

Carter sat with his rifle across his lap, waiting for morning.

Eleven

The slopes of Mount Challenger were treacherous but the continual rain had made them even more difficult to negotiate. However, as the Paras climbed, yard by yard, using the outcrops of boulders for cover, they were at least grateful for the fact that the rain had stopped for the present. The wind was there, naturally, to blast them and make the ascent that little bit more difficult, but they struggled on towards the places where they knew the Argentinians were entrenched. The slopes were grassy and Moss could smell the rich odour of dampness and wet earth as he clambered along beside Carter and Wallace. The men held their weapons in one hand, in places using tufts of thick grass to pull themselves up the slopes.

Grey fingers of dawn were beginning to poke across the sky when they reached the first of the enemy outposts.

The Argentinians were taken completely by surprise as Carter and three of the others tore open the flap of their tent and burst in, guns levelled. However, one of the grey-clad men went for his rifle, rolling over in an effort to get a clear shot at the British. The shot went wide, striking one of his own comrades in the back. The man pitched forward, knocking Morris over, but Carter reacted quickly, firing point-blank at the other Argentinian. The bullet caught him in the chest and the men heard the strident snapping of bone as the heavy grain slug shattered his ribcage before erupting from his back.

'Bastard,' snarled Carter.

The remaining Argentinians threw their arms up into the air, all too eager to surrender. However, the shots had been enough to alert their companions and now the Paras suddenly found themselves under fire as the Argentinians further up the slopes were shaken from their slumbers and leapt for their guns. There were about half a dozen dug-outs on the forward slope, each one barricaded with lengths of wood, two of them covered with sheets of corrugated metal. It was from one of these that a stream of tracer spattered through the semi-darkness, leaving red flashes in the gloom like supersonic fireflies. Moss heard the chatter of machine-guns, the harsh crack of rifles and he threw himself down behind a boulder, swinging his rifle around on one of the dug-outs. He was joined by Turner who swiftly flipped down the legs of the GPMG and tightened his finger around the trigger. The heavy machine-gun thundered noisily and the sound almost deafened Moss, but he too kept up a steady fire.

A mortar shell, from one of the British 51's a little to the right, landed ahead of them and exploded with a loud bang. Chunks of rock and hot metal scythed out in all directions, one particularly large piece of rock spinning towards an enemy dug-out. It hit the rampart and shattered it like a bowling ball hitting the tenpins. Men sheltering behind were catapulted across the narrow opening by the impact and Moss heard screams from inside. The mortar crew seemed to have discovered the range now, for, a second later, another shell fell to earth. This time right in the middle of the wrecked dug-out. Bodies were sent flying by the blast and a tin helmet landed close to the youth. It spun round for a second then was still. Moss noticed that there was a crimson lump of something inside it but he didn't bother looking to see what it was. With Turner at his side, he dashed on up the hill. Major Fulton and half a dozen men found themselves pinned down by a withering salvo of small arms fire and the officer looked around for some way to extricate himself and the group from the hollow where they lay trapped. He spotted Carter about twenty yards away. The private had three other men with him and they were sheltering safely behind a large outcrop of rock. The Major cupped both hands to his mouth in order to make himself heard above the rattle of the machine-guns' fire;

'Carter,' he bellowed.

A bullet zinged off the Major's helmet and he ducked lower. Two of his men opened fire on the dug-out, trying to give him the chance to communicate with Carter and, for brief seconds, the Argentinian gun fell silent.

'Carter!'

This time the private heard him and turned. He saw Fulton motioning towards the dug-out, which immediately sprang into life again, a line of slugs dotting the earth just in front of the officer. But Fulton remained where he was, pointing towards a shallow gulley which ran from where Carter and the others were sheltering, right up to the side of the offending bunker. Carter understood. He got to his feet, and followed by Moss and three other men, scurried along the gulley towards the Argentinian machine-gun nest which continued to blast away at the men pinned down in the hollow. Moss could feel the perspiration clinging to his back as he ran and his breath came in gasps. The bunker loomed ever closer and he tried to blot out the thought of what would happen if the gunners suddenly turned their fire the other way.

The men with Fulton fired back as best they could, bullets ricocheting off the corrugated steel which covered the dug-out. Only the muzzles of the Argentinian rifles and the barrel of the M2 poked out, almost defiantly. Moss watched as Carter tugged a grenade from his belt, primed it and, with lethal accuracy, tossed it into the very heart of the machine-gun nest. There was a second's silence; then an explosion which ripped the sheet steel off, tearing it back like the lid off a can. The Paras hit the dirt as debris rained down. A battered rifle landing next to Moss. Then, suddenly they were up again, dashing towards the wrecked bunker, zig-zagging just in case there was anyone left in there who still felt like a fight. Fulton and the men with him also scrambled to their feet and raced forward. The Major was first to reach the wreckage and he glanced briefly at the destruction wrought by the grenade. Bodies lay sprawled in impossible positions amidst the broken wood and ruptured ammo boxes which, he assumed, must have gone up in the initial blast. There wasn't a man left alive in there and the Major counted four dead. He looked across at Carter and nodded. Then, the men scuttled off up the slopes towards the next bunker.

Argentinian mortar crews dropped the odd shell, but to little effect. Most fell well beyond the attacking Paras, the explosions erupting harmlessly many yards behind them. The British crews on the other hand were having more success. Plumes of earth and fire funnelled into the dawn sky, blowing men many feet into the air and ripping open the breastworks of dug-outs. Smoke drifted lazily across the slopes forming a kind of fog as it mingled with the early morning mist. Shell craters hissed and Moss watched the plume of smoke rising from one like some kind of grey ghost, swirling in the wind. Once again the stink of cordite was strong in his nostrils. He ran on, firing his rifle every so often. He saw Turner lying prone behind a rock, peppering a dug-out with fire from the machine-gun; he saw Brent firing carefully and purposefully with the LSW, and he saw Fisher and Wallace leading groups of men forward, the spent shell cases flying from their Sten guns as they charged. So caught up in the sights and sounds was he, that the youth almost didn't notice several Argentinians fleeing up the slope towards the crest of Mount Challenger. Indeed, many of the Paras failed to realize that, in at least five of the bunkers, firing had ceased altogether. Grey-clad troops were hauling themselves out of their bunkers and running hell for leather in the wake of the British onslaught.

Wallace saw the retreat.

'They're running,' he shouted.

Other eyes followed his pointing finger. The hail of mortar bombs ceased abruptly, as if a switch had been thrown and now only the odd crack of a rifle or sub-gun could be heard on the slopes. Most of the Argentinians had reached the summit by now and were hastily disappearing over the top. A few Paras chased them but Major Fulton called them back.

'God knows what's on the other side,' he said, ominously.

'The Paras were now amongst the remains of the enemy bunkers. Wallace leapt down into one to find a fire burning, a bubbling pot of foul brown liquid suspended over it. There were magazines scattered about inside, helmets left discarded, full boxes of ammo with the lids still screwed down. The Corporal smiled as he inspected what the Argentinians had left behind. One of the magazines had a picture of a black haired woman on the front, she was dressed in an army uniform which was undone at the top to reveal a pair of mountainous breasts.

'Jennings,' the Corporal yelled, holding up the magazine. 'Here's something for you.'

His companion hurried across and let out a lecherous grunt when he saw the magazine cover. He snatched it from the Corporal and began leafing through it, muttering appreciatively at each new picture.

Major Fulton found half-eaten food in another bunker and, as he was inspecting a discarded pistol, Carter held up a pair of boots.

'They really were in a hurry,' said the Major, smiling.

Turner was collecting some biscuits he found in an enemy pack, greedily shoving a handful into his cavernous mouth as he did so. Mugs of weak looking coffee lay all around the fire, some spilled. There was even a uniform lying nearby. Its owner, who had obviously taken it off whilst trying to wash in a tub of freezing water, lay nearby. Most of his face had been obliterated by a mortar explosion. The story was the same in every dug-out. Food, ammo, arms and even boots all left behind in the Argentinians' mad dash for safety. Moss looked on in amazement as his companions went amongst the debris, checking over the weapons, seeing if there were any wounded to be attended to. The youth saw Granger and Crane walking about, the newsmen pausing here and there. He heard the click of Crane's camera as it focused on the carnage, committing forever to film the slaughter and horror of war. Granger had his pad out and was scribbling notes.

Anderson wandered amongst the dead, gazing down at the faces of his foes, most of them teenagers. All carried that familiar frozen look of fear and pain. He saw a boy with his left arm severed at the elbow, the remains of the limb lying a few feet away. Close by him lay another grey-clad soldier, his body riddled with bullets, one hand clenched tightly into a rigored fist. The slopes were stained with blood but the smell was carried away by the powerful wind which seemed to act as a cleanser, driving away too the odour of cordite and smoke. It was as if nothing had ever happened. The battle had been so short. They'd attacked at 4.00 am and now Anderson looked at his watch to see that it was not yet 4.25. He walked over to Brent who was busily looking over an enemy machine-gun, checking its firing mechanism and squinting down the sight. He looked up at Anderson and held the gun before him almost as an accusation.

'It's an AA52,' he said. 'The bloody thing is French.' Brent tossed the weapon aside. 'More help from our "Allies".' He added sharp emphasis to the last word.

Captain Hansen strolled across the slope, seemingly oblivious to the wound in his arm. A bullet had nicked him just above the left elbow. It wasn't a bad wound but it had bled a lot and his uniform was stained a dark rust colour below the place where he'd been hit. A medic scampered after him, trying to get the Officer to keep still long enough for him to attend to the wound.

Fulton turned to greet him and saw his arm.

'Are you all right?' he asked, watching as the medic finally caught up with Hansen and set to work on the injury.

'It's only a flesh wound,' Hansen said, yelping in surprised pain when the medic applied some antiseptic to the wound before hastily bandaging it.

Fulton smiled.

'I didn't expect them to run as easily as that, sir,' said Hansen.

The Major nodded, stroking his chin contemplatively.

'Perhaps it was a little too easily,' he said. 'I wonder what they've got lined up for us on the other side of this bloody hill.'

'We caught them napping,' Hansen insisted. 'There's nothing sinister about that, sir.'

Fulton was unimpressed.

'Well, we'll have to check it out before we move on. I want you to take fifteen men up to the crest, just have a scout round.'

Hansen saluted and hurried off to collect the necessary complement of troops. This done, Moss watched them as they made their way cautiously towards the top of Mount Challenger before disappearing over the top.

He also saw Fulton relaying information to Private Regan who was fiddling with the knobs on the radio. All around, the other men of the battalion were collecting up discarded weapons and ammunition from the dug-outs, piling them in one huge cache beside an outcrop of rock about a hundred yards from the top of the ridge. Bodies of dead enemy troops were dragged to the largest of the bunkers and bundled in. Moss saw Father Driscoll standing over them, speaking words which were drowned out by the mournful wail of the wind. However, the sun had actually managed to battle its way from behind the clouds and now the morning was bathed in a cool golden hue. Moss thought how strangely unpredictable the weather on the island was. One minute it was raining, the next snowing and then there was sun. But always, no matter what the conditions, there was the wind. As he helped collect up some boxes of ammo, it lashed his face and made his wet clothes feel even more uncomfortable. There were still white patches of snow on the slopes—the sun wasn't strong enough to melt those—but, on the whole, the day was shaping up to be a pleasant one although Moss could have thought of better ways to start it.

He almost stumbled over the corpse of an Argentinian private who had been shot in the eye, the torn socket looking as if it had been filled to overflowing with thick red ink.

The cleaning-up operation continued well into the morning and it was about 10.00 am when Captain Hansen returned with his reconnaissance party. Moss saw him go over to Major Fulton who was studying a map, leaning against the remnants of a bunker breastwork. The two officers spoke animatedly for a while and then Hansen saluted and strode off to join a group of men who were being attended to by a couple of medics. As far as the youth could see, none of them were badly hurt and one or two were even joking with each other.

Harris, who had been in the recon. group walked over looking tired. He sat down on a piece of rock and exhaled deeply.

'Well,' Sergeant James wanted to know. 'What *have* the bastards got lined up for us over the other side?'

Harris smiled.

'Nothing. Not a bloody thing. We couldn't find hide nor hair of them for about half a mile. We found some more rifles and even a few more boots but not an Argie to be seen.'

The men gathered round about looked at him disbelievingly.

'I'm telling you,' Harris reassured them. 'They've buggered off.'

'Anybody got a map on them?' Wallace wanted to know.

Brent had one in his pack and he hastily unrolled it, spreading it out on a large flat boulder nearby.

'Where did you get this?' said Wallace, noticing that all the words at the bottom were in Spanish.

Brent shrugged. 'I picked it up off some dead Argie officer at Goose Green.'

The men gathered round while Wallace traced their route with his finger. 'Now, we're here,' he said, jabbing the digit at the spot marked Mount Challenger. 'The next few miles are flat then it's all uphill until we reach Port Stanley.' He glanced at the names printed across the map.

Tumbledown Mountain. Sapper Hill. Wireless Ridge. Two Sisters.

'The marines will take the hills to the north,' said Carter. 'We're left with these.' He poked a finger at Tumbledown and Sapper Hill.

'How far to Stanley?' Fisher wanted to know.

'About eight or nine miles,' Carter said, scanning the map.

'According to this,' Brent said. 'There should be roads leading into the capital.'

'The Argies will have mined the fucking things,' said Turner.

'I heard that there's still civilians in Port Stanley,' Anderson said, softly.

'Oh Christ,' murmured Harris.

The men were still considering the prospect of having to fight their final battle in a town full of non-combatants when the air was suddenly filled with the whirring of rotar blades.

They turned to see half a dozen helicopters flying in low from the west. The large Sea Kings hovered over the plateau at the top of the ridge, something dangling from the bottom of them. It was Brent who realized they were bringing in artillery. The massive 105's swayed precariously beneath the choppers, blown by the wind, looking as if they would either break loose or drag their carriers down with them at any moment. But the Sea Kings hovered steadily, dropping lower and lower one at a time until they had unloaded their huge cargoes. More of the choppers flew in, also carrying cannons. Those already grounded were hurriedly being dug in by their crews. The Paras watched mesmerised as the big helicopters dipped and checked, ensuring that the 105's were landed safely. Artillerymen jumped from the bellies of the Sea Kings and guided their huge weapons down to the security of the grassy plateau. There were about a dozen cannon in position by the time the choppers had finished. But still more came on. The next batch had boxes dangling beneath them and Carter assumed that they were ammo for the guns. He was right. The gunners unlatched the heavy crates and struggled across to their guns with them, tearing off the lids and heaving out the large brass-cased shells which they stacked neatly beside each gun. Netting was set up over the 105's and pieces of stick and grass spread over them for camouflage. The artillerymen worked ceaselessly to protect their precious weapons, knowing that one sweep by Argentinian aircraft would be enough to expose them. Moss saw an officer squinting through a pair of binoculars towards a range of low hills which the lad knew to be Tumbledown and its foothills. What he didn't know was that the Argentinians had their own artillery set up there, just waiting for the order to fire. But, at the moment, the Paras were blissfully unaware of the danger and when the order to dig in came, they went about it spiritedly. The sun continued to shine and the wind even dropped slightly. Carter rolled up his sleeves as he dug and Moss found that he was able to forget the fighting he'd just been through as he worked hard to make a secure bunker for himself and the rest of the platoon.

One of the Sea Kings had actually touched down and Harris glanced up to see men unloading several boxes and hessian bags which they carried back down the hill.

'Looks like the rations have arrived,' he said.

'I hope so,' echoed Turner.

'I wonder if there's any mail?' Harris pondered aloud.

'Come on, keep digging,' bellowed Sergeant James.

'Aren't you expecting any mail, Sarge?' asked Fisher.

'My bloody old lady can hardly write,' he said. 'Still with a mouth like hers she could probably shout to me and I'd hear her.'

The men laughed.

'How long you been married then, Sarge?' Fisher persisted.

'Too bloody long,' said James. 'Anyway, what fucking concern is it of yours?'

'Just curious,' said Fisher, smiling.

'You're curious about everything,' the Sergeant told him.

'Life's full of mystery, Sarge,' said Fisher, haughtily.

'I just like to discover the truth behind some of those mysteries.'

The other men laughed.

'You'll discover my toe up your arsehole if you don't shut up and keep digging,' James told him and walked off. He was heading in the direction of the Sea King. The rotar blades swept heavily through the air, the persistent 'whump, whump' of the propeller sounding like a large fan. Moss saw the Sergeant talking to one of the crew who was crouched in the doorway. The two men were laughing although it was impossible to hear the sound. Like watching a silent movie, Moss thought. He saw the crewman hand James a hessian sack, then the Sergeant backed off, watching as the chopper rose majestically into the air. It hovered a second before turning full circle and heading off back the way it had come.

All over the hillside, the Paras were digging in, aware of the banks of cloud which were gathering to the east and also realizing that they would be exposed to any aerial attack should the Argentinians decide to launch some aircraft. As yet, they were oblivious to the fact that, a mere half mile away, 155mm enemy artillery were trained on them.

The weather which looked like changing had by noon reverted to the type which the men had almost come to expect. The banks of cloud which had hung so menacingly in the eastern skies earlier that morning finally drifted in, unleashing a torrent of rain that threatened to wash the Paras right off the plateau. They huddled in their trenches, listening to the icy cascade hammering against the groundsheet, one or two of them pulling their sleeping-bags around them in an effort to keep warm.

'I wouldn't want to be a bleedin' weather forecaster out here,' said Fisher. 'I mean, you never know from one minute to the next whether its going to be sunny or pissing down.' He shrugged and took a drag on his cigarette.

Carter was cleaning his rifle, oiling the firing mechanism and checking that it was working all right. That task done, he began sharpening his bayonet on a piece of flat stone which he'd picked up on the slopes earlier on. Brent was also in the process of cleaning the LSW. He sneezed twice and cursed.

'I think I'm getting a bloody cold,' he said.

Wallace, warming his hands around the portable stove, pushed two more of the fuel tablets into the flames and stirred the large bowl of soup which hung over the fire. He sniffed appreciatively and stirred the concoction around with a spoon, sipping a drop.

'Perfection,' he said, grinning.

'Never mind that,' said Turner, holding out his mug. 'Just get it served up, I'm bloody famished.'

Jennings was huddled in one corner of the slit trench, his head buried in the Argentinian porno magazine which Wallace had found in the enemy bunker. The men could hear his grunts and chortles of delight as he thumbed through it.

Moss blew on his hands, trying to restore the circulation. He eagerly held out his mug when Wallace offered him soup, allowing the warmth to seep through his damp gloves. He was shivering and the mud on which he sat was rapidly becoming saturated as the rain somehow found ways to seep beneath the ground sheet. The youth drank his soup, dipping a piece of stale bread in it as he did so. The bars of chocolate which had come in with the rations he had stored in his pack. There had also been some tubes of Rolo which everyone seemed to appreciate. Turner, needless to say, had already eaten his.

The tent-flap was pulled back and Sergeant James stuck his head in.

'Wake up, you dozy sods,' he said, grinning.

'Oh shit no,' grunted Turner. 'Not bloody guard duty, Sarge.'

'No *not* bloody guard duty you gutsy bleeder,' said James producing a sack which he dropped into the trench. 'Mail.'

Moss looked up. (Please let there be a letter from his parents.) He held his mug tightly, watching as James opened the sack. He rummaged around inside and came up with just seven letters and a small brown parcel. The sack looked incongrously large for the small amount of correspondence it contained. The other Paras too looked up expectantly.

All except Carter. He just continued sharpening his bayonet, as if the anticipation around him were alien to him. Which indeed it was. He had no need to wonder whether or not there would be a letter for him. He knew that there wouldn't. After all, there was no one back in England, no one in the entire fucking world for that matter who gave a shit about him. But that didn't bother Carter.

'Fisher,' James called out. 'One for you.'

The lance-jack caught the letter as it was tossed to him.

'Jennings. Two for you. Popular little bugger aren't you?' He tossed the mail to the private who dropped his magazine and hastily tore the first letter open.

The roll went on.

'Harris. Brent.' He paused. 'There's one for "Robbo". I'd better hang on to that.' The sergeant continued. '"Knocker".' He shrugged. 'Well, that's that.'

Moss froze, looking almost disbelievingly at the Sergeant. James suddenly remembered the brown parcel and scanned the name on it.

'Moss,' he said, smiling. 'Sorry, son, nearly forgot you.' He tossed the parcel across the trench and the youngster caught it. James smiled at him and balled up the sack, carrying it with him when he left the trench. Those men with mail tore open the envelopes, those without crowded round to see what their comrades had received.

Carter leant across, watching Moss struggling to undo his parcel.

'It's from my mum and dad,' said the youngster. 'I recognise my mum's writing.'

The older Para smiled, looking on with faint amusement as his younger companion wrestled with the thick wads of sellotape which held the parcel together.

'You'll be lucky if you have that open by the end of the war,' said Carter, grinning.

But Moss finally managed it. It was a small tin and, when he opened it, he found a piece of fruit cake inside. Amazingly, it was still fresh. Like some kind of human food detector, Turner shuffled over and peered at the cake. He made an appreciative noise and reached out to touch the cake which Moss hastily withdrew.

'If you've got any of that spare . . .' Turner let the sentence trail off, backing away when Moss turned his attention to the letter. He recognised his mother's careful hand. Written in ink, the letter was splashed in places, some of the words difficult to read, but he did his best—feeling a strange mixture of happiness and sorrow as he did so. He was pleased to hear from them, pleased too that they had received *his* letters but somehow, the sight of that familiar script made him shudder even more than the icy wind and rain which beat about the tent. Nevertheless, he read on.

As did the other men. There were laughs, groans, curses and all manner of exclamations as the Paras read their mail.

'Fucking bitch,' rasped Jennings balling up one of his letters and ripping open the second.

'What's wrong?' asked Morris.

'This bird I was knocking about with,' Jennings explained. 'She's given me the elbow. Bloody cheek.'

'Does she say why?' Morris wanted to know.

Jennings shrugged, then a wry smile creased his face.

'She found out I was screwing her sister too.'

The men laughed loudly.

'My old man's out of the Scrubs,' Fisher announced proudly. 'They've shifted him to Parkhurst.'

Once more the men laughed.

'But that's maximum security isn't it?' asked Turner.

'Yeah,' Fisher said. 'But he says it's getting overcrowded in the Scrubs, besides the food's better in Parkhurst and he says the sea air's good for him. He's never been overseas before.

'I'd hardly call the Isle of Wight overseas,' grinned Brent.

Fisher looked him directly in the eye.

'You try walking there,' he said, dryly.

The men erupted into fits of laughter once more, a chorus of merriment that was ultimately overshadowed by a long whooping yell from Harris. He scrambled to his feet and did a little war dance in the mud, yelling like a maniac.

'I'm a father,' he shouted, happily. 'Can you believe it? I'm a bloody dad. Look.' He held up a photo, a simple polaroid of a little bundle of pink and white which was his son. 'My boy, I've got a son.' He clenched his fists in triumph and the other men gathered around to congratulate him, passing the photo from hand to hand. They slapped him on the back, they embraced him. 'Oh Jesus, I can't believe it,' he beamed. 'And my old lady's fine too. They're both in great shape.' He let out a whooping yell once more.

'Time for a celebration lads,' said Fisher. 'Fill up your mugs.'

The other men of the platoon did so and there and then, in that filthy, rain-pounded hole in the ground, they toasted Harris's child. With soup, tea and hot chocolate they toasted him and, for fleeting moments, the men actually managed to forget the vile surroundings into which they'd been pitched. Harris got the photo back and kissed it. There was another one of his wife holding the baby; it must, he guessed, have been taken just after she had given birth for she was still in a hospital bed.

'What are you going to call him?' asked Carter.

'Fuck knows,' said Harris, laughing idiotically. He felt like a schoolkid who's just got drunk for the first time. Everything seemed amusing to him. Maybe he had been touched by that elusive, that most elusive of emotions, happiness.

'If it had been a girl, you could have named her after the Prime Minister,' said Anderson.

'Leave it out,' said Fisher. 'Who wants a kid called cunt?'

Once more the men broke up into gales of laughter, as if Harris's joy were contagious. Moss laughed as loud as the rest of them.

Harris held the photos before him, tears in his eyes.

'My son,' he whispered and tucked the pictures into the top pocket of his combat jacket, patting them gently. He squatted down again, reaching for his mug of hot chocolate. The initial euphoria still enveloped him like a warm glove, but something was nagging at the back of his mind, gnawing away that cover of expectation, pulling off the blanket of relief to expose the naked fear beneath. Thoughts began to tumble through his mind. What if he was killed in the forthcoming conflict? What if he never got the chance to hold his child? What if he were blinded, unable to see it even if he did survive?

What if?

What if . . .

He tried to force the thoughts to one side but they refused to be pushed. Harris closed his eyes. No, he told himself, it'll be all right. He *would* get home no matter what. He swallowed hard, feeling the slight film of perspiration on his forehead despite the cold. It was like discovering something worth living for; he had two reasons for wanting to go home now. He had always been anxious to get home to see his wife, but, until she had the child he had not felt this kind of fear. He turned his eyes skyward, speaking a prayer inwardly to a God he didn't believe in. He sipped at his drink, the fears subsiding slightly. Yes, everything was going to be fine.

He patted the photos nestled in his breast pocket.

It was at that exact second that the British artillery opened up.

The entire ridge seemed to shudder as the first withering salvo was let loose. The guns rocked wildly and the artillerymen stood back as the massive barrels hurtled backward in recoil. Immediately the breeches were hauled open, spent shell cases dropping to the ground where they rasped on the wet grass. Fresh rounds were slammed in and the guns roared once more, their deadly cargo arcing across the valley to explode on the high ground which marked the enemy positions. Great funnels of earth and stone were thrown up by the exploding shells but the gunners didn't stand around to admire their handiwork, they heaved shell after shell into the 105's, into breeches which soon began to heat up. The thunderous roar of persistent cannon fire was deafening and the men had to shout to make themselves heard, even from short distances. Smoke drifted across the ridge, thick and grey, brightened every few seconds by a brilliant red and white muzzle flash as another round was fired. The deadly shells whined down onto the Argentinian positions, catching the grey-clad men by surprise, and it was some time before their own artillery began to reply.

Then, the big 155's unleashed their own brand of fury. But the British gunners continued unflinchingly as the shells rained down on their positions. Massive plumes of fire rose screaming into the sky, sending lumps of earth flying in all directions. Clouds of smoke began to form over the top of both ridges as the artillery of the British and the Argentinians kept up a devastating fusillade.

The Paras, atop the ridge, hugged the ground, crouching helplessly in their slit trenches as the bombardment seemed to intensify. One shell landed particularly close and tore away part of the ground sheet. Carter and Fisher scurried across to try to secure it, glancing out as they did so. They actually saw the Argentinian guns blaze and, a second later, they were ducking down as a series of massive explosions showered them with wet earth and tiny pieces of stone. The ridge itself seemed to move backward slightly at each titanic impact and, coupled with the ceaseless firing from their own guns, the Paras were dazed and deafened by the furious artillery duel. Moss coughed as the banks of smoke filled the slit trench, the smell of cordite strong in his nostrils. He felt the back of his throat turning raw and it was difficult to see in the mist of fumes. He sat huddled in the trench, listening to the incessant tirade, his ears ringing.

An Argentinian shell landed near to one of the 105's, the furious blast catapulting two gunners into the air. Another was disembowelled by a spiralling lump of shrapnel which sliced through his stomach like a hot knife. Shrieking insanely, he stumbled about, blood bubbling on the red hot piece of metal which had eviscerated him. The remaining gunners kept up their fire though, only two of them ramming shell after shell into the hungry breech which swallowed each brass offering greedily before spitting it out in the direction of the Argentinians.

Despite the size of their guns, the enemy troops were not as quick as their British counterparts and many of the big 155's fell silent after a while. An artillery officer could see one or two being dragged away by huge lorries. The remaining ones, however, and some smaller 88mm cannon continued to return the withering fusillade which the British poured forth. It was becoming difficult to see on both the ridges, so choked with smoke were they and, the men found to their chagrin, the wind whipping in from the east was bringing snow with it. The icy particles only made it more difficult to see and visibility was badly reduced. Nevertheless, the firing continued, both sides blasting away until it seemed that both ridges would just disappear beneath a rain of high explosive.

Moss hugged the side of the trench as three blasts rocked the ground in quick succession. He felt as if he had been beaten about the head with a lump of metal and, as each fresh explosion came, the feeling grew worse. All the Paras were crouching down, trying to find shelter in a few feet of peaty earth but of course it was little or no help. Entire earthworks were obliterated by a single shell and, even through the ear-splitting cacophony of blasts and muzzle discharges, the sound of men's screams could be heard.

Sergeant James appeared in the trench, cupping both hands to his mouth to make himself heard.

'On your feet, quick,' he yelled.

The men needed no prompting. Snatching up their equipment, they followed the Sergeant up and out of the trench towards the rear slope which would offer them some cover at least. They ran as fast as they could, conscious of the fact that any second a shell could fall right in front of them. As Moss struggled along, he thought he was going to faint. Everything swam in a haze before him—then he realized that it was a heat haze set up by the furious series of blasts which were tearing the ridge apart. He saw sweating gunners pushing fresh shells into their weapons, saw one man, his hands red raw from constantly hauling open the breech. He saw medics attending to wounded men amidst the hail of shot and shell. He saw bodies blasted into unrecognisable pulp by the powerful detonations, shell craters that bled smoke into the freezing air like dancing ghosts. The snow stung his face and the smoke made his eyes water, he felt one ear-drum pop as the thunderous barrage seemed to grow in intensity and, once or twice he felt himself slipping over as the very earth beneath his feet seemed to move in protest. Such was the ferocity of the bombardment and the counter-fire.

If anything, the Argentinians were faring worse than the Paras. Told by their officers to sit tight in their trenches, they could do nothing but wait and pray as the 105's sent their lethal load crashing into their positions. Bunkers were torn apart by multiple explosions, the breastworks of trenches blasted into matchwood by the accurate fire. Men screamed in pain, some in terror as the unceasing curtain of fire and hot metal smashed down on and around them. Trucks which had been sent to tow away the 155's were particularly vulnerable and one was hit by a stray shell. It exploded with a roar of almost seismic proportions, the driver being blown to pieces in his cab. Wheels and other parts of the shattered vehicle spun into the air. Mudguards and hub caps became deadly weapons, whizzing like razor-edged frisbees from the exploding truck.

One of the hub caps hit an Argentinian officer, the metal disc catching him just above the left eye. It shaved off a large portion of his skull as neatly as a bacon slicer, exposing the sticky grey brain matter beneath. He pitched backward and lay in the mud beside one of his men who was screaming for help as he tried to tear a length of shrapnel the size of a car bumper from his body. It had pierced him like a spear, entering his chest just below the sternum, ripping its way through him before erupting from his back. Another private, fleeing from the terrible cannonade was scythed in two by a flying lump of metal from one of the mashed trucks. The top half of his body toppled sideways into the mud while the legs ran on for a few yards, tottering about like a decapitated chicken, before falling into the mud.

Another of the trucks was hit, the cab disappearing beneath a ball of white and orange flame. The men in the back dived for cover but there was none and the entire group were obliterated as two more shells fell to earth amongst them.

The Argentinian gunners in many places had left their guns and were sheltering in trenches with the infantry but a dogged few kept up a steady fire. Officers screamed at their terrified men as the British continued to pound the ridge but, already, some of the grey-clad troops were beginning to crawl from their bunkers to seek the safety of the rear slopes just as their opponents across the valley had done—but few made it. Some were hauled back bodily by their superiors, others blasted to atoms in the merciless bombardment. Freezing cold and screaming in terror, they could only sit helplessly as the shells continued to pour out of the sky like high explosive, brass rain.

The Paras meantime had found relative safety in trenches about twenty yards from the crest of the ridge. The only troops left exposed were the artillerymen themselves, who now seemed to have gained the upper hand. In fact, one of them counted that for every seven shells the British fired, the Argentinians replied with only one. But still, that one was too many and men went down every now and then, some only because of the shock wave, others because of hideous injuries. Nevertheless, the barrage was unceasing, the big guns jerking in their positions every time they fired, so fierce was the recoil. The camouflage netting around them shivered with each discharge and fresh ammo was carried up by the gunners to replenish that already fired.

'I've never seen anything like that in my bleedin' life,' said Fisher, still deafened by the onslaught.

'It's like the beginning,' said Moss, quietly. 'When we first landed at San Carlos. When the Navy bombarded the Argies.'

Fisher grinned.

'Well, the bastards cleared off after that lot. Let's hope they do the same this time,' the lance-jack said.

Every so often, a stray Argentinian shell would fall beyond the plateau, causing the Paras to duck down but, for the most part, the large projectiles hit the forward slope of the plateau itself. The British gunners kept up their ceaseless fire.

'They're softening them up,' said Carter.

'I shouldn't think there'll be anything left of that fucking mountain by the time our blokes have finished,' Turner said, almost hopefully.

'Good,' Harris said. 'I'd rather walk into Port Stanley than have to fight my way there.'

Some of the other men echoed his sentiment.

'What's the matter, Harris?' asked Sergeant James. 'Don't tell me you've lost your top after all this lot you've been through.'

Harris shrugged.

'No Sarge, it's not that,' he said. 'But, I mean, wouldn't you rather have it easy?'

'You get nothing easy in the Army, son,' he sighed, wistfully. For a moment that hard edge to his voice softened. 'You're worried about your kid aren't you?'

Harris looked puzzled.

'How did you know about that, Sarge?' he asked.

James winked at him.

'I hear things,' he said, smiling. 'Don't worry. We'll make it. It's going to take more than a bunch of fucking cowboys to stop us now.'

The men ducked instinctively as another shell exploded nearby.

'You're not the only one who's worried you know,' said James. 'I mean, if I don't get back who's my old woman going to nag?'

Harris smiled and the other men managed a laugh.

'Just sit tight, now,' the Sergeant told them. 'Major Fulton's called a meeting of all officers and NCO's; we're getting our orders for tonight.'

'Do you think we'll be attacking tonight, Sarge?' asked Moss.

'Well, the fucking artillery aren't putting on a show for *our* benefit are they sunshine?' said the NCO hooking a thumb over his shoulder in the direction of the ridge where the 105's continued to blast away. He turned to Wallace and Fisher. 'Come on you two, the Major's not going to wait all bloody day.'

The three men scrambled up out of the trench and scuttled away to a bunker-like construction a little further down the hillside. It was an ordinary slit trench much like their own but fortified with large rocks. The three men disappeared inside.

Moss looked at his watch, noting that it was 11.15 am.

Five hours later, the roar of cannons was still filling the air.

Harris sucked a last mouthful of smoke from the cigarette and crushed it beneath his boot.

'It's this sitting around that drives me up the wall,' he said. 'If we've got to go in why the hell can't we do it now and get it over with?'

'Do you fancy charging Argie machine-gun nests in broad daylight?' said Carter.

'We've done it before,' Harris countered. 'At Goose Green and Fitzroy.'

'Well, it's a bit different this time isn't it?' said the older man.

He was referring to the fact that these particular enemy positions were mined and fronted by barbed wire too. Reconnaissance had revealed that the trenches on top of Tumbledown and Sapper Hill were heavily fortified and had a high concentration of machine-guns and artillery backing them up. As for the number of Argentinians holed up there, they could only guess. The Paras now sat around in their trench, some of them wrapped up inside their sleeping-bags to ward off the freezing cold, cleaning their weapons in preparation for the attack which was to be launched that night. Each man had fitted a Starscope to his rifle, the ingenious little devices enabling the British to see in the dark by squinting down the sight. Moss looked through his but everything looked normal. Only in the darkness, and with the help of special flares did the scopes really come into their own as invaluable aids.

The orders had been simple, relayed to the men by Sergeant James about an hour ago. They, under the command of Major Fulton, were to attack Tumbledown Mountain. At the same time, supported by Scots and Welsh Guards, the other half of the battalion would assault Sapper Hill. Whichever stronghold fell first, the victorious troops were then to go immediately to the aid of the other unit. Radio contact between different branches of the army had told Fulton that the Marines and Ghurkas would take Two Sisters and Wireless Ridge. There was to be both air and artillery support. Indeed, even as Moss sat writing yet another letter home, he heard the familiar whirring of rotar blades signalling the arrival of another Wessex. The choppers had been arriving steadily for the past two hours, bringing in fresh ammunition and medical supplies. (Something which a few of the men found ominous to say the least.) The youngster paused in mid-sentence, listening to the steady flapping which reminded him of the wings of some great bird. The blades sliced through the snow-filled air, the engines idling as the cargo was unloaded, then, moments later, the unmistakeable change in pitch as the Wessex took off, its rotars spinning quickly now.

'I hope old "Windy" remembers to send in his bloody Harriers tonight,' said Wallace, smoking a roll-up and watching as Turner attached a Starscope to the GPMG.

'I heard someone say the SAS were going to be involved in the attack,' said Anderson.

'They've been involved in everything since this bloody war started,' said Wallace. 'Nobody ever knows where they are.'

'I hope to Christ everything goes all right tonight,' Harris sighed, taking the photos of his wife and child from his top pocket.

'After the pounding the Argies got today,' said Fisher, 'they've probably already pissed off back to Stanley.'

Moss continued writing, vaguely aware of the chatter going on around him.

'. . .for the present. The snow is back. It is freezing here. I have never known a place as cold in my life, I don't know how the islanders stand it every day of the year. We are attacking tonight. Everyone thinks it will be an end to the war after this. I do hope so. I'm sick of all this fighting. Everyone is frightened even if he doesn't say so. "Bomber" got a letter from his wife and he's now a father. He can't wait to get home to see his wife and kid. It's a little boy. I pray that everything goes all right and that no one gets hurt . . .'

He chewed the end of the biro for a moment, listening to the howling wind, the steady spatter of snow on the groundsheet. There was a puddle of water at the bottom of the trench, it was frozen solid and the youth tapped it with his hand, hearing it whine and wheeze under his touch. Then, he remembered his letter and began writing again.

Carter sipped at his mug of soup, warming his hands around it for a second before returning to the more urgent task of cleaning his rifle.

'What happens after tonight?' asked Anderson.

A number of the men looked up at him in surprise.

'What do you mean?' asked Carter.

'Well, even if we beat the Argies tonight. There's still Port Stanley to take, that won't be easy with civilians still in there.'

'Yeah, those fucking bastards,' snarled Wallace. 'They could have let the islanders go. I just hope none of *them* get hurt.'

'They could use them as hostages,' said Anderson.

The words hung in the air for long moments. It was something the men had not thought about before. What *would* happen if General Menendez threatened to kill the islanders if the British troops didn't pull out? Moss chewed the end of his pen once again, the thought making him shudder.

'It's going to be a bleedin' sight harder taking Stanley if we've got to keep our eyes open for civilians all the time,' said Fisher.

'We've got to get through tonight before we can start thinking about that,' Jennings added, anxiously.

Moss finished his letter hurriedly and folded it up, stuffing it into a damp envelope he had in his pack. One corner was dog-eared and there was a dark stain on the back, but it was the only one he had. It would have to do. The gum tasted sour on his tongue as he sealed the letter, pushing it back into his pack after he'd addressed it. Once more he had that feeling that it could well be the last letter he ever wrote.

He settled down in an effort to catch a couple of hours' sleep. Some of the other men were doing likewise but it was almost impossible in the sub-zero temperatures. The frost stuck icy daggers into them and even their insulated sleeping-bags did little to combat the horrendous cold. The men kept their gloves on at all times when handling equipment. Only a matter of days ago, in another bout of freezing conditions, a Para from another platoon had lost the skin off his fingers picking up his rifle. The frozen metal had welded his flesh to its surface as surely as acetaline to steel and, when he tried to pull his hand free, it had stripped the skin away as cleanly as if it had been flayed off with a knife.

So, Moss lay awake thinking about his parents and his home, wondering if he would ever see them again. He glanced to one side and looked at the SLR which was propped against the wall of the trench, its bayonet already fixed but covered with grease to prevent it reflecting any light should flares be fired. Nothing could be allowed to give away the British positions as they advanced.

Harris lay on his back almost unconsciously touching his top pocket where the photos were. He whispered his wife's name once and closed his eyes.

Wallace finished his roll-up and settled down to sleep, nudging Turner in the ribs to stop the big man snoring.

Fisher was flicking through his pack of cards, each of which bore the picture of a naked woman. He held up one the cards and looked at it.

'W.here do you reckon she lives?' he said.

Jennings looked up and raised an eyebrow questioningly. He didn't speak. Fisher put the cards away and lay down beside his companion. The men huddled close together, aware that their shared bodily heat, what little there was of it, might help to warm them somewhat.

Brent cradled the LSW on his lap, giving it one final check before propping it up beside Morris's SLR.

Carter sipped his drink, looking around at the men of the platoon. He wondered how many of them were going to die in the forthcoming conflict. He wondered if *he* was going to die. The fact that he didn't care either way should perhaps have been disturbing to him but it wasn't. Perhaps it would be best if he went down on some windswept, snow-blown piece of grass, his rifle clutched in his hand. He knew the war was reaching its final stages and he knew that his time in the army was similarly running out. He looked down at Moss and felt a twinge of something akin to sadness. The boy was still frightened, a lot of them were, but during the past few weeks Carter had seen his young friend transformed into a perfect killing-machine. Gone was the naivety which he'd shown on the ship travelling across from England when the Task Force had first set out. The lad was a professional, skilled in the art of death. Perhaps that was the true horror of war, Carter thought, it turned frightened young men into killers. It changed them as people too. It had changed him. He could face an enemy soldier, dive for cover when some filthy Irishman skulking in a Belfast doorway shot at him, but he couldn't face life without those things. He had lived with death for so long it had become a part of him. The army had given him a home but, more importantly, it had given him a channel for his aggression. Without it he would probably be locked up in Parkhurst doing bird with Fisher's old man. Somewhere deep inside Alan Carter, a hidden and unwanted truth had risen during these past few weeks. He *needed* the violence, the surge of adrenalin which came with each fresh engagement. It was something he could never regain in civilian life and he wasn't sure that he could live without it.

On those snowy slopes, as the darkness drew in, he was probably the only man who actually relished the idea of the battle to come. He looked at his watch and nodded.

It was 7.30 pm.

Twelve

The night was moonless, it lay like a shroud over the land. Impenetrable, almost palpable. A nearly physical creature. The wind blew powdery snow into the faces of the Paras as they advanced, their boots crunching loudly on the frosted ground. In places they crossed small snow drifts and it was like walking over broken glass. Moss, his face thick with grease, moved slowly, the SLR held across his chest. He could feel his heart beating heavily and his pack and webbing belt seemed unaccountably heavy. Admittedly the pack weighed sixty pounds, the belt another twenty, but up until now he had not realized just how heavy the gear was. The men moved slowly across the open ground that led them to the foothills of Mount Tumbledown and, to Moss, it seemed as if they were moving in slow motion, each step taking an eternity.

There was a crack and anxious eyes scanned the area to their left.

Someone had stepped into a frozen puddle, breaking the surface ice.

There were audible sighs of relief, and the men continued on their way. Moss was finding it difficult to breathe and each breath had to be sucked in through clenched teeth. The snow peppered his face, stinging his eyes and he wiped it away with the back of his hand. It was then that he noticed a glowing arrow which shone on the ground ahead of them. A few yards further on there was another, and another.

'What the hell are they?' whispered Harris.

'They're fluorescent markers,' Brent told him. 'They give off a mild radioactive glow.' He looked at the arrows which reminded him of large cats' eyes. 'That's what the SAS must have laid.'

'Quiet,' hissed Sergeant James, who was slightly ahead of them. 'Just keep in single file, follow those arrows and shut up. We're passing through a minefield.'

Moss felt his heart jump and then begin beating just that little bit faster. He kept his head down, his eyes firmly fixed on the luminous arrows. So intent was he on watching them he failed to notice that the column had stopped. He banged into the back of Carter who looked round at him.

'Sorry,' said the youngster, apologetically.

'We're clear of the minefield,' the older man told him.

Major Fulton passed quickly from unit to unit talking in hushed tones to their officers, giving out orders. Moss looked up and saw the outline of Tumbledown towering over them. Up on the battered slopes he knew there were hundreds of Argentinians all of them entrenched.

And waiting?

Fulton looked at his watch. The attack was supposed to begin at 1200 hours. It was 11.55 pm. The Major guessed that Captain Hansen and his men must be nearing Sapper Hill by now. Radio silence was to be maintained throughout the attack so the officer could only hope that his second in command hadn't run into any trouble. The second hand ticked round.

'Stand ready.'

The order was flashed along the front, the Paras readying themselves for the assault. Invisible in the blackness, they waited for their officers to fire the flares which would signal the attack.

'Come on, come on,' murmured Harris.

Eleven-fifty-seven.

Fulton pulled the flare gun from its holster and cocked it. Moss closed his eyes momentarily. The moment was approaching. He felt icy fingers of fear clawing at the back of his neck.

Two minutes.

Anderson crossed himself.

The wind seemed to blow stronger and the Paras stood as stiff as trees as it spattered them with snow and icy rain.

One minute.

Carter touched his trigger lightly, surprised to find that his fingers were shaking. He told himself it was due to the cold.

Fulton looked at his watch for the last time and, as the second hand swept past twelve he fired the flare gun, watching as the Starscope flare rose into the air and exploded. Immediately, all along the line, other officers imitated their CO and the heavens were transformed into a Fifth of November firework display as the brightly coloured projectiles burst, showering the battlefield with a green light. It was like looking through a haze of pea soup, Moss thought. The Paras dashed forward towards the first of the enemy dug-outs, ducked low to guard themselves against the furious onslaught of fire power. They had got half way up the slope when they realized that nothing was moving ahead of them. Fulton, leading a platoon of men reached the dug-out and dashed in.

'Jesus Christ,' he muttered.

The dozen or so Argentinian soldiers inside were sound asleep. One or two of them looked up dreamily to see British soldiers staring down at them. Sergeant James, who had crashed into the bunker with his commander laughed in shocked amazement. The enemy troops merely threw up their hands in surrender, making no attempt to reach for their weapons which were piled up in one corner of the dug-out.

Fulton left a couple of privates to shepherd the prisoners away while he and James ran on towards the next bunker which was already surrounded by Paras.

The sight which met him was, unbelievably, the same.

The grey-clad men were fast asleep, only awakened now by the prodding of bayonets in their backs. They sat up, yawned and automatically placed their hands behind their heads as if that were the natural response at meeting enemy troops. Fulton couldn't believe it. But now, as he emerged from the second dug-out, he saw fire away to the north. And, suddenly, bullets were ploughing up the ground around him. Further up the slope, the Argentinians had been alerted to the British presence, but they were firing at an invisible foe and all their action served to do was pin-point their own positions. Using the Starscope, Turner rested the bipod of the GPMG on a boulder and opened up. The thunderous rattle of machine-gun fire ripped through the stillness, shortly joined by the crack of rifles and pistols as the other Paras easily picked out their targets using the lethal scopes. The bewildered Argentinians could be seen running about behind their ramparts, trying to get a fix on their foes but it was impossible for them and as the British fire grew more concentrated, many simply turned and fled.

A mortar battery opened up, its shells falling with devastating accuracy into the midst of the panic-stricken enemy troops. The night was lit up momentarily by explosions and the Paras saw men hurled high into the air by the blasts. Bunkers were obliterated by the concentrated barrage and smoke began to fill the air, mingling with the snow.

From Two Sisters in the north, to Sapper Hill in the south, the British swarmed forward.

Carter, crouching behind a boulder, heard the unmistakeable sound of jet engines and looked up to see the dark outline of aircraft hurtling out of the east. A moment later he saw them drop something. The sky was filled with blinding white light which lit the entire battlefield for long moments and he realized what was happening.

'Parachute flares,' he called, directing Sergeant James' attention to the slowly falling lumps of cold light. The entire hillside was lit by an eerie glow which reminded Carter of faulty neon. But the flares gave the Argentinians the light they so badly needed. Now machine-guns and rifle fire began to dig up the ground around the Paras, spent slugs singing off the outcrops of rock. An M2 opened up, its rattle momentarily drowning out all other sounds. A private nearby went down clutching his face, another crumpled up not far from Carter, blood spurting madly from a wound in his thigh. In the half light cast by the flares, men dashed back and forth trying to find cover. But the British still had the upper hand, with their Starscopes they were able to pick out individual targets. Brent, in particular, shot down half a dozen enemy troops in rapid succession before dashing on up the slope.

But now mortars were beginning to fire back from the slit trenches and dug-outs of the Argentinians. The bombs came whistling in, sometimes way off target, sometimes right in the midst of the advancing Paras. Men were tossed about like leaves in a gale and Moss stumbled over the body of a corporal who had been left legless by a blast. He sat on the slope helplessly, blood jetting darkly from the shattered stumps of his legs, both of which had been torn off just below the knee. He sat silently, gazing ahead of him with glazed eyes. Moss ran on, firing in the direction of the next dug-out. Harris appeared at his side and both of them suddenly found that they had been singled out for machine-gun attack. The heavy grain slugs tore through the air above their heads and the two Paras hurled themselves down, trying to escape the fearsome fusillade which spattered around them. Harris pushed the youngster towards a boulder nearby and both of them dived for it, a bullet tearing through Harris's boot, ripping the heel off.

'Fucking hell,' he gasped, inspecting the damage.

Both of them pulled grenades from their belts and, in unison, threw them towards the offending machine-gun. There were two terrific bangs and the M2 was mangled by the blasts, the men around it peppered with pieces of shrapnel. Squinting down the Starscope, Harris picked a couple more off then vaulted the boulder, rushing towards the bunker. He was joined by two or three other men, Moss amongst them and they found that four of the Argentinians were very much alive. The first of them reacted quickly and shot the leading Para in the face but, even as the grey-clad man was turning his weapon on Moss, Harris drove his bayonet forward, skewering the man to the back wall of the bunker. He whipped the bloodied blade free and spun round. Moss shot another of them in the chest, finishing the job with his bayonet. The two remaining Argentinians immediately dropped their weapons, arms held skyward.

Fulton raked a slit trench with fire from his Sterling then, supported by half a dozen men, dashed forward. Holding the SMG in one hand he squeezed the trigger. The savage recoil nearly broke his wrist but he kept his finger tight on the trigger until the hammer slammed down on an empty chamber. Seeing his chance, an Argentinian sergeant launched himself at the officer, attempting to wrestle him to the ground—but Fulton was too quick. He brought the Sterling up with terrifying ferocity, using it as a club to smash it into the man's face which immediately dissolved into a bloody ruin. As his opponent staggered, clutching what was left of his face, Fulton whipped the Browning pistol free of its holster and fired twice. The bullets powered into the sergeant from point-blank range, catapulting him several feet across the trench. The Major slammed a fresh magazine into the Sterling and ran on.

He and his men were about half way up the slope by now, still fighting their way up, beneath the eerie white light of the parachute flares. Two Skyhawks had dropped some more and the Paras could hear their powerful engines as they wheeled away. The aircraft, fortunately for the British, were no good in an attacking roll that night for fear of hitting their own men. The battle was an infantry one and it was proving to be tougher than anyone had dreamt it could be. Further up the slopes, as they neared the summit, Argentinian resistance seemed to stiffen.

Grenades were lobbed at the oncoming Paras, mortar bombs fell amongst them and the machine-guns and sub-guns sent red-hot hails of lead into the camouflaged ranks. Men went down in heaps.

Anderson screamed in pain as a bullet tore through his shoulder shattering the clavicle. He staggered, finally hurled into the mud beside Brent when a second slug hit him in the thigh. It caught him just below the left testicle and erupted from the other side, splintering his femur as it did so. He blacked out immediately and Brent pulled his companion to safety behind a rampart of sandbags from which several Paras were firing. He bent close to Anderson, listening for breathing and was thankful to hear it, although it was faint. Brent screamed to a medic to help but the medic himself was hit as he dashed across to help. The bullet hit him in the side of the face, staving it in like some giant super-powered fist. Teeth and a portion of his tongue fell from the open mouth which gaped for a second before filling with blood, the bottom jaw hanging at an impossible angle.

'Oh Jesus,' gasped Brent and looked around for help.

He heard Anderson groaning softly, the blood running freely from his wounds. Brent felt so helpless. With teeth gritted, he pressed the LSW to his shoulder and peered down the sight, blasting away at anything that moved.

'Bastards,' he roared.

Carter, meanwhile, was beside Moss and Harris, the three of them faced with the prospect of another machine-gun nest. They saw Fulton, James and several other men approaching it from the left and at a signal from Carter, the three of them opened up a withering cover fire. Bullets tore into the breastwork of the trench, splinters flying up from the impacts. But the Argentinians inside the fortified hole continued to rake the oncoming Paras. Harris took careful aim and fired at the man who held the machine-gun. The bullet took half his head off, but the muscles went into spasm immediately and, instead of falling back, the fingers of the corpse remained tight around the trigger. To his horror, Harris saw the body fall sideways, held up by the firing handles of the gun, turning the fire-spitting barrel on Fulton and the other men.

'No,' he shrieked.

Fulton was lucky, He saw the barrel whizz round onto them and dived for the dirt. James wasn't so lucky. The Sergeant took one of the slugs in the chest, another in the throat. He remained upright for long seconds then fell backward beside a private who had been hit in the arm. Then, an Argentinian Captain pulled the rigored corpse free of the M2 and took over himself, swinging the barrel back on the three Paras pinned down behind the boulder. Bullets skimmed off the rock. chipping chunks of it away and the trio kept low. When the shooting finally ceased momentarily as the Argentinians hurried to feed a new belt into the machine-gun, the Paras leapt up and charged forward. Fulton, still lying on the ground, hurled a grenade into the bunker but, to his horror, found it was a dud.

The bloody thing didn't go off.

And now the new belt was threaded, the M2 was set for firing.

'This is it,' Moss thought. 'I'm going to die.'

He found himself staring down the barrel of the HMG which yawned only twenty feet from him.

There was a deafening roar as it opened up.

Harris screamed as a bullet hit him in the groin, shattering his left testicle, ripping away part of his inner thigh. Blood gushed down his leg and he fell to his knees where a second slug powered into his stomach, a third into his chest. It tore through his pectoral muscle and erupted from his back, spattering Moss with grey and red gobbets of lung tissue. The boy blenched and hesitated for a second, watching helplessly as Harris fell backward.

The photos of his wife and child fluttered from his pocket and lay in the mud beside him.

A searing explosion brought Moss back to his senses.

A mortar bomb had landed in the machine-gun nest blasting the crew to smithereens. He and Carter vaulted the breastwork, into a stinking mist of smoke and cordite fumes. From out of this mist, bleeding like a stuck pig, came an Argentinian corporal. Carter never saw him, never even heard the arc of the shovel as it flashed towards his head. But Moss did. He threw himself in front of the enemy soldier, lifting his own rifle to block the shovel blow. There was a dull clang and Carter spun round, immediately aware of what had happened. He saw Moss kick the injured Argentinian in the groin, bringing the butt of his rifle down with terrifying force as the man crumpled up. There was a strident snapping of bone and the enemy corporal's head split open like an overripe peach. He crashed to the ground at Moss's feet and the boy stood there for long moments. Carter touched his shoulder and their eyes locked briefly. A look that answered a thousand questions, that said a thousand thanks. Carter realized that his life, his worthless, miserable life had been saved by a boy of eighteen and Moss understood it also. There was nothing to say. There was nothing they *could* say.

'They're running,' roared Fisher, firing a blast from his Sten gun.

Carter and Moss looked up to see groups of grey-clad men racing for the crest of Tumbledown. In places they were rallying, fighting back. But, for the most part, they were throwing away their weapons and legging it as fast as they could.

A cascade of mortar bombs followed their frantic flight.

The Paras did not chase after them, they merely took up safe firing positions amongst the wreckage of the enemy posts and shot at the rallying troops.

Moss saw a private turn his sub-gun on a corporal who was trying to force him back into the fray. The terrified Argentinian was screaming something, the PAM 1 gripped in his shaking hands. An officer who tried to stop him got the same treatment. Mown down in a hail of fire. The enemy troops were fighting amongst themselves now, the officers and NCO's physically hitting men who tried to run, but it was a losing battle. Like trying to stop a flood with a piece of cardboard. The young Argentinian privates threw away their weapons and fled and, as the Paras continued to fire, the officers eventually joined them in their flight. Now the Paras moved forward, moving cautiously towards the crest of the mountain. As they reached it, Carter again heard the loud roar of jet engines and, from the west, six Harriers came screaming in, their Aden guns blazing, strafing the battered Argentinians. They flew in low, bringing the defeated men down in heaps, and the darkness was dispelled once more as a murderous hail of bombs was dropped on the terrified men.

The night sky was filled with reeking smoke, the brilliant plumes of fire from the multiple blasts acting as gigantic flares. The Paras advanced a little way down the slope, watching for any signs of continued Argentinian resistance, but there were none. The Harriers swept over the fleeing men and on towards Port Stanley itself. Carter and Moss, the breath rasping in their lungs, stood and watched as they saw more explosions in the distance signalling that the planes had dropped the remainder of their load on the capital itself.

On the horizon, the first minute threads of light began to creep across the sky like spiders' webs, gradually coming together until they formed into one large grey line which signalled the coming of dawn. Moss, his eyes stinging with the smoke, his throat raw and his ears still ringing with the sound of machine-gun fire and explosions, slumped down on the wet gorse and took off his helmet, running a hand through his hair. He was panting like a dog, his mouth hanging open. He felt as if he'd been running some incredible marathon race. He had a pain in his chest which felt like a stitch and there was perspiration on his face. He coughed and spat, a bitter taste in his mouth.

Carter put a hand on his shoulder and helped him to his feet. They both saw Major Fulton, his uniform spattered with blood, talking to a couple of men who had been wounded. Then the officer crossed to Private Regan, who himself was clutching at a bullet wound in his shoulder. Blood was seeping through his fingers and he was kneeling beside the radio. Fulton asked him if he was all right and Regan announced that he was. Words were exchanged and Moss saw the radio operator speaking into his set. Fulton stood over him relaying instructions, receiving information back again from the other units who'd taken part in the attack.

'What's the time?' asked Moss, his voice a harsh whisper.

Carter scraped some mud from the face of his watch.

'Just after four,' he told his young companion.

'Christ,' muttered Moss.

Incredibly, they had been fighting for over four hours. Fisher joined them, the Sten gun still gripped in his fist.

'Time flies when you're having fun doesn't it?' he said, mirthlessly. 'Where's the Sergeant?'

Carter shrugged.

'I think he's dead, we saw him hit.'

'Oh fuck,' grunted the lance-jack. 'What about Knocker?'

Carter shook his head.

'I haven't seen him,' he said.

'Harris is dead,' said Moss, his eyes misting over.

Fisher didn't wait to hear more, he turned and headed back towards the crest of the hill, pushing his way through the Paras who were still flooding over the captured ridge. The cockney found Wallace quite close to the top of the reverse slope. He was lying face down beside a dead Argentinian private. There was a dark puddle of blood around both bodies but Fisher couldn't tell which of them it came from. He rushed over to the motionless figure of the corporal and pulled him over onto his back.

He bowed his head as he looked at the corporal. Wallace's eyes were still open, tiny flecks of wet grass sticking to the bulging orbs. He had been shot twice, both bullets catching him in the chest and, as Fisher cradled the body in his arms, he felt blood dripping from the exit wounds in his companion's back. He shook his head and gently laid the body down again then, with a vengeful cry, he began kicking at the body of the dead Argentinian laying beside him.

'Fucking bastard,' he rasped, driving his boot into the corpse. 'Fucking bastard.'

He kept on kicking until he could no longer raise his leg, then he sank to his knees beside Wallace's body, reaching for the corporal's Sten gun. Fisher discarded his own weapon, throwing it away with a grunt of disgust. Then he called a couple of men over who were busily collecting up the wounded and dead. He watched as they lifted the bullet-torn corpse and carried it away. Medics were hastily attending to the wounded of both sides. Other men were escorting prisoners to the rear. Fisher watched for long moments, the grey dawn casting a dull light over the proceedings, making it look like a monochrome film. Then, he turned and walked wearily back to re-join the remnants of what was now *his* platoon. He found them grouped on the other side of the crest, some squatting on their haunches, others standing exhausted, watching as the last remaining Argentinians fled towards the relative safety of the capital itself.

From their position on the hillside, the Paras had a clear view of Port Stanley, in particular the red roof of the church. It looked so small.

'So, that's what we fought all night to get to eh?' said Brent. He was dragging his left leg slightly, having been hit on the kneecap by a lump of shrapnel which, luckily for him, hadn't broken the bone, only given him one hell of a bruise. The damn thing hurt like mad every time he put his foot down and Morris had to support him when the order finally came to move forward.

All along the front, Paras, Marines, Ghurkas and Guardsmen advanced towards their final objective. On all fronts, from every piece of high ground around Stanley, the Argentinians had fled and now, as dawn took command of the sky, the British saw the destruction they'd wrought during the night of fighting and with the ceaseless artillery bombardments. Pockmarked ground, discarded helmets and weapons, packs thrown away. It all looked so familiar.

Moss saw a group of Argentinians walking slowly towards them and he felt that old fear rise momentarily, gripping his rifle in his hands until the knuckles turned white. But, as they drew closer, he saw that the grey-clad men had their hands placed behind their heads. The one leading them carried a white flag which was merely a bandage tied to the end of a rifle barrel. The bandage was flecked with blood and it fluttered mournfully in the early morning breeze. The Paras passed the dismal little procession, moving off the hillside and onto the narrow road which had been churned into liquid mud by the comings and goings of enemy troops and with the constant rain and snow. White patches still dotted the ground here and there and, even as the men began their slow trek along the narrow quagmire, the sky began to weep icy tears once again.

A couple of Scorpion tanks drove past, a number of commandos clinging to their hulls. The armoured vehicles moved slowly through the oozing muck, their tracks spinning in the slime, sending up sprays of thick brown sludge as they passed by.

Moss looked across to his right and saw another platoon of Paras, led by Major Fulton, advancing parallel with them. Beside the major Private Regan marched and Moss managed a smile when he saw that the radio operator had attached a small Union Jack to the antenna of the radio. It flapped proudly in the strong wind. Moss looked across at Carter and tried to smile but neither of them could manage it. As if the gesture was just too much of an effort.

Moss felt tears welling up in his eyes as he thought about Harris, the photos of his wife and child lying in the mud beside him.

Victory suddenly seemed a very empty word.

Thirteen

Moss had no idea how long he and the rest of the battalion had been in Port Stanley. He sat on the floor of the church now, his head lowered, surrounded by his comrades who were crammed into the small building like so many camouflaged sardines. Each man held his helmet in his hands as he listened to the words which floated gently through the church. They seemed hollow, echoing around the small building, echoing inside his own head as the chaplain spoke.

Father Driscoll was standing in the pulpit at the far end of the church, dressed in his uniform, his red beret lying before him. He was holding a Bible in one hand, flipping it open every now and then. Moss thought how different things were now to how they had been at the mass burial at Goose Green when no one had been able to hear what the chaplain was saying. Now each word came across with crystal clarity. They had already sung two hymns and now they listened as Driscoll spoke, each man wrapped up in his own thoughts but aware of what the chaplain said. The church smelt of dampness and sweat but no one seemed to care.

'I'd just like you to think for a moment about the men who are *not* with us today,' Driscoll was saying. 'About the men who we left behind at Goose Green and Fitzroy and Tumbledown.'

Moss closed his eyes, that image of Harris and his photos surfacing yet again in his mind. It was an image he knew that would haunt him for many months to come. Perhaps for the rest of his life. But there were other things which had made their mark on him too. He thought of the way the sun had come out from behind the clouds as he and his companions had entered Port Stanley, as if it too were pleased to see them. He remembered with pride seeing the Union Jack being hoisted once more over Government House and how he had felt that swell of pride yet again. But, balanced with that were the scenes of utter degradation which he had seen. The streets of Port Stanley (re-named in Spanish for the benefit of the Argentinians) littered with discarded equipment, houses painted with red crosses to prevent them being bombed even when they contained ammunition. The floor of the Post Office covered with three months worth of rotted, stinking excrement which two men had hosed clean. Moss had almost thrown up at the sight and smell of that. Anti-aircraft guns had been placed in the children's playground, and between two houses stood a massive 155.

Carter, who now stood behind Moss, had been both surprised and disgusted at how easily and how gladly the Argentinian troops had abandoned their arms and surrendered.

'No bottle,' Fisher had said.

Even now, as the Paras crowded in the church, the defeated grey clad men were being rounded up by Marines and Guardsmen.

'What did *you* think about when you were charging into the mouth of an Argentinian machine-gun?' Driscoll was asking them.

(Fear.)

'What did *you* think when you heard a shell whistling towards you?'

(Help me.)

There was a subdued silence hanging over the men as each cast his thoughts back to the things of which Driscoll now spoke. We were scared, thought Moss, all of us. Scared to death. He felt a tear run down his cheek and wiped it away, almost in surprise. A tear of relief perhaps? Relief that he was still alive. Or was it a tear for the men who had died? He wasn't sure. His stomach felt as if someone had knotted his intestines together. More tears came and he fought them back.

'Did you think about your friends, your family, your wives?' Driscoll continued.

'Or did you just think about what it would be like to die?'

(All the time.)

Moss didn't attempt to fight back his emotions now and, through blurred eyes, he saw that other men too were crying.

The chaplain paused for long moments before continuing.

'Let us pray,' he said, softly.

And they did. Each of them saying a silent prayer, thanking God that they were standing in this damp, smelly little church on a windswept island in the South Atlantic. They wept, some of them and Moss, raising his head for a second looked out of the window.

He saw the devastation, the long ranks of prisoners filing past, the islanders watching in shocked bewilderment as their captors were hustled away. Moss watched for long seconds, one thought plaguing his mind.

Had it all been worth it?

He thought of Harris, of Sergeant James, of Wallace, of the men who had died at Goose Green, Fitzroy and countless other places on this Godforsaken lump of rock. The tears flowed again.

Had it been worth all the sacrifices?

Then he watched as a little girl, perhaps no more than six, wandered up to a Marine sergeant and threw her arms around his neck as he bent to pick her up. She kissed him on his stubbled cheek and Moss felt a smile beginning to crease his face.

The answer to his question was there before him, in the grateful face of that little girl.

It had *all* been worth it.

He lowered his head once more.

Fourteen

There were about two dozen Falklanders gathered around the simple cross which stood atop The Hill of Gorse, just beyond Goose Green. They stood in the wind, their faces peppered with snow which was falling in thin sheets. They stood silently, looking up at the cross, old and young alike. The man with the wreath walked slowly towards the base of the simple monument and laid the small circlet of flowers there; then he backed off and joined his companions. They stood there for a few more minutes, just listening to the wail of the wind. Then they turned and headed back towards Goose Green.

The breeze stirred the wreath, blowing against the flowers and causing their petals to shiver. At the centre of the wreath was a plaque, almost incongurously small amidst the welter of colour which surrounded it.

It bore just three words;

Lest we forget.

AFTERTHOUGHT

To *Sun, Express* and *Telegraph,* our "Democratic Press":
You make me sad I'm British, and that's something to confess.
And here's a word for Thatcher and the Great New British Right:
Next time you want to have a war, why don't *you* go and fight?

Attila the Stockbroker.

STAR BESTSELLERS

0352 309350	**WHISPERS** Dean R Koontz (GF)	1.95*
0352 310804	**ROGUE OF GOR** John Norman (Sci. Fantasy)	1.95*
0352 310413	**AFTERMATH** Roger Williams (GF)	1.60
0352 310170	**A MAN WITH A MAID** Anonymous (GF)	1.60*
0352 310928	**A MAN WITH A MAID VOL. II** Anonymous (GF)	1.60*
0352 395621	**THE STUD** Jackie Collins (GF)	1.60
0352 300701	**LOVEHEAD** Jackie Collins (GF)	1.50
0352 398663	**THE WORLD IS FULL OF DIVORCED WOMEN** Jackie Collins (GF)	1.60
0352 398752	**THE WORLD IS FULL OF MARRIED MEN** Jackie Collins (GF)	1.50
0352 311339	**THE GARMENT** Catherine Cookson (GF)	1.25
0426 163524	**HANNAH MASSEY** Catherine Cookson (GF)	1.25
0426 163605	**SLINKY JANE** Catherine Cookson (GF)	1.25
0352 310634	**THE OFFICERS' WIVES** Thomas Fleming (GF)	2.50*
0352 302720	**DELTA OF VENUS** Anais Nin (GF)	1.50*
0352 306157	**LITTLE BIRDS** Anais Nin (GF)	1.25*
0352 310359	**BITE OF THE APPLE** Molly Parkin (GF)	1.35

* Not for sale in Canada

Prices are subject to alteration

STAR Books are obtainable from many booksellers and newsagents. If you have any difficulty please send purchase price plus postage on the scale below to:-

Star Cash Sales
P.O. Box 11
Falmouth
Cornwall

OR

Star Book Service,
G.P.O. Box 29,
Douglas,
Isle of Man,
British Isles.

While every effort is made to keep prices low, it is sometimes necessary to increase prices at short notice. Star Books reserve the right to show new retail prices on covers which may differ from those advertised in the text or elsewhere.

Postage and Packing Rate

UK: 45p for the first book, 20p for the second book and 14p for each additional book ordered to a maximum charge of £1.63. BFPO and EIRE: 45p for the first book, 20p for the second book, 14p per copy for the next 7 books thereafter 8p per book. Overseas: 75p for the first book and 21p per copy for each additional book.